CONTEMPORARY AMERICAN FICTION

THE REST OF LIFE

Mary Gordon is the bestselling author of the novels *Final Payments*, *The Company of Women*, *Men and Angels*, and *The Other Side*, as well as a collection of stories, *Temporary Shelter*, and of essays, *Good Boys and Dead Girls*. She has received the Lila Acheson Wallace-Reader's Digest Writer's Award and a Guggenheim Fellowship. She teaches at Barnard College.

THE REST *of* LIFE

THREE NOVELLAS BY
MARY GORDON

PENGUIN BOOKS

PENGUIN BOOKS
Published by the Penguin Group
Penguin Books USA Inc., 375 Hudson Street,
New York, New York 10014, U.S.A.
Penguin Books Ltd, 27 Wrights Lane,
London W8 5TZ, England
Penguin Books Australia Ltd, Ringwood, Victoria, Australia
Penguin Books Canada Ltd, 10 Alcorn Avenue,
Toronto, Ontario, Canada M4V 3B2
Penguin Books (N.Z.) Ltd, 182–190 Wairau Road,
Auckland 10, New Zealand

Penguin Books Ltd, Registered Offices:
Harmondsworth, Middlesex, England

First published in the United States of America by Viking Penguin,
a division of Penguin Books USA Inc., 1993
Published in Penguin Books 1994

1   3   5   7   9   10   8   6   4   2

PUBLISHER'S NOTE
These are works of fiction. Names, characters, places, and incidents either are the product of the author's imagination or are used fictitiously,
and any resemblance to actual persons, living or dead, events, or locales
is entirely coincidental.

THE LIBRARY OF CONGRESS HAS CATALOGUED
THE HARDCOVER AS FOLLOWS:
Gordon, Mary.
The rest of life: three novellas/by Mary Gordon.
p.   cm.
Contents: Immaculate man—Living at home—The Rest of life.
ISBN 0-670-83828-4 (hc.)
ISBN 0 14 01.4907 4 (pbk.)
I. Title.
PS3557.O669R46   1993
813'54—dc20   92–50753

Printed in the United States of America
Set in Simoncini Garamond
Designed by Francesca Belanger

Acknowledgments

I would like to thank Dr. Eva Sperling, and Meryl Segal and the staff of the Forum School, Waldwick, N.J., for all their time, their generous advice, and the opportunity to observe them at their work as I tried to learn about autistic children in preparation for writing *Living at Home*. I also consulted many books about autism. Particularly useful were Bruno Bettelheim's *The Empty Fortress*, Mira Rothenberg's *Children with Emerald Eyes*, and *Communication Problems in Autism*, edited by Eric Schopler and Gary B. Mesibov.

I got the idea for the suicide of a young man in Turin in the late 1920s from an incident recorded in Davide Lajolo's *An Absurd Vice: A Biography of Cesare Pavese*. I read Pavese's diaries and letters, from which I took some of the details I used in *The Rest of Life*.

And my thanks to Victoria DeGrazia, who has helped me in more ways than I can name.

Contents

IMMACULATE
MAN

For Maureen Strafford

What happened to me on the bus wasn't unusual. The person sitting next to me was surprised and even outraged and that made me wonder for a moment at my own lack of outrage and surprise. It's very easy for me to think that other people are right, more right than I am anyway, or that at least they have more right to things, which is why I always give up arguments. I'm easily swayed and along with that I don't expect too much. Why would I go on with something—anything, a conversation, a debate—when it seemed clear that the other person wanted so much to be winning? When it meant so much to them?

When I was a teenager, I liked reading Russian novels. I wanted to study Russian, but the sixties came and I decided I should help the poor. I became a social worker. I think I was right.

I must have read thousands of pages of Russian novels, but of all those words, only one sentence still stands out. It's spoken by a married woman who goes to a priest every week to confess adultery. Every week she cries and cries. She seems distraught; her whole body is racked with sobs. The priest asks her why she goes on doing it, sinning this way, since she is so contrite. Suddenly she stops crying. She sits up straight. She dries her eyes. I could always

3

see this very clearly: how suddenly she got hold of herself. It must have seemed to her all at once that the priest had never understood a thing. It must have been a bad moment for her: suddenly to feel she hadn't been understood. She must have felt disappointed, and quite lost. But at the same time, contemptuous. At that moment, she must have felt that she could have turned over the whole institution of the Russian church with one flick of her foot. That's how insubstantial it must all have seemed to her.

She looked up at the priest with clear, dry eyes. "I do it because it gives him so much pleasure and me so little pain." Then she left. The priest said nothing. I'm sure that she went right off to her lover.

I don't know why I began talking about all that. I want to talk about what happened on the bus. But, after all, it's not so bad to start out with a story about a priest. This is a story about one. And, I suppose you could say, about adultery. I don't know yet how all this will turn out. I know that whatever will happen, everybody tried.

I was on the bus that day because my car broke down. Otherwise, I never would have gone through it: the trip through Port Authority, the smelly bus with the bathroom door that kept opening and shutting. The only seat was near the bathroom door—I got there late and every other seat was taken—I kept having to smell the disinfectant, and pretend I didn't see people disappearing into that little place.

The walk through Port Authority warned me that there might be marginal types on the bus. But that doesn't bother me, I've worked with lots of different kinds of people. I'm used to dealing with out-patients, or ex-patients, or people who should be patients but there's just no money or no room. I could tell that the guy across from me hadn't been taking his medication. I knew all the signs, and I was ready for an outburst, or at least some inappropriate remarks.

I was wearing a black knit jumpsuit. Nothing special, nothing to make remarks about. But the guy across from me just seemed to love it. "I love what you're wearing. I just love what you're wearing. What do you call that material. What would you call it, cotton?"

"Cotton knit," I said.

"Well I just love it." He took the material of my pants between his thumb and forefinger and fingered it like a tailor.

"Look," I said. "You can't do that. It's one of the things you can't do, touch people when they don't want you to. And I don't want you to, so you can't. It has nothing to do with what I think of you as a person."

I knew how easily people like that can feel devastated. And I didn't think less of him, I really didn't. I just didn't want him touching my clothes. I thought it would be possible for me to make him understand that, and we'd both be no worse off. I'm a great believer in that, it's what I hope for: not to leave people worse off.

"Well," he said, "it's not that I really like the material so much, it's that I really wanted to go to bed with you but I thought it was better to talk about the material."

This is the kind of thing that often happens. I try to make things better, or at least not worse, but the worst seems bound to happen. I often wonder whether the worst will happen anyway, whether it's useless to try and stop the worst from happening.

After the man had told me that what he really wanted was to go to bed, what was there left for me to do? Nothing. Nothing but to stare ahead at a fixed point in space and pretend, like most of the people in his life, that he didn't exist. I suppose I could have talked to him about it. But, you know, that would have required a very different kind of person.

What kind of person would that have to be? Woman, I mean. Someone more unusual, more confident, more detached. What would the woman be like who could have a conversation with a man, an unacceptable man, an undesirable man, a man she didn't want to go to bed with, after he'd told her that what he wanted was to go to bed. Not like me. I've said that. So like what? I'm not sure. I have two ideas, completely different from each other.

One idea is about a kind of woman who didn't know much about sex, the other is about a kind of woman who knew a lot, had been through a lot, perhaps even been abused, and wasn't very interested. So she could say, about herself and sex, "Well, yes, he wants that but I don't. Let's go on." Someone who'd had a bad time with sex, or even too much of it, but still kept her interest in life. This does happen. The other kind of woman I thought about, who didn't know anything about sex yet, would be bound to run into trouble sooner or later. Probably she would end up abused.

I see her, maybe a religious girl, someone who has faith in people, someone brought up to have faith in people, someone who wants sex, but has been brought up not to think about wanting sex, that might be selfish, someone brought up not to be selfish, to be helpful. This kind of woman can get into really dreadful trouble with the worst men. Can fall so easily to the bottom of the pit—unrecognizable, even to herself. But how do any of us recognize ourselves? By being around familiar objects, by performing actions that have some similarity to the actions of the past. I think that's all.

I tell you I've seen trusting girls, well-brought-up girls, girls who were trying to be unselfish or thought that there were things that they should learn, I've seen girls like this end up at the bottom of the pit. Some of them climb out, leave it behind, all that—by which I mean sex, sex with men at any rate, some of them find happiness with women—and go on, still interested in life, in stories.

I know about these women because it's what I do: I work with abused women. I used to run a shelter; now I'm a consultant.

I have never been abused. But I know that someone who could go on talking to an unacceptable man after he'd told her he wanted to go to bed with her would be on one or the other side of abuse. Before or after.

Or maybe not. Maybe there are some women who are so interested in hearing stories that they forget about protecting themselves. They know they could be in danger, but they'd rather hear the story. There must be women like that, women who went to Africa or joined the army. What was sex like for them, when they had it? Another story? You can't imagine a woman like that abandoning herself. Turning the machine off so the story stops being told or recorded. To have sex, you have to be willing to give up the line of the story.

I like stories, I've always liked stories, and I've never been abused. Perhaps because I married early. So the things I know about the painful kind of sex I only know from other people's stories.

What would it be like to think of sex as just another story? Your own story, but only one of them, and maybe not the most important.

But I was talking about what happened on the bus. I'd given up talking to the guy, I was staring straight ahead of me, and I heard some kind of kicking going on, someone kicking the back of one of the seats.

"Cut that shit out, man," I heard someone say.

"I'm not doin' any shit," said the guy who wanted to go to bed with me.

"You move that seat back up. I don't have room for my legs. You keep moving it up and down. Just keep it where you had it. I don't want trouble."

It was a young black man who was speaking, quite well dressed. He wasn't going to take any crap. I thought what he'd define as crap and what my friend would think of as his rights had a good chance of colliding.

"I have the right to move my seat back. You can't take away my rights."

7

"There's no room for my legs, man. Just move the seat up and leave it where it is."

I thought each of them had a point, and it didn't matter, something bad was going to happen soon. And there was nothing I could do to help.

I expected some kind of fight. But no, what came next was a perfectly civilized threat.

"You better cut that shit out, man, or I'm going to tell the bus driver you cracked that window banging your beer can on it."

"Bullshit, man, that window was cracked before I got on this bus. And you know it."

"I know that I saw you crack that window with your beer can. Some kind of crazy behavior. So just cut that shit out or I'm telling the bus driver about all that."

That quieted my friend, my admirer. He pushed his seat upright. The young black man had enough leg room. He put his Walkman phones into his ears. He was satisfied. Then my friend (I'd already begun to think of him that way: he seemed so familiar) lit up a cigarette. When the first hint of smoke got to the middle of the bus, a woman wearing a long full cotton skirt and black Reeboks popped up, as if the smoke signaled real fire, not a cigarette. She walked up to the bus driver; righteousness was on her side. She whispered something in the driver's ear.

He pulled out of the traffic lane and stopped the bus on the shoulder of the road. He stood up. He had short black slicked-down hair, and he pulled his pants up, putting his thumbs through his belt loops. He walked heavily, rolling, lurching up the aisle as if he were aboard a ship. He stopped heavily at my friend's seat.

"Now I've had all the crap from you I'm about to take. We're just going to get off the bus right now and wait for the troopers."

My friend began to cry. "Please," he said. "I'll get sent back.

I'm on probation. I swear to God I won't make any trouble. Whatever I've done here today, it's not so bad that it's worth what's
going to happen to me."

I thought he was right. I wanted to tell the bus driver to give
him another chance. But I could tell that the passengers weren't
on my side; I thought it would be a useless gesture. I thought of
the position I'd be in for the rest of the ride if I made an unsuccessful plea. And it was bound to be unsuccessful. At least I convinced myself of that. I've never been sure; I've never quite forgiven
myself for not trying.

"The trouble with scum like you is you have too many chances
to ruin the life of decent people like my passengers here."

I could feel the passengers come together; each breast swelled
with a sense of group pride. Except mine. I was ashamed.

The boy was sobbing as he walked down the aisle and out of
the bus. I saw how handsome he was. He had a high color—from
emotion, perhaps, or sun. Maybe he was part Indian. His thighs
were strong and he had James Dean hair that fell into his eyes. I
wondered what it would have been like to go to bed with him
after all. Sometimes women like me do go to bed with men like
that. Someone I used to work with married one of her clients
who was a prisoner. Of course it turned out badly. But so many
things do.

The troopers came and handcuffed my friend and made him
spread-eagle against the car. All the time he was crying and begging
for another chance. I could see how dirty his hands were, and his
trousers. I was wondering how he lived.

One of the troopers, a woman, came on the bus to take statements
from anyone who'd seen the man outside "engaged in acts of
disruptive behavior." The young black man who'd been annoyed
by him testified that he'd been annoyed, and that he'd seen the
guy crack the window with his beer can. No one else had seen it

though; no one could remember whether or not it was cracked, as my friend claimed, when he'd got on the bus.

The woman who sat next to me, a small, oldish woman who was knitting, poked me with one of her needles.

"Aren't you going to tell her what he did to you?"

"What?" I said. "I don't remember what he said. It was no big deal anyway."

"Well, what is it?" she said angrily. "Either you don't remember what he said or it's no big deal."

"I guess I mean it's no big deal."

"You should speak up," she said. "You should always speak up."

"I just don't feel it's worth it," I said.

She looked at me with real hatred. "It's people like you who are the cause of everything," she said.

It took the trooper an hour and a half to take down all the statements. Then they drove away with my friend in the car. I wished that I were handcuffed in the car with him.

I saw everyone's position; I thought everyone was right.

That was the day that I met Clement.

But I don't want to talk about meeting him, what he said, what I said, how we seemed to one another. That would get things off on the wrong foot, as if this were the sort of story that would end well. I suppose it won't end well.

It was such strange weather when I met him. I'm from Southern Illinois and we lived near a river; I grew up in fog you might say. My parents were good people. I'm not sure of that. Can you say someone's good if he or she hasn't been tested? That's the kind of thing Clement and I talk about. Perhaps it's better to say they were nice people, my parents. But that's not fair, that says too little of them. It certainly seems fair to say that they were kind. I know that's true, even though I believe they were never tested. They never met anyone too different from themselves, anyone who behaved really outrageously, or made demands on them that they had no reason to expect. But maybe they thought they were sorely tested; maybe they thought they'd lived their whole lives on the rack. Maybe my mother was in love with someone else; maybe my father nursed a secret thirst he subdued at great cost each day. I'll never know. She's dead now.

I'm forty-eight; my mother's dead, my father has Parkinson's disease. This is slightly on the dark side of the national average, I suppose, but it's not tragic. You could say the same thing of the fact that I'm divorced, after a marriage that went on for fifteen years and ended when he met somebody else. But we weren't in love; it all seems a long time ago. It's worse than what my parents wanted for me, my life that is, but not nearly so bad as what a lot of people have.

I've seen what a lot of people have, have done to them, or visited upon them. The kind of work I do has given me that. And I know this about myself: I've never been outside the web, never been in extreme circumstances: danger, degradation, absolute abandonment. I have two children and they're both healthy. That's the only thing I couldn't bear. If anything should happen to them. A lot of people don't get that: to be spared the one thing they couldn't bear.

Something almost happened to my daughter once, and I was with her, and I couldn't stop it. No, it was worse than that. I didn't stop it. As it turned out, I didn't need to, but it's a good thing, because in the moment that we all fear, the extreme moment, I failed her. And I have to live with that.

We were swimming at Nantucket. We were on vacation at the beach; it was a perfect day. My daughter was ten; this was a while ago; she's seventeen now. And my son's fourteen. There we were on the beach, and everyone was in the water. People's voices rose and fell; little screams, echoes, a flat buzz of talk, all of it so far away. We were vacationing with my best friend and her children. We would all wake at different times, eat anyhow, clean up haphazardly, read, talk. It's not important that you know any of that.

My daughter and I went into the water. I ought to have known. Now I know: a riptide makes a channel in the other water, a clear stream, as though it were fresh water in the thicker foaming water of the ordinary waves. The children were in my charge. I ought to have known it, I ought to have known about the riptide. My daughter could have died, it would have been my fault if she had. She didn't, and I had nothing to do with that.

We were laughing, swimming. Then we understood that we were being carried terribly far out. We tried to swim back but it wasn't working. However hard we swam, it didn't matter. We just kept being pulled out.

This is the shameful part. I saw my daughter and my friend. I saw that my daughter was much nearer to my friend than she was to me, and that they were both nearer to the shore than I was. It seemed to me that it was my friend's job, and not mine, to save my daughter. An immense peace came over me. I heard a voice— it could have been a teacher's, no one I knew intimately, no one in my family, and not the voice of God or my own death. It was saying, as if it were reading from a book: "Keep calm. The most important thing is to keep calm when you're drowning."

I was very calm. I was annoyed at other people for not being calm. I felt impatient with my daughter for flailing; when I heard her terrified bleats, I was annoyed. I wanted to strike her, to strike her farther away from me so I couldn't hear her. I didn't want to stop what I was doing: floating calmly, being carried out. I was very happy. It was as if my daughter were calling for my attention when I was in the middle of making love. It was a bit like that, being carried out was absorbing like that, like the calm you feel before you're taken over by arousal in the hands of a lover you rely upon to be expert. Or when you give yourself up to an overpowering scent: the scent of freesias in a cold room heated by a fire. No need to worry, no need to question. Just a giving over, in one case to pleasure, in the other to death by drowning. Where is obligation in two states like these? Far from you, where you lie pillowed and quiescent in the milky peace of giving up.

Someone came out with a Styrofoam board to save my daughter and my friend. People keep telling me all this took less than half a minute, that what I did was right, that if my daughter had been in mortal danger I would have acted to save her. But I don't believe them. I know I didn't save her, that I left her, that I wanted to be apart from her, alone, wherever I was, in a trance of selfishness, survival, drowning, wherever it was that was not mother love.

And yet I've always said that I would die for her. I always said it would be easy. I don't say that anymore.

I'm ashamed to think about this incident, but I have to, in case it's the one thing about myself that's most important, the truest thing.

I've told Clement this story many times. As if, in telling him the events in different words, slower or faster, in a slightly different order, I might come upon some gratifying and redeeming truth. He always says, "It's not the most important thing about you." Once he said, "It might not even be about you."

"Who would it be about?"

"A drowning person."

"That was me."

"No. The story didn't end. You don't know if it was you."

"If the story ended, someone would be dead."

"Or saved. So you don't even know the story, do you? What the story really is. And besides, you couldn't help it. You were panicked. What you thought was calm was really panic, a very extreme panic. I've read a lot about drowning. You couldn't have done other than you did."

You see, he can say things like that, and then say things that are really stupid. Unbelievably stupid things that make you think there's something wrong with him, or you're embarrassed for him, so embarrassed you never want to see him again. He's a terrible judge of character. He makes mistakes with women at the shelter all the time. He gives them money; he believes them when they couldn't possibly be telling the truth. Well, he made a bad mistake in choosing me. He ought to have chosen someone simpler, like himself, or more impermeable. Not like me.

It was so foggy when I stepped down from the bus that day, it was impossible to see him. Not that I knew who I was looking for. Father Clement Buckley. I had never spoken to a priest. It was a job, he was another man I'd have to speak to about setting up a place to hide women who'd been hurt by men, women who think that men might kill them. I have to talk to men about these things, because we need money, or a building, or the know-how for the locks, the secret telephones, the secret codes.

The bus station was near the river. There was a fence that separated the parking lot from the steep bank, the scrabble, the kind of mean slant down to nothing where people throw bottles, a terrible kind of place where nothing has ever bred. One of those awful cyclone fences, braided diamond-shapes of wire with barbed wire on top. In case anyone would want to get—to what? that black godforsaken slope. Those broken bottles.

That's the kind of thing Clement and I talk about. The term *godforsaken*. How terrible it is. The meaning of *forsake*. Or why it is that cyclone fences, especially the barbed-wire tops, always make me think of the Rosenbergs. He can be so quick at understanding things like that and so infuriatingly slow at understanding something obvious, that anyone could understand. Like the fact that he should close the door if he's making a call using his credit card, so none of the women will hear the credit-card number and copy it down and use it. He just doesn't see how something like that could go on.

That first day he called my name out; I could barely see him. We agreed that we should sit in his car a while until the fog lifted—and it would have to lift—enough for us to see where we were driving. He put his hand on my shoulder to guide me to the car. It was really that bad, things really were invisible. Was I the first woman he touched like that? Of course not, he had a mother and sisters. He said much later that he'd liked the feel of my shoulder under the cloth. I told him the guy on the bus had liked the cloth too, it was a real winner, I told him. He laughed: he understood. Sometimes he doesn't get jokes. But the story of the man on the bus whom I did not defend is another story I've told him ten, maybe fifty times. What is there about him that allows me to repeat stories, hoping they'll end differently, believing that they will. Why does he listen each time, as if it's a story he's never heard?

The fog came up around the car like water. It was as though we were drowning in silver air. It was like a sweet dream moving into waking, an early-morning dream, half torn from life. I loved it in that car. He asked if it was all right to turn on the radio. Maybe we'd get the weather. I didn't want to say: "What for?" It seemed to me we'd know when the fog lifted. That we'd be the first to know. But I said, "Of course, turn on the radio." A song came on that we both liked. We both started singing. It was a Muzak orchestra. A song from *Oklahoma*. He said he'd sung the songs from *Oklahoma* in his high school glee club.

"That was before the seminary, of course," he said, as if it were important to make that clear.

"Of course," I said, pretending I knew why he'd said it.

There was so much I didn't know, that I still don't know. But I was happy with him that day in the car, singing, enclosed, invisible to everyone, the whole world indistinguishable. I knew no one could see us and we couldn't see a soul. I remember saying to myself, "All bets are off," not knowing what I meant, what bets.

He can do things like that. Make you feel it's fine that you're stranded in a parking lot in fog and listening to the radio. That it's good that you're there, it's the right place, he's made a place for you, this place, and it's the right place because he's made it right.

There was so much I didn't know that he assumed I knew because he so rarely met people who didn't know about all that. All that. I keep calling it "all that" because I don't know what to call it. The Catholic Church. That way of thinking. That whole world, gone now, and what was implicated in it. I guess I mean implied by it. Maybe Clement would be better off with someone who knows more about it. When I tell him that, he says, "It's all gone away. What it was is gone."

And then I feel it's my fault, that I destroyed it all, "all that," and I would put it back, rebuild it if I could, or I would leave him if he thought that would help. "Please don't leave me, I will never leave you," he says. I don't know why he doesn't want to be without me, why, when he says "please" it is a word so full of hope, belief, a word that swoons from its own heaviness. So I don't leave him, so we stay together, even though "all that" weighs on us like the bricks and stones of a basilica. Even though it's over and I can't know very much about it now, except for what he tells me. There's nothing left to see with my own eyes.

Sometimes he'll make a point of something, like saying he sang songs from *Oklahoma* in the glee club, but that, of course, was before seminary days, and I won't get the point. I know that there's a point but I don't get it. Sometimes I pretend to get it, and sometimes I ask him to explain.

He tries to explain it all to me. But there's so much of it. It's as if he were an émigré and I a naïve girl, unseasoned by misfortune. Or not that, not only that, an American girl abroad, brought up on plain food and objects valued only for their usefulness, meeting up with a young prince, or not a prince, a member of the aristocracy, now impoverished, who takes her to his room and shows her what his family brought out. He unpacks pigskin cases with expensive receptacles of crystal and silver held in by leather straps. He shows her programs of famous concerts he attended in the famous opera houses of his travels: he makes distinctions between singers and performances. She's never heard of the singers or the opera houses; she doesn't know if the receptacles held in by leather straps are meant for perfume or for gin. But she listens, she keeps listening, and slowly, a picture forms. Of a life: objects and characters, fuller, richer, more adorned than hers, but over, gone.

There's a lot I don't know, and he isn't used to talking to people who don't know. If I said something to him, in the beginning, when he'd do anything for me (he kept saying that, "I'd do anything for you—anything, you know that, don't you?—anything"), if I'd said, for example, "What are final vows?" or "Who do you mean when you say the provincial?" he'd blink at me, like an animal, a patient animal, a little stupid, and then seem embarrassed. "Oh, well, final vows, you see." Or, "What we mean by the provincial." Then he'd go on much too long, because he was embarrassed, until we'd both be embarrassed, and sad somehow, because of that gulf between us, that emptiness, misinformation, all that space that had to be filled in. If we'd been younger, or different, or felt we had more time, if we hadn't had to spend so much time covering up, the task of filling in the blanks might have been fun, or even sexy. As if the time we hadn't known each other was a long mist, through which the other could see dabs of color only, purple, red, orange, but the muddied versions of those colors. All the events of the past—standing there, a little smirched, a little tainted—until familiarity had made them pure again. So you could say the names, the places of the lover's past without feeling you'd stolen or you'd lied.

But we're not younger, freer. We've always been in hiding, always worried. I'll never meet his family, although he's met mine. My children, of course, know him very well. We'll talk about my children later. And my father knows him, though he's puzzled, he thinks he's some kind of minister, he doesn't see the difference.

And what is the difference? That's what I didn't know before. I didn't know it in the car that day when we sat, trapped and yet enjoying ourselves in the fog listening to the radio, as if there were no place we needed to be, although I'd traveled all that way. I'd been paid to be there.

Now I know the difference, even though I don't believe in it. I don't know if he believes in it, Clement, but he has to live as if he does. He's thought of himself as that way for so long, he can't think of a new way now.

His mother cried when, at age fifteen, he told her he was going to preparatory seminary (the *prep:* I can use that word now, rightfully, I've filled it up with objects, faces). Of course she cried. But let me tell you now what those tears meant. It wasn't just that she was sad at losing him, her youngest and her favorite. And it wasn't like she was giving him up to be a soldier. Although there was pride in it, a little like a soldier's mother. But it wasn't that: she was giving him up to God. But that wasn't it, either, it wasn't as if he were dying. It was almost that he was becoming God. When

I said this to him, he was shocked. "She'd never feel a thing like that, that would be blasphemy," he said. That's the kind of thing he says. I've heard him say it so many times: "She'd never do that, she doesn't even believe in it." About some woman at the shelter who'd gone back on drugs or out on the street, or back to her husband. There is in him some habit of belief in belief that I don't understand.

I try to understand. What does belief mean to him? What do any of us mean by belief?

I've come to see, I think, that what we call belief is a kind of situation, some creation of a face, a street, a building in which, next to which, we imagine ourselves rightly placed. We can recognize ourselves, or we imagine we can. And this is who we say we are.

But for believers, such as Clement, it's difficult to think a person isn't who he says he is. I try to tell him: People don't know themselves. They may be acting in good faith, and yet they may be self-deceived.

Faith and *deceit* aren't words Clement can place together in a sentence, keep in his mind at one time.

His is a way of thinking that, in the end, I can't know. I never can. How can I know him, then? I ask myself. Or is it just that he is my invention?

When a man invents a woman, he invents an emptiness. Some place to disappear inside. He hollows out, he scoops out what's already there: the wet seeds of a melon. He discards, he darkens, he obscures. For us, it's much more difficult. What must we invent? From nothing, from whole cloth? A fortress, a stone monument, a face to fill the gap, Virgil, Orpheus, a steering wheel, an engine. A solidity. That's why Psyche couldn't stand it there with Eros: the invention in the dark. A man might have enjoyed it. We do not enjoy the dark. We aren't after emptiness. Why would we be, housing our own emptiness, or knowing that at any time someone may be getting ready to empty us, or getting ready for the emptiness, to fill or to deny it, to inhabit it or wall it off.

What did he find when he first put himself inside my body? It was more difficult for him, in the beginning, to touch me than to enter me. Now I know why. His hands. He *was* his hands. His penis was only a part of him.

I didn't know about blessed hands, anointed hands. Oil, linen, men in shining vestments, music spilling down, light falling straight to the floor through amethyst- or emerald-colored glass. How could I know about all that? On Sundays we sometimes went to the Congregational church where Mrs. Hastings, who was married to the druggist, played the small organ right in front of us, right in our sight. The sight was clear; the words were comprehensible. Things were as visible as possible. Plainness was urged and prized. We were banishing the darkness: it was what we were about, large, fair Americans, hacking our way through dark woods to a simple architecture and an honest way of life. We didn't believe in darkness. If you shone a light, the darkness would disappear. Or if you shone it in the right place, the shadows would be seen to be only shadows. Nothing.

Clement talks to me about praying in darkness. (Am I a darkness to him?) He was a sixteen-year-old boy asleep in a room of older boys, and they were woken up to pray. He loved it: on his knees on a stone floor, the damp smell of the walls, the first blue light replacing blackness. It's all gone now, he says. Am I meant to make up for it?

His mother is still alive. "If she knew about us it would kill her." Would it? She's active, healthy, only her hearing is a little bad. Suppose he said, "Mother, do you know what my sacred hands have touched?" Would he say *who?* It wouldn't be the thing he meant if he said *who*.

They bound his hands with a linen strip. Oil was poured. His temples shone as if he were a god. He saw his mother's face, and it was shining.

Once we were going through old papers in a box and he showed me a poem he had written to his mother the same month he was ordained. September 1974. Vietnam was over. Even Watergate. And this is how the man was writing:

A Priest's Hands: To His Mother

Hands that you held mom, mother, maker,
Made for play, grime-smeared, and sweat, dirt, soil, all
In a day's play-work. I was that boy
And why, why, why was I of all
Alone, the one, your son, picked, plucked
From your bosom to the face of Him who was a Son
O not alone am I mother, does it matter,
That I roam, far, and the home,
Loved last, only seems lost to me.
Hands, mine, mother, Make Christ's blood
Flesh, from the bulk of bread, real stuff
Earth-stuff, food-stuff, God
Your son this does. Hands that held boys'
Toys, child's things, play things, held yours,
Now God's toys, your boy's no more.
His. Hands. And not by bread alone.

He told me he'd been influenced by Gerard Manley Hopkins. I hadn't read Hopkins very much; apparently Catholics did. He was a priest himself. I didn't know what to say about it all: his poem, his hands, his mother. I tried to forget about it.

Does he forget about it when he touches me, when he goes in the darkness, looking for something, the thing that's gone. That I'm supposed to stand for or replace.

I was the first woman he slept with. He was forty-three.

I suppose that's the interesting part of the story. Except it only happened once: I mean his sleeping with me for the first time. We have a life, it knits itself up, it unravels. It goes on. As the night goes on when you're awake in it, only the darkness gradually lifts. You realize you can turn the lights off, you can read by the bright light of day. We have a life. He had this thing: virginity. He was a man who had it. That's only part of the story.

What could you say he *had*? There was no membrane to be ruptured, given up. And what was it I had? The habit of not having. A forgetfulness. At one point you realize you've forgotten the details of sex; it's harder to make up the picture in your mind. You have to remind yourself: what did it feel like to have a mouth on your breast, a hand between your legs, traveling upward?

He had nothing to forget; he hadn't known anything. I'd felt undesirable. I believed I knew what men desired. Everywhere around them there are pictures of what's obviously desirable: beautiful large round breasts, small firm behinds, long legs, sleek hair, unmarked skin, red-nailed fingers, supple, willing. Every man knew what was *out there,* what was there to be got *if only he could.* And I, too, living in the city, kept seeing images of those bodies, of those women, I had to see them, I regretted it, they made me feel so bad. Why would anyone want me when they could see so clearly and so often what was the true desirable. They knew what was *out there.* They had to know.

But Clement didn't. There was no *out there.* He'd stayed inside. And there was only me.

He didn't know about pornography because he'd never been able to make that kind of purchase. If someone had given him some, he'd have looked at it, he'd certainly have looked at it. Sometimes he longed to. But he didn't know anyone, or he believed he didn't, who would have been able to make a purchase of pornography, to walk up to someone, ask for it, pay for it. There's no better way to describe the extreme strangeness of his life: he believed that no one he'd ever known could buy pornography. Certainly not himself. In the small town where the monastery was, where he was known as Father Clement, where he'd lived for twenty years, he certainly couldn't have.

Do you understand what this means for a woman? That your lover has never looked, in rapt, private avidity, at images of strange women, offering themselves, I have to say, in degradation, to his eyes. He has always been very far from the objects of degradation. It makes an enormous difference. It makes him different from all men.

He lived in a world that managed, for quite some time, to replace sex with a desire for pure emptiness. They took these young men (Clement was sixteen when he entered) and convinced them that by heroic effort they could rise above sex. They could replace it. By what? This is what I try so hard to understand.

I read the kind of books they read, I look at the kinds of art they looked at, I listen to the kind of music that's been suggested to me. Not by Clement, but by Father Boniface. It's hard to talk about Boniface. I don't always like talking about him. When I think of what we do to Clement, what we *have* done, Boniface and I, the two of us, it makes me a little sick.

It can seem dreadful, but in other lights it seems benevolent. I suppose there are a lot of things like that. Neither Boniface nor I is a bad person. We would probably be considered quite good people. Exceptionally good.

Boniface gave me a tape of the monks of Solesmes singing an Easter service. He insisted that I go to the Cloisters on a winter day at twilight. Don't get there before four o'clock, he said. I took a day off from work.

It's not that I have problems talking about Boniface because I dislike him. I love him. I admire him as much as I've admired any man. I know that he loves me. Not in the way that he loves Clement. But I'm a woman, that would be impossible for him. This is one of the many things we keep from Clement. Both of us believe that he must never know.

Father Boniface Lally has known Clement since he was thirteen. Clement joined the Paracletists because of him. They lived under the same roof, in the same monastery, for over twenty years. Boniface was Clement's confessor, his superior, his father, his brother, his best friend. Now Boniface is in a nursing home. He's had a series of debilitating strokes. You might say, you wouldn't be at all wrong to say, that Boniface's going into the nursing home made everything happen. Or was the end of everything, depending on your point of view.

One day he said: "I don't know if you understand that for a long time everything held. You don't know what it means to live like that."

"You're right, I don't."

"I want you to know what it's like. It's important for Clement."

He wanted to show me, but he could hardly walk, he was confined to his bed. Some days he could sit up in a wheelchair. He had to try to describe a whole world to me in words, and sometimes he became aphasic so he lost his words. Or sometimes there were peculiar gaps between them, or reversals, or misplacements that could make it hard to understand. He said, "It doesn't matter that I have to tell you everything. There's not much left to show."

"It was complete. It stood. It helped us for a very long time. And then it went away. It only took twenty years from the first slip. There's no place I could take you to now that wouldn't be dead. I must make you believe: it used to be alive. You can only understand him if you know that."

We both loved him. We wanted him to be understood.

"In the mornings sometimes I would open up the church. This was when I was in Springfield, in St. Sulpice. It was over a hundred years old, so I felt people had been there for years, praying, whatever people do when they say they pray, mainly asking for what they wanted, but also in despair, and then they'd been married there, and seen their children baptized, and the people they'd loved brought there as a last stop. It was both heavy and insubstantial, that place in those mornings. The cold of the stone floor would be pulled up toward the sunlight. This little space where so much life had gone on. And I had this little space, the time I was alive between the time I was born and I would die. The time, the space in that church was something in between, not life, not nonlife, unhectic, uncrowded, almost unalive, but not frightening. The light was quiet, as if it weren't from the sun but from the moon. The sun, the full sun, triumphant, and I never wanted that.

"I'm not sorry it broke up. It wasn't really the truth about life. So many lies to keep it up. Too much left out. They insisted that it be left out. It's better now. More truthful. I'm very hopeful about the way things are. Even here, in this place. Maybe especially here."

Hope. It's not something I'd thought of, that we think of nowadays. For them, Boniface and Clement, it's one of the touchstones. They think a lot about what hope might be. They believe in it. And they are hopeful. That is to say they believe in open situations. This is what they put their weight behind. Most of us feel we're on a precipice, looking down at a torrent; behind us are the hordes who don't even see us, who would simply, to get wherever they're going, push us over. This isn't what they believe. They believe in a parade, not orderly, but going somewhere. I don't know how they can believe in it, how they can look around at the world and still believe in it: they say they do. It gives them hope. I know I'm not a hopeful person.

Only sometimes I have an idea of the kind of thing they believe in, that they hope for, and then I myself believe and hope. But it has nothing to do with God. It happened once, for instance, when we were out with people, dancing, listening to samba players. We'd been asked to go by a nurse at St. Gervaise who's quite attached to Boniface. She keeps wanting to confess to him: her sins, her sexual misconduct. Boniface won't let her confess. He says that he'll listen to her as a friend, but she must stop thinking of herself as sinning. As someone who sins.

Susanna, who wants to confess to Boniface, tends him with the devotion of a beloved daughter. Or is it all expiation? Feeding him on the days when his hands shake too much to get a fork to his mouth, walking beside him, chattering about her neighbors or her children, or the price of green peppers or beef, while it takes him ten minutes to move twenty feet, doing all this, does she feel she's been absolved? Or does she just feel happy with him, for no reason, or because he's good to her, he listens to her all the time, he helps her make sense of her past. Who knows? What can be known is that she cares for him with a tenderness that makes all the difference. We'd do anything for her, Clement and I. So when we visited one night, Clement and I together, and before she gave us the report of Boniface's week (always trustworthy, the report of a connoisseur), she told us that her uncle was up from Brazil and playing in a famous concert hall, would we please come, would we bring Boniface, it would make her so happy, what could we say, but yes, of course?

Taking Boniface anywhere outside St. Gervaise is always a bit of a horror. All the equipment! The world of the permanently ill is a complete world, a real culture, with its own rules, its own standards, and perhaps above all its own artifacts. All the objects made of plastic, rubber, metal, held together with pins or screws or clamps or tape, to do what the body is meant to do by itself. Pulleys to do the work of the legs, tubes for eating, shitting, pissing, straps to keep the spine upright, bandages to do the skin's work, pumps, and endless small receptacles, a nightmare image of the body, what we force ourselves to forget it is, a machine that keeps us (what do we mean *us?*) alive.

We rented a van with an elevator that could lift Boniface into it. We got the equipment packed up and arranged. Or I should say Susanna did. Then we set off.

Susanna was beside herself with happiness.

She isn't beautiful. She's squat, dun-colored like a hen, around twenty-eight, with wide hips and a bad complexion. I'm always surprised at the extent of her amorous adventures given her plain looks, but Boniface laughed at me and said I was naïve to be surprised. She'd bought a Panama hat with a blue band for him.

Many of her friends were at the concert. She kept introducing Boniface to all her friends. "A priest," she kept saying, or I think that's what she said, holding his chin like he was one of those Hindu baby gods, sacred and helpless.

All kinds of people came into the hall, people wearing nylon shirts and electric blue pants, well-dressed men with fashionable, slicked back hair, women with hair pulled back against their expensive skulls (I kept thinking about all that cosmetic surgery in Brazil and wondering who'd had what done), white people, people with brown skin, black skin, blue-black skin, everyone polite, pushing a little but not dangerously, calm, expectant.

The leader of the group came out onstage. He had beautifully cut silver hair and was very tan. He was wearing a plain white shirt and well-tailored black pants. He introduced the others in his group. Some people in the crowd began cheering as familiar faces appeared on the stage: a short woman in a navy blue pantsuit, two old men, looking strained (one was Susanna's uncle), a tall black man, smiling.

At first, the music began slowly, it rose up like a curve or an upward spiral. Everyone was thinking of a time they had made love and had been happy at it, a time when there was no rush, it was warm, you had all day. The audience was sighing, they were almost silent. Clement and I held hands. We were proud to be part of it: the human race that had sex and liked it. I felt Clement's gratitude to me for bringing him into all this, but I wanted to forget it. What can you do with sexual gratitude? There's nothing you can do.

The squat woman sang about men who loved and left her. Then she sang about nights of flowers. At least that's what I like to think. We were all drowsing animals, hypnotized together, as if we shared one pulse. Then suddenly Susanna's uncle picked up a tambourine and a stick. The rhythm changed. It was still curvy, uninsistent, but more joyous now, no longer about languorous love, but about street life shared: the world outside we were all a part of. Everyone. No one was left out. People were dancing in the aisles. Susanna and her friends held Boniface's hands as they danced. Clement and I held each other and danced, right in public, unafraid as we had never been. Women in their sixties danced together, a girl in a red dress with many ruffles twirled alone in the front of the balcony, men danced the game of playful dares, everyone was with everyone, everyone was at home. Then the squat woman began singing about home and people started weeping. All the home songs, reminding them of the familiar food, the trees, the names of the streets, the houses, their mothers, the children they'd left behind. Everyone was weeping: we all knew what it was to be bereft, unmoored, and strangers. Then the music became lively again and people danced up and down the aisles in lines, danced out of the hall, not wanting the musicians to leave the theatre and go back to their lives, we loved them so, we all knew we'd never again be this happy.

I watched the people who knew how to move so beautifully, who probably didn't do so well in this world, who were poor, or criminal, or victimized, or overworked, and then I watched the people more like me who did well in this world, who moved un-beautifully, but who weren't poor, away from home, in danger. But it was all right. No one made fun of us. No one was excluded.

I knew that in a few minutes it wouldn't be like this. People would make distinctions. They would once again be rude or snob-bish, they'd push each other and perhaps hurt each other by harsh words or blows. Perhaps men would fight with knives over the dancing women. Perhaps in nine months, because of the arousal of this music, children would be born into miserable lives. But for a few minutes I had belief, that life could be like this, that the gift of moving beautifully, spontaneously to music would be honored, would be the important thing, that everyone, including Boniface and the old people who looked as if dancing like this would cause their bones to break, the beautiful, the unbeautiful, the lucky, the unfortunate, would come together. I wanted a world that was more like this more of the time. This is the closest I can come to faith.

But there's no one I can say this to. Not Boniface. Not Clement, certainly. They might understand, or think they did, but to them-selves they'd be saying, "That's not it. That isn't what we had at all."

And they'd be right.

What was it I was talking about? Oh, I remember, Boniface. The kind of conversations Boniface and I would have.

"If he leaves, if Clement leaves the priesthood, if he's no longer what he is, that's not good. He can't be what he is without being a priest. What would he be without it?"

"Less." We both knew that.

"He's the best of it. He took the best it had to offer. What else could he be?"

A professional?

My husband?

An ordinary man?

I didn't suggest any of these things.

I don't need him to be my husband. But I don't want to be without him. I don't want to live like that again.

Do you know what it's like when you give up the idea that you'll ever again be prized? In a way it's not so terrible. But all the songs, the stories, are about someone else. Some other kind of person.

You hear songs or stories, you see lovers, any age, any people, just walking arm in arm. On any kind of street. The wind can be blowing, it can be lifting sheets of newspaper, throwing whole clumps of pages into the river. You can be by a river or else on a dark street, where there are looming buildings. The sun can be bright, or not; it can be morning, evening. It can be a bit cold or else tropically humid. If it's cold, for example, you'll see a man take a woman's hand and chafe it. You'll see his lips saying, "You're so cold." On a languid day, she'll lean against him. "I'm so tired," she'll be saying, or "It's so nice to lean against you like this." Or teenagers will be kissing in a shopping mall. An old woman will help her husband across the street because the light is beginning to turn. Anything can do it. Anything you see, or read, or hear on the radio and you think, "That's not me. None of that is me. I won't have that anymore." You feel a bit self-pitying, a little angry, but it passes, it's not terrible, many people live that way, a number of my friends. I expected to live that way the rest of my life. Living, knowing your body is of no concern to anyone except yourself. You worry that one day you might get sick, that you'll become a nuisance or a burden. But that's all. You know that's all your body will be to anybody else: a nuisance or a burden. No one will look at you again attentively or lovingly. No gaze will ever rest on you for anything but the merest second. Then it will move on. You grow to expect that, you give up expecting anything else.

Mine was the first body Clement ever looked at. How happy he was, looking at my body. He would thank me for my body, as if I had invented it for him. In his eye, I was a gift, and gifted.

But I wasn't talking about that. I don't want to talk about it yet. Before that, there's much more to understand. Particularly about Boniface. Or Boniface and me. Or Boniface and me and Clement. I put myself, the small female word *me,* the motherly, the calm, sororal me, between the two male names. It looks like it belongs there.

Boniface met Clement when Clement was thirteen years old. It was 1959. He was preaching a mission in Clement's parish. Do you hear how easily I use those words, *mission, parish.* Two years ago, I would have used them as I used a foreign word, a technical expression. But no more.

"I was preaching a mission in this awful town, in western New York State. It was still in our province, though. I liked it when there were those long drives. You know those towns with the ugly names, Fischs Eddy, or Occam or Vestal, Roscoe or Fort Wells. Towns far from the water, with no thought given to the look of things, everything practical, except the few large houses with those windows that were supposed to show prosperity. Now if a Catholic family got hold of one of them, watch out. Walking into one of those houses made me sick. I'd lived in Europe. I'd studied in the order's college in Rome. That's where I first had sex. With another young American priest. Not from our order though."

Boniface would talk like that, tell you about the first time he had sex, but make it seem like the important part of the story was that his partner wasn't a Paracletist. That was their order, Clement's and Boniface's: the Paracletists. I should say it still is their order. But that doesn't seem right. Not the way things are with Clement.

"I guess I was a snob about Americans, but there was something about those houses, those windows in western New York State built with money sweated out in mills or factories. Self-loving money, the worst kind. And the ugly churches. I could pack them to the rafters. 'This year once again, Father Boniface will be preaching our Lenten mission.' That was all they needed to hear. The wives would get their husbands out. God knows what they were making them pay for.

"And there I was, up there in front of them, hating myself, accusing myself of bad faith. (I had no faith then. Clement restored my faith.) Knowing I was mediocre. But I was eloquent. I had them in the palm of my hand, all kinds of families, businessmen with briefcases, workmen with lunchpails, on their knees every night saying the family rosary. And I didn't believe a word. I'd have these poor souls coming to Confession, and all I'd say was, it's all right, don't worry, don't be so hard on yourself. God loves you. And I didn't believe in anything. God or love.

"There I was in that town, Wellsberg, St. Theresa's Parish, ready to do another false, disgusting trick. And then I saw him. Clement. He was thirteen. He was the head altar boy. He helped me vest. I felt I was being dressed by an angel.

"He could move so quietly and do everything so well. You know what I'm talking about."

We were both silent, dreamy, thinking about Clement's body, its movements, the body we both loved, whose slowness, whose thoroughness and deliberateness of gesture, whose insistent stillness could be painfully arousing. So that you felt pale and insubstantial, like a moth endlessly circling a warm globe.

"And then I watched him kneeling in prayer. The sun fell on him, the light hit his gold hair. He was a perfect form, like something in mathematics. He disciplined himself to kneel perfectly, he told me later, not to slouch, not to lean back on his heels. He was an athlete. He thought it was the least that he could do.

"At night, I lay in that awful bed in the smelly rectory, wanting to hold him, thinking I was defiled and vowing that I would never defile him, never, but that I would have him with me. Just to be with me. So I could look at him, be near him.

"And I did.

"If you knew his family, you'd see I wasn't wrong, that nothing about what I did was wrong. They had an awful farm a few feet off the highway. You know how Clement loves things to be run well, needs them to be, it's a hunger. Nothing on that farm or in that house ran well. The porch sagged. The sills on all the windows rotted. The animals got diseases. The fireplace didn't draw. Slates were missing from the roof. The windows in the barn were broken. Clement worked like an animal to try to make it right. But he was only a child. His father was a bad, nasty drunk. Clement couldn't make up for it. And the rest of his brothers and sisters weren't worth anything. They were like the father. All six of them. All of them with those mean mouths and those dead, dark eyes."

"Clement says his mother was a saint," I told Boniface.

"I don't know, but I know she was different from the rest of them. She wanted something better. She did the best she could. Maybe that means she was a saint.

"When I came along, she knew it was Clement's way out. She let me have him. She knew he'd never be hers again. Sometimes I think she knew about me, what I felt for Clement, Frank his name was. She was like that. She might have known. You never knew exactly what she knew.

"I never saw her, afterward, except at Clement's ordination, when she was embarrassed about her bad hat, her bad teeth, her bad dress. They weren't that religious. I don't think they got much out of his being a priest. Even her, though Clement doesn't like to think of that. She lost the only child who understood her, who was any comfort to her. The father lost his best worker. And we got him. We won him. He was ours. The church's. The order's. Mine.

"I took him away from all that ugliness. All that coarseness. All that hopelessness. I wasn't wrong. Do you know what that house was like? A house without a kind word, or a joke, or even a jar of flowers in the middle of the table."

I said to Boniface, "What would he have been like if you hadn't come along?"

He said, "I think he might have joined the army. He liked defending things, standing for things. Maybe I saved his life."

Occasionally, Boniface and I, both of us, hear voices telling us that we have stolen something, lied, or at least misappropriated, that we are misers, usurers, embezzlers. We don't allow ourselves these thoughts. Or not for long. But it isn't that we don't know what we do.

I love Clement and I love my children, we're connected by ties of flesh. Other than the three of them, I can truthfully say I love Boniface most in the world. I know that he loves me. I guess that you could say our tie is fleshly too.

We both love Clement in the flesh. But only I have been his lover. What do I mean by that? That I've been penetrated by him. Brought him to orgasm. These are the ways in which my loving Clement is different from Boniface's. All those years.

I wonder, both of us wonder, how it's possible, or if it is, that Clement never knew.

All the years that he desired Clement, lay on his bed yearning, used the image of Clement as he lay with other men or brought himself satisfaction, Boniface never, as they say, laid a hand on Clement. Sometimes when Clement was very tired, after he'd done a lot of physical work, Boniface would massage his shoulders or give him a back rub. "My joy was very great then," Boniface said when he told me. "I was tremendously happy to be able to do that. For him. For myself."

He didn't approach Clement sexually because he was afraid that Clement would respond, or comply, rather, only out of obedience. "An obedient lover," Boniface said to me once, "who could imagine anything worse? I was his superior, his confessor. I didn't think that he loved men. Or perhaps I didn't want to. You see, for us, the way we were, it may be different now, it was important to feel that a 'regular' man, a straight man, found you acceptable as a human being. Our self-hatred was very great. I wasted too many years in self-hatred."

Boniface and I love each other in this way: as if our love for Clement were a house built on a cliff overlooking a rough sea. Outside the waves beat, the stars are brilliant in a dark, wet sky, but we're dry and safe. And in this house, we house our treasure. We keep it pure and safe from danger. It is always at our reach, and to our use. We sit near each other in the house and listen to the buffeting outside. We talk late into the night. Watching. Keeping watch. There's nothing we can't say.

We ask each other, Boniface and I, if it's possible he doesn't know that we do this to him. If it's possible that he's never known the real story of Boniface's love. Clement is like that; it's often difficult to know what it is he knows. If he knows what's been done to him. What's being done.

Supposing that he did? What would that mean about him?

We don't think of that: we tell each other it's impossible, and we believe that it must be.

Clement misses enormous numbers of clues about the world, and yet he is a kind of genius about human suffering, for going to the heart of it, searching it out, like a heat-detecting missile. I've seen it again and again. He'll walk into a room, it could be any kind of room, he can be in any situation, and someone will see just him. You'll feel that when you're with him: the force of his having been seen. There'll be a kind of flicker, or a click, like a candle being lit, or a bone breaking, and you'll see Clement carried up on a wave of someone's sadness. Sometimes nothing will be said. But often, very often, people speak to Clement in extraordinary ways. As if all their lives they'd been waiting for him to arrive, to walk into a room where they just happened to be, waiting all their lives for him to walk in, to arrive. So they could tell their story. The one story of all the stories they needed to tell to the one person, him, they had been waiting for.

Sometimes I think it's just the way he looks. Or anyway that's a big part of it. This is the kind of thing I say to Boniface, "Supposing he just had different hair." Clement is forty-five years old, but he has a child's hair, still unruly, hair you almost never see on an adult. It sticks up in the back. I suppose he could spend a certain amount of money and it would be different. But to spend money on his physical appearance, Clement would have to change completely. If I ever saw that he was spending money on something like that, clothes or barbers, after-shave, things for his hair, I'd know that I had lost him. I'd tell Boniface about it and we'd both know we had lost.

It's very possible I'll lose him, we both will, and the church will, and the world. I know just what the danger is. And almost who, and though who isn't important, it's a type of woman, what she represents. And maybe it would be the best thing for him. To lose everything. To be lost. I just don't know.

I was talking about his hair and how he looks. He's large-boned, the hair on his chest and legs is sparse. He takes very long strides; his walk is always purposeful, at once young and as if he'd never been allowed a youth. In bed he's like that too: both boyish and unyouthful: a bit heavy, slow, deliberate in his love for me, a son and father over-responsible for my pleasure, his own taking him, each time, by surprise.

I would hate to think his body was no longer mine. No, I don't mean that, it's impossible, I'm a woman, how can I talk about possessing a man's body. How can you possess what you can't enter? What you don't invade, penetrate, fill with the unfamiliar, fill with the outside world, fill with yourself, the product of your body, all those swarming colonies of creatures: protozoans, tadpoles, fish, homunculi. How could a woman be said to possess a man?

And is this what I want? Or is it just that I want him to be beside me in a way I can depend on?

I don't want him to belong to anybody else. I want to be the only body he lives a bodily life beside. I want to be the only body that he enters. I hope this isn't too much to ask.

If he stays with me, and me alone, he still can be a priest. The world needs him to be a priest. Because of the way he can be with people as a priest. I'll tell you something I saw him do that he could only have done as a priest.

We met John and Jean Mobley and their daughter Jeannine for the first time at a conference. The diocese had sent both Clement and me, as well as the three other women on the staff, to the conference on the treatment of abused women. It was in Kansas City. We stayed at a Holiday Inn. Late that night, Clement came to my room and we made love on the rough, toxic sheets of the king-size bed. On the second day of the conference, the Mobleys gave a presentation. John Mobley introduced himself as a recovering abuser. "There's no such thing as an ex-abuser," he said. "I struggle every day. All I have to do is look at the scars on my poor baby's body and I know all about that struggle, and how I have to take it one day at a time."

Then his wife patted his hand and rubbed his back. Their daughter stood up and walked around the room. The father stood next to her and pointed out how one of her shoulders was lower than the other. "See this?" he said to the audience. "I did this to my little girl. I broke her shoulder, but she didn't want to go to the doctors, to protect me. And her shoulder's like this forever because she loved me more than she loved herself."

Jeannine wasn't a baby. She was twenty-three. This was what she and her parents did for a living. They conducted workshops for abusers and their families. They'd learned a lot from AA and various other therapies; they put it together and traveled around the country charging twenty-five hundred dollars for a weeklong workshop. They also addressed church and civic groups, and did local TV and radio. They spoke at conferences like ours. I don't know how much they charged for that.

They billed themselves as an all-American family. John had been in insurance, Jean had been, as she said, "A full-time homemaker. Why I was never out of my kitchen, and now, with the road life's taken us on, I'm never home more than two days at a time. But I believe we're needed out there, that's what keeps me going." Jeannine, they said, had been a cheerleader and an honors student. She loved to write poetry.

They were probably right that what they were doing was important. They reminded people that abuse wasn't limited to the poor. Maybe somewhere, someone would admit he'd hurt his wife and children after seeing them. I don't know, maybe. They looked so much like what so many Americans seem to want to look like. Their model must have been the daytime soaps. Jean was forty-eight, but tall and slender. Her hair was long; it had a coppery tinge; her eye shadow was coppery and she outlined her brownish lipstick with a thin copper line. Jeannine's hair was cut the same way as her mother's, it was lighter, flatter, thinner, with much less bounce, as if she'd been denied whatever force sprang from her mother's body. She looked at her mother the way a younger plainer girl looks at a striking older girl: with despair and self-hate. I suppose Jean always hoped people would say, "Why that can't be your daughter. You look more like sisters." But no one would ever say that because Jean always seemed younger than her daughter.

Jeannine was one of those flat-chested girls with too light eyelashes and shoes that make you think she'd bought them in the A&P. You worried when you looked at her that those shoes weren't enough support, with their thin straps and overly flat soles, that she'd turn over on her ankle and her ankle would just snap. She had thin, straight, birdlike legs. When she stood up and said, "I just want to say how proud I am of both my parents, and our journey together and our healing love," I wanted to get on a plane for some fancy resort where I'd have drinks brought to me at poolside and dive under the blue water where I'd never have to hear a word about abuse or families of any sort again.

But I assumed that was my fault; everyone else seemed to admire them. I looked around me and I thought all eyes but mine were filled with tears. I didn't dare ask Clement what he thought.

After the presentation, the diocese hired them to give a workshop at our center for a week. I tried to remember that it was likely they could do a few of the women and the kids some good. Although it didn't seem to me we were exactly the right place, since no husbands or boyfriends were allowed even to know where their women and children were. But the monsignor from the family life office liked the idea, and he didn't give us a choice.

I'm never comfortable with public confessions or displays. The part of my job that involves sitting in circles with people holding hands and telling intimate things to groups of strangers is the part I like least. I know it's my fault: some legacy of Midwestern propriety I don't value in myself. I have to say I've seen cases where this kind of group thing has done enormous good, where it's the only thing that has done good. It's just that I don't like it; I know it's my fault. Clement doesn't like it either, but he tries. I don't even try.

Belle Riggs, the senior staff person, had no use for the Mobleys either, but I only found that out after they'd been around a day or two. Belle thinks the whole white world is crazy as a matter of course. She thought the Mobleys were some white folks on to a good thing. But she didn't think it was worth bucking the diocese: she figured they'd be gone soon enough. We'd hide in her office and she'd imitate them. Once she said, "I wonder who owns more jewelry, him or her." John wore a gold ID bracelet and a gold chain around his neck. Usually, he didn't wear a tie, so you could see the chain grazing the neck of one of the pastel shirts he liked to wear.

John and Jean saw they weren't making it with Belle and me, so they kept trying to flatter us. When that didn't work, they acted like we weren't there. Some of the women would come to us and tell us how wonderful the Mobleys were. We didn't know if they'd been sent. Most of the women just ignored them.

The Mobleys didn't know quite what to make of Clement. They left him to Jeannine. They asked if she could be with him and the children when they worked, in the garden or with the animals. "Jeannine just loves nature," they said. "Particularly animals. I wouldn't be surprised if she worked for a vet someday."

That was the most that had ever been said about Jeannine's future. She couldn't have been in college; she traveled with her parents all the time. I asked Clement if she really seemed to like animals. He looked up at me. "I don't think she can like anything. Her heart is dead."

That's the kind of thing Clement says. That's the kind of language he uses. Comfortably. As if everyone else did.

I don't know what Jeannine said to him, if anything. She must have said something. But, without consulting anyone, certainly none of us on the staff, Clement called the Mobleys into his office. From what I gather he told John and Jean that they must stop taking Jeannine around with them. It was bad for her, couldn't they see that? She was sad all the time. She was a young girl, and young girls should be happy. She should go to college. She should be with people her own age. Later she could decide what it was she wanted to do with her life.

I heard Clement's door slam. I saw Jean pull her daughter by the arm. "What'd you tell him? Just what'd you tell him?"

"Nothing," I heard Jeannine say.

"He must've got that idea from somebody, young lady. Where'd he get an idea like that if not from you?"

"Nowheres," Jeannine said.

The Mobleys left early. Clement said Jeannine told him she liked her life the way it was. She was helping people, that's what was important to her. She said she was sorry she'd given him the wrong impression.

Did Clement do the right thing? I don't know. I almost never know about these things. But I think he did. Perhaps for a few minutes Jeannine Mobley felt not alone. That somebody could see her and would speak for her. Even if it didn't do any good. Even if he didn't have the right to.

He felt it was his right to, as a priest. As a priest, he felt he had to. I don't know what he'd feel he had to do if he weren't a priest. I don't know what he'd think of as his place. It would certainly be different. For a priest, boundaries aren't important. They mean nothing, in fact less than nothing: it's a kind of duty that they be ignored. A priest can say anything as long as it's the truth. He never has to worry if it's his place to say it: every place is his place, since he has no place of his own. It doesn't matter that what he says or does might not do people any good. If he sees it as the truth he has to say it. Or at least I think that's what Clement believes.

And I think that being my lover has displaced him. I feel it most when his being my lover doesn't go well for him. He's forty-five but like a teenager in some ways. Of course there are bound to be some bad times. Once he said, "I hate it when I feel too young to give you what you need. People have been calling me father for twenty years."

I don't know who he wants to be when he's with me, or who he thinks he is. He keeps saying he loves being my lover but I don't know exactly what that means. Something romantic.

Coming to it so late, he's very romantic about sex. Like a boy new at the game. The game, it is a game, but he can never see that. Sometimes the seriousness of our lovemaking is a burden to me. Sometimes I want to say to him: "Haven't you ever heard of love *play*. Fore*play*." By which, of course, we mean that which happens before penetration. Before orgasm. By orgasm we mean the male orgasm, that shaping punctuation. Everything stops, or changes when he comes.

But Clement's always serious about sex. This is a legacy of poverty: he was sexually poor, and he wears his legacy like a winter coat passed down by a dead brother. Sometimes I want a romp: athletic, careless, and desanctified. Slang words for body parts. Something fast, and jokey. A quick slap on the ass, then up and dressed.

This will never happen with Clement. He's reverential about my body. The one body he has ever seen. By which I mean looked at. The one body from which he hasn't felt it was his duty to avert his eyes.

At first he wouldn't look at me at all. He wanted to be inside me: he'd thought about that, being inside a woman, for so long. He was famished for the inside of my body. Any body, really. It just happened to be mine.

Does that sound harsh? Sometimes I think that for Clement I was only this: I was at the right place at the right time. The time when everything broke up, collapsed. And then Boniface approved of me. The circumstances were correct. My body was just incidental.

I should tell you what I mean when I say everything was breaking up.

Clement joined the Paracletists, which is to say he left his family, his home, the world, in June of 1962. John Kennedy was in the White House. Pope John was in the Vatican. The air was shot through with ideas like silver nitrate. He was on that farm in Biltz, fifteen miles southwest of Elmira, in the west of New York State that is, with the drunken father and the overworked mother, the too-numerous and undercared-for children, the rotten hasps on the barn doors, the broken panes in far too many of the windows, the animals with coughs or mange or difficult births the vet wouldn't attend because too much was owed him. There he was, working like an ox trying to keep it all together. In came Boniface, aged thirty-eight, with his silver hair and movie-star blue eyes, his eloquence, his passion when he said that grace was everywhere and that Jesus came to tell men that they were to have life and have it more abundantly. Who'd been to Rome and knew people in Africa. Who loved Clement from the first moment he saw him kneeling in the church with the light on his hair, who believed he was saving him, who wanted above all to have Clement near him, or perhaps it's best to say, to have him for himself.

And did Clement want that as well? What did he really want? What did he want that he could never know he wanted?

He wanted to have life, and have it more abundantly.

He wanted to get away from home.

Only Boniface could have made it happen. Could have made it possible, no, could have made it *not impossible* for Clement's father to have let him go. Boniface is physically helpless now, but I understand what his power was. I've seen pictures. I've heard him talk. He was someone who walked into a church, walked into a crowd of people, and got them to love him and to want to do whatever it was he said. He was used to making people do what he wanted. He said it was very bad for him when he had sex: corrupting and distorting. He couldn't give up that habit, that skill, that expertise. Even in bed, he told me. You see, we can speak like that.

Boniface said that Clement's father worked him like a slave. In order to let go of his slave, the father had to be made to believe in hellfire, to believe that hellfire awaited him if he did not. Boniface, at that point, hadn't believed in hell for fifteen years. But he made Clement's father believe in it. Or rather Frank's father. He was still Frank.

This new woman, who I'm so afraid that I'm losing him to, calls him Frank to tease him. She dances into his office waving her hands with their long pink nails, clicking her shoes with their high heels, spinning around him, putting her hands in front of his eyes saying "Guess who," then crying about her husband who has beaten her and almost killed her son, then dancing, clicking, waving, darting out from hidden and surprising places, calling his name. Frank. I wonder how she knows. He must have told her. I wonder how that happened.

Frank's mother had to be made to believe not in hellfire but in her son's sacredness. His sacred hands. She had to make her husband feel he owed her this, for all the drunkenness, the poverty, the disappointment, the abuse. He owed her a sacred son. He owed her not standing in the way.

Clement, Frank, could only leave his family—or leave them in the lurch—if he believed that he was called to do so and that to ignore the call was not only perilous to his soul but, what would have moved him more, ungrateful. It wasn't hard for Boniface to make him believe that. He'd done it to a lot of boys.

So that by 1962 there was a whole cohort of them: shining like bull calves whose horns had been painted gold, joining the Paracletists so they could be like Father Boniface.

It was his personal force that made it happen. The Paracletists were a mediocre order, and not glamorous. Their specialty was Parish missions and retreat work. They'd had some foreign missions once, but they'd concentrated on China, and when Mao came to power, they had been killed or banished; this had so alarmed the general council of the order that they had decided to give up foreign missions altogether.

I told Boniface that being part of the church allowed him to put a face on a lot of history. He could hear the words *Long March* and attach them to a body of someone familiar. "Not so many bodies anymore, and not the same history," he said. "The old guys aren't quite so free to send the fresh-faced boys around the world. They're not going out so readily, not quite so quick to pass on the dead Roman ways. Not quite so quick or quite so happy with their own salvation. Better now: We stole too much history. Time to give it back."

When Boniface says things like that, I'm not always sure whether or not he's become aphasic. Talking about the past, the past whose moorings he was happy to be free of, makes his mind wander, and his tongue. I can't always follow, but he doesn't seem to care.

When the foreign missions were given up, the Paracletists lost whatever allure their work might have brought. It was only Father Boniface who drew young men. If there were others, I've never heard about them. Maybe it's Boniface's one remaining vanity: to believe there was no one else like him. But by the late sixties, the drama of the parish mission was the thing of the past. The star preachers, even Boniface, were like star vaudevillians, a bit embarrassing, invited to perform out of an instinct of old charity on the part of some pastor, or his guilt or anxiety for what he felt he was allowing to slip away.

Most of the boys Boniface recruited didn't stay. Some of them went off to universities and never came back. Some of them fell in love. No new men joined up. The older ones began to die. In 1980, Clement was the youngest Paracletist in the Northeastern Province by twenty years. Between 1980 and 1985 two new men joined. Neither of them stayed. One became a Trappist, one made money in cellular phones.

The cellular-phone man is probably Clement's best friend. Besides Boniface of course. Clement visits Charlie and his wife and children on Long Island. They have two girls named Kelly and Shannon. The house is huge: a prefab house they say they put together from a kit. I don't know what that means. I keep imagining a little box with thousands of tiny pieces that, put together, make a house. Or an enormous box shaped like a pirate's treasure chest with a few very large pieces in it. Charlie and his wife don't have what seems to me enough furniture for this big house: their living room chairs look like they're from Alice in Wonderland; you sit on them and you're afraid you'll be reduced to a miniature, and pretty soon you'll disappear. Charlie's wife says that when the girls are grown, she'll go back to teaching school. She organizes the town soccer league, and swimming lessons in the summer at the public pool. She's very clean. Her hair is very short. When we visit them, Clement introduces me as a good friend he works with. I don't know what they really think. Sometimes I see Charlie (Clement has a hard time not calling him Bonnie, Bonaventure was his religious name) squinting a little in Clement's presence. As if the light of his own broken promises (leaving the order as Clement did not) were too strong for him to fully open up his eyes.

By 1988, when Boniface went into the nursing home, there were only seventy-six men in the order. Boniface asked to be put in the nursing home. He didn't want the shame of having Clement care for his grotesque body. He saw that Clement was becoming a slave again. He thought he'd freed him from slavery in bringing him into the order. Now he was a slave to a house and property that was too big a job for one man, a slave to the older priests who complained and demanded things like ruined courtesans. Clement was the only able-bodied one among them. And he served them all: old men, house, property, and animals. Boniface couldn't stand to be part of it. After his second stroke, when he asked to be taken to a nursing home, he said it was because there was a chance for rehabilitation there. But he knew there was no chance, or very little, he'd be rehabilitated. He just couldn't stand to see Clement turning into his slave.

In 1989, Father Marcellus had a heart attack and died. In 1990 Father Luke, aged eighty-three, died in his sleep. Clement was all alone in the big house. The Motherhouse, they called it, that odd poetry of ecclesiastical bureaucracy. Motherhouse. And then the diocese stepped in.

Although they're ninety miles away and in the middle of the woods, the Paracletists' Monastery of Our Mother of Sorrows is under the jurisdiction of the Archdiocese of New York. Clement was summoned to the chancery. The priests on the governing council were in the office too. They told Clement the truth. Gave him the dope, in Father Louis, the provincial's, words. Showed him the lay of the land, according to monsignor. They were going to close down the Motherhouse. Or, really, they told him, that wasn't the best way to think of it. They were going to reuse the space in a way that had to do with the church's expanding, ever-changing ministry. The church is a living thing, the monsignor said. If it gets stuck in the past, it dies.

They told him they'd like him to stay around to facilitate the transfer. They were sorry if it caused him pain. They suggested counseling. But they hoped he'd see in time that it wasn't the end of something: it was a new beginning. They hoped in time, they said, that he'd get around to seeing it like that.

I know what his face must have looked like. It must have made them feel awful. Don't get the idea that I feel sympathy for them, any of them, I don't. I hate them, they were crude in the handling of the man I love. They hurt him, and I can't forgive them. You can see how that would have to be. But even so I feel sorry for them, having to look at his face after they'd told him something like that.

I've never seen anyone who can look so miserable as Clement, whose features can be so entirely saturated by misery, and then be saturated in the self-same way with joy. I can imagine what his face looked like in that room in the chancery (more poetry, I hear polished teak boxes slipping into one another, *chancery*). What it looked like on the bus trip down, and later on the trip back up. I know his face better than I know any face except my children's. Better than my children's. I have seen his face in the contortions and abandonment of what's called love, but isn't love, because at that moment you are always the most alone. No one else matters at the moment of orgasm. A second after, yes perhaps. But at that moment you are very far away. Why would you call it love?

Why should we call anything about sex love? I've loved only some of the people I've had sex with. I haven't had sex with most of the people I have loved. And I know this about my love for Clement, the man with whom I have been most intensely sexual, whose body has known mine, who's given me the deepest pleasure of my life (how did he do it, knowing what he first knew about sex—nothing—and given the fact that everything doesn't always go perfectly well?). I know that if something happens, which it quite easily could, so that we were no longer what is known as lovers, we'll go on loving each other in some way until one of us dies. Even as Clement and Boniface love each other. I know that to be the case.

Or maybe that's not right at all. It won't happen if she—one of the women I can well imagine losing to—speaks to him like this. If, raising her dark pink or her blood-red nails she says, "You are never to see her again. Over my dead body. It's her or me."

The woman whom I could very well lose him to would be capable of words, phrases, sentences like that. As I am not. Maybe that means she deserves him more than I. That she's more womanly than I, more generous, more natural. I often think that I'm neither generous nor natural. Except sometimes with my children. There are times when I know for certain that I have been both with them.

I could never marry Clement since he doesn't understand my children. He thinks they don't appreciate me, don't respect me, that they're ungrateful, lazy, spoiled. (He'd never say I spoiled them. He'd never criticize me in that way: not in any way. We've been lovers two years and he's never criticized me. If he has to tell me I've done something wrong—failed to change the oil in the car, been too harsh with someone at the shelter—he tells me as if his words were some gnarled root he needed all his strength to pull out and expose. It's a bad thing for both of us.)

Nevertheless, he's harsh, much too harsh with my children. I couldn't place the harshness at first: not in this man who seemed so loving, so responsible, so free of judgment and the will to dominate. I should have sensed something watching him with his dog.

He has a dog, named Buddy, whom he rescued from the woods. The dog was starving; who knows where he came from. Clement was out doing some winter chore: now I remember what it was. There'd been a storm the night before, a heavy snowstorm, and a branch had fallen on the roof of the shed where the tractor and the snowplow were kept. There was an inch of snow on the ground, but Clement had to get up on the ladder to see if the branch had made a hole in the roof. He had to check on it before another storm came up. I guess it was important to do that; I can only believe what Clement says about the care of the property. If he says it was important to put a ladder up against the shed while it was snowing, I know it must have been important.

I can imagine what his life must have been like then. Walking around the property, the nearly empty house, the unused outbuildings: the one living creature tending the ghost village. The last survivor of a plague. The house itself is enormous: twenty-seven rooms, or cells as they were called originally. A kitchen big enough to see that all of them were fed. Parlors for middle-range spiritual crises, too casual for Confession. Offices where the money was kept track of when money was coming in. Which both Clement and Boniface assured me it once did. There was a thriving business in Mass cards. And there were things called Purgatorials: for five dollars, you could buy, in the name of the dead, a share in all the order's prayers. But in the last years there was nothing in those offices: emptiness and dust. I can see Clement going from room to room, cleaning, polishing, dusting (he had no help: the order couldn't afford it). Empty rooms need as much care as ones that are lived in: more, because the emptiness itself is a reproach: neglect on top of that would be unbearable.

This is how Clement spent his days. He did chores. Chores. What a demanding, unexalted, childish word for that hard work. He fed and cared for the old priests, he did repairs on the house and the property. In winter he plowed the snow and in summer he mowed the grass. Not lawn, mind you, but meadow. He cleaned and mended, hammered, dusted, oiled, patched. He shopped in town. He began each day saying Mass in the empty chapel, then he would walk over the property to see what needed to be done. The afternoon was left for inside work. He prepared dinner and he served it. In the evenings, he watched television in the huge common room. Usually he was alone in there: the old priests fell asleep soon after dinner and would often take themselves upstairs after the news.

I don't understand how this situation was allowed to go on so long. There are things I'll never understand about the church, the order. Perhaps they didn't want to dislodge the two old priests. Perhaps the superiors didn't want to face the fact that what they'd given their lives for was finished. And what would they do with Clement?

What they came up with was really dazzling. They'd use the building. They'd use Clement. They'd have a place for people who needed to hide and to recuperate. The provincial remembered that Clement had been a farm boy: he thought it might be good for the children who'd be living there to work with animals. He knew that Clement was physically strong. There had to be a man in the shelter in case an irate, potentially murderous husband or boyfriend tracked his wife and children down. It had to be a man who could be trusted not to go off the rails with a house full of women. He'd had no reason to distrust Clement on this score. (He doesn't know about me, the provincial, none of the order or the diocesan officials do. Or maybe I'm wrong, maybe they do know about us, but Clement's of use to them, and I am, so they turn a blind eye. I suppose the Catholic Church is famous for that sort of thing.)

Clement has always been of use. To his family, to his order, to Boniface, now to the women and their children. And to me. He gave me back my life, one part of it, I mean. He gave me hope. Making love to him is such a hopeful thing for me. It would be terrible to lose that, to have to admit that the thing I called hopefulness was just misnamed. Should have been called foolishness, delusion, self-deceit. And exploitation too. Clement once more being of use.

I don't want this to happen. But I can see how likely it is that it will.

Every time Clement tells the story of Buddy, he gets excited at exactly the same point. He was standing on the ladder sweeping the snow off the shed roof with a long broom. He was concentrating on keeping the ladder steady and worried that it might slip because of the inch of snow. "There I was," he says, "on top of this ladder, sweeping the snow off the roof with my broom and I heard this whimpering. It was the sorriest thing you ever saw. This poor old character like a drowned rat. I took him right in and wrapped him up in some old rags and blankets and laid him down by the wood stove. I gave him some bread dipped in hot milk with whiskey in it. At first he'd only take a little bit, then a little bit more. I took him to the vet. The vet said he was fine, he'd been on the point of starving, but I'd gotten to him in time. I put signs up all over town. I took an ad out in the local newspaper. Nobody claimed him. After two weeks I figured he was mine."

Clement loves that dog as much as he loves anything. Poor Buddy, poor clumsy, dumb mongrel. Clement literally goes everywhere with him. I guess he had to leave him home the day of his appointment at the chancery, but that may have been the only time. At one time, Buddy was Clement's life. He probably would die for him. I'm sure he'd die for him. And yet I've seen him violently angry when Buddy misbehaves, when he gets into the garbage or breaks a screen in a thunderstorm or steals food or chews something up. Clement turns into someone I don't know. He hits the dog over and over with a rolled-up newspaper. He's furious; he's out of control. He does it too long and too hard. The dog whimpers and cowers. Afterward there are tremendous reconciliations. The whole thing makes me sick.

Once I spoke to him about it, but that was a mistake. Like interfering in a lovers' quarrel. He was adamant. "Buddy's a dog. He lives in a human world. He's got to know what's what."

I think Clement thinks my kids don't know what's what, and that's why they behave as they do. Rudely, he would say. It's true that Buddy is tremendously well behaved. But I can never relax around Buddy because he seems to have only two ways of being: eagerness and despair. Eagerness to please and despair at not pleasing. That's exactly what I didn't want for my kids.

I was brought up to be well behaved. Brought up to practice all the minor virtues: thrift, honesty, politeness, temperance. All forms of moderation. Above all not to make a fuss. No hint of heroism, grandeur, exaltation touched my upbringing: neither did the crueler and more pleasurable forms of self-assertion, which might lead to self-regard. Clement says he grew up being told why he was put on earth, and he never doubted it. He was put on earth to know, love, and serve God in this world and to be happy with him forever in heaven. What I want for my children is different both from Clement's way and mine. I'd like them to live fully, not to victimize but to be witnesses against victimization, to have some sense of beauty and pleasure in their lives. I'm not sure any of that will happen. I didn't become what my parents wanted. They were shocked at the kind of work I chose to do. Among people whose lives were so disorderly, as if disorder in a life were a disease that could rub off, a disease they thought they'd inoculated me against, like whooping cough or smallpox. They hated the way I dressed. They were mortified that my husband left me for another woman. They thought I didn't know what's what. I didn't know the score. Maybe my children don't because I never have.

But I've never known who's keeping score. Clement thinks the score is visible and legible. He too veers between eagerness and despair. My children are very different from him. They never believed that their lives were at stake. I've wanted them to enjoy their lives, to do more good than harm. If, in the course of that, they occasionally tell me to go get fucked, if they refuse to pick their clothes up off the floor, if they slam doors at me and at each other, I don't mind.

Maybe that means that I don't know the score.

I do know that Clement can't live here, in my apartment, with my children.

As a mother, I am unrecognizable to him, maybe dangerous or shocking. He doesn't see what happens between me and the children when he isn't there: their kindness when I come home dead tired, their discussions on my bed late at night about injustice or their fears, our singing in the car, their fierce defenses of each other, the comfort they go to each other for that they can get from no one else. Jokes, favorite foods, remembrances of babyhood or childhood: all that happens only when he isn't there.

We live, my family and I, in what is called a railroad apartment. The bedrooms give onto a central long corridor. There is no natural light, no one has a window that looks out on anything, we're on the wrong side of the building. There are too many books, framed drawings by the children that embarrass them but that I won't take down, musical instruments left on the floor beside their cases, socks on the coffee table, anybody's sneakers anywhere. Often it's quite chaotic.

Clement has never lived in chaos. Even in the ugliness of his family's house, his mother kept chaos back. If his father came home drunk, there was a space for that. A hiding place, a room, like the rooms in old houses in France for storing nuts or cheese or drying out windfall fruit, to keep old toys, to do the ironing. I didn't want to live like that: with hiding places, securely closed doors. I don't know what I wanted. I wanted my children to be able to have solitude without shame. It's force that makes children ashamed. My children seemed born good to me. That idea was always in my mind when I corrected them. They resisted me, God knows they still resist me, but I've always felt their goodness, and I base my treatment of them on this faith.

But they're not good to Clement's dog. I can't bear to see that, which is another reason I don't like him to come here and why

I've convinced him to rent a studio apartment in my neighborhood where we can be together. Where I don't have to watch my children being horrible to my lover's dog.

They do to Buddy what they'd like to do to Clement.

Buddy is so obedient, so anxious in his desire to please he nearly trembles with it. Of course he brings out the sadism in people who would otherwise be decent human beings, who might otherwise be called good. I've never understood it, but I know it's very strong. This instinct for abuse.

I see it all the time in men and women: it's the foundation of all my work. If only I could say it stopped at that, that it was only sex, or only men and women. But it's more than that. I know it. What I don't know is why. Why this need to persecute, like hunger for a bad smell, like our love for the stink of our own shit (but no one else's), or our own rank armpits (but no others). Like an animal's urge to roll in what is rotten, dead. All we need to see is the hint of a cringe, and we begin to raise our arm. To punish. Whom? For what? Each one of us must see ourselves always ready to fold into a cringe, always crushed underneath some heel. And we must be determined, every one of us, that this won't be our final resting place, crushed under some heel. Do we feel we have to punish the cringer since he reminds us of the place which could all too easily be ours? Or is it only by imagining someone else under our greater force that we feel free?

I see the instinct in myself. There's a woman in an exercise class I take who's very plain and has long stringy hair the color of orange pop. She goes to the front of the class and smiles at herself in the mirror. She wears flesh-colored panty hose; you can see the darker shaded area of the thigh part. Every time I see her, I have to force myself not to insult her, to insist that she not stand in front of the class, not smile at herself in the mirror, not wear those flesh-colored tights. Sometimes I dream of striking her, knocking her unconscious on the floor. Because of the way she smiles at herself in the mirror. I want to say to her: "What have you got to smile about? How dare you smile at yourself like that?"

I'm sometimes like that about some of the women in the shelter. It's why I think I'm not good for this job, or I've been doing it too long. I'm too fond of the ones who get themselves together, I'm too quick to call them heroic, to compare their brave generous children to my own, putting my own in a bad light. And I'm too quick to want to lash out at the manipulative ones, the victims who wallow in their victimization, or who use it as a base from which to be seductive, to suggest that since they've been beaten by a man they're the true women among us. To parade their scars. I must admit it: I feel quite angry at some of the women I'm supposed to help. I judge them harshly; I feel they've gotten away with something. Or is it that I feel they've taken something from me? The honored female place. The true, ancient name of woman? That in their supine posture, they arouse in men (I guess that I mean Clement) the instinct to reach down and lift them up. I see the women who are tough, suspicious, a little cold, a little quick on the trigger with men as on the same side of the line as I am: the side of the line that men will not cross over. Perhaps all of us on that side of the line would like to crush the other women, lying weeping, whimpering, "Save me. Save me. I have suffered. And only you can."

Knowing this about myself, how could I condemn my children?

My children say they love all animals. But I've seen them shout at Buddy for tracking mud onto floors already filthy from their boots, for lying on the furniture, already stained with their food, ink, fingerprints. I've seen them take away his food before he's really finished (he likes to eat in stages; they say leaving the food around draws ants, which we have never had). I've seen them refuse to walk him when he's clearly desperate. They call him stupid, smelly, ugly, old. They vilify him when he's not around. Only near Buddy do they become fastidious. "Jesus, I've been vacuuming all day. There's enough dog hairs to make a rug." Overworked. Houseproud. In no other case would it occur to them to touch a broom.

They ignore Clement, or speak to him as though he were a fool. They think that they're polite. There's nothing I could accuse them of. How could I say to my beloved children, "I accuse you, like the rest of humankind, of the bald desire to inflict pain, spread misery, exclude, punish, cast out. I, your mother, accuse you of this."

Well, I couldn't do that, could I? You can see why I talked Clement into a studio apartment. I lied. I said we'd discovered my daughter was allergic to dog hair. If he knows I lied, he's never told me.

Does he know I lied? Does he know about Boniface? This is the thing about Clement, you never know what he knows. And you're afraid to ask him. Because if he does know, what's left? A stranger.

Perhaps having a room, and one room only, where we do nothing but make love is one more thing that I've arranged to suit my purposes in the name of protecting someone else. My children. Clement. Perhaps I've arranged everything to suit myself as I've arranged the room. The blue sheets. The striped fold-out couch.

Clement had never bought anything for himself but food and machinery, and what was needed to keep it going, materials for the prosperity of the property and the house. I guess that he bought clothing. Underwear and work pants. Sweaters. Winter coats. Until he knew me, he didn't own a suit. I went with him to buy the first suit he'd bought since he left for the seminary.

We went into a men's clothing store in lower Manhattan, some place I'd read about in the newspaper. Old-fashioned service, the ad had said. Incredible prices. We were both nervous. How could we conceal the fact that, at the age of forty-five, Clement was buying his first adult suit? I didn't know how to coach him. He thought I knew and was withholding information. Being tough. I wasn't withholding anything: I didn't know about men's suits. All the time he was taking jackets off and putting them on I was dumb with longing. Because of Clement's body, and the old, unchanging fabrics of men's clothes. Herringbone, pinstripe, chalk stripe, Harris tweed, Glen plaid. I stood in a sea of a hundred years of maleness. All the push and thrill and safety of men in offices: decision makers, moneylenders, "I'll-take-care-of-that, I'll-take-care-of-everything." My father. Everybody's father. The government. What kept things going. And underneath it all Clement's body, the body I knew so well. Putting on jackets. Taking them off.

The salesman was a kind man, defeated-looking, sad that men weren't dressing like they used to, deferring to me, calling me the wife, making chalk marks on the shoulders and backs of jackets. He tugged at the trouser legs, and all that I could think about was Clement's cock, and the delicious soft dark hair around it. I wanted to say to the nice salesman, so full of suffering, like a minor clerk in Dostoyevsky with a shrewish wife and a daughter dying of consumption, I wanted to say to him: "May I please go into one of those curtained rooms with this man? The place between my legs is soaking wet. I just need five minutes with him. I know you understand."

Clement stood in front of the long mirror, pleased with himself as if his own looks were a surprise. I came up behind him and embraced him. The unhappy salesman smiled.

In the cheap room, painted light blue, on the fold-out couch covered with gray and white striped cotton (everything my choice), we lie beside each other many hours, taken up with only this: the work of love. It is work. At first it seemed more job than pleasure, and it wasn't easy.

You must remember that I was the first woman he'd ever touched. Almost literally. I suppose he'd kissed his sisters. And his mother. There was no other woman with whom his relations would have sanctioned even a casual, social embrace. The whole life of the order enabled him never to come near a woman. It was structured like that, and the structure held for a remarkable number of years. It held itself up outside history. Then it collapsed. The order died. The Paracletists died a natural death. That is, old life took over, new life could no longer graft itself on the old body. Clement must have wondered what he would do next. I think that I was the next thing. I was in the right place at the right time. The Motherhouse was no longer a motherhouse. There was no place for him to go. What could be more obvious. Why shouldn't he go with me?

We worked beside each other for three months. And then there was the day that I got sick.

I'm very good at my job. And he was good at what he was in charge of. We worked well together. Each day, I'd drive up from the city, leaving my apartment at five-thirty. It was spring, the leaves were thin and yellow green, you could see anything through them, everything, the sky, or houses: mountains springing up. As I drove I would listen to the radio. WNEW. AM radio. Old songs. Frank Sinatra made me happy before six a.m. "In the Wee Small Hours of the Morning." "Come Fly with Me." I was thinking about Clement, all that time. I was sure it was impossible. We'd walk around the grounds, we'd look at heating bills, we'd make plans for refurbishing the kitchen, we'd think about communal gardens. Sometimes we'd bump into one another or our hands would touch. I knew we wanted each other, but I believed nothing could happen. He was very handsome, and he knew all about the boiler, the storm windows, the deep freeze. He made me feel that whatever I did, it would be fine. He makes everybody feel like that. Now that annoys me: I want to say, "Tell her she has to change, that she'll ruin her life if she goes on like that." But people leave him thinking everything they do is fine. Sometimes they change because of this. I don't know why.

All the time we were working together we were talking. Or I was talking more than Clement: he never talks much. But some of the things he said amazed me. Some of the things that he believed in were ridiculous. He thought that welfare families should be given small parcels of land and taught to farm them. He believed that everyone should be required—required by law—to work an hour a week in shelters for the homeless or in hospices for AIDS patients. He believed that the rich should be taxed and taxed and taxed. He was a fiend about recycling, and he wrapped food in wet cloths or waxed paper instead of plastic.

At the same time, often minutes after he'd said something preposterously naïve, he'd say, "Human beings need so much comfort." That's the kind of thing he says. I can't remember much of what he says. He doesn't live in language; language baffles and confuses him. It's one of the reasons why they never sent him out to preach, why they kept him at the Motherhouse, in charge of things and property. It's why he didn't get out and meet women. It's why he's with me.

One day, as we were sitting in the kitchen going over plans, I got a terrible pain in my stomach. I vomited, right in front of him, into the kitchen sink. I couldn't stop vomiting. He put me in a room set up for the retreatants. It was a room for prayer and for reflection: an iron bed, white sheets, and a white chenille spread, a scratchy mud-colored blanket. A black cross on the wall. I kept vomiting. I vomited for seven hours. I couldn't be left alone. I thought that I was dying.

And there he was, so clean and helpful. His freshness seemed so beautiful to me. I felt filthy and weak. I wanted to lean against him for a minute, just for a minute. I had worked so hard. Leaning against him, I felt I was saying these things aloud: "The weight of my body is yours. I don't want the responsibility. For too many years I've held too much up. I want to be prone now, but more than that, immobile. Not forever. Just for a minute. Let me enjoy my weakness. I am feverish. I wouldn't mind dying. I would prefer though, to lean against you. The top of your shoulder smells like hay. I know that there is nothing about you that wills me harm."

I don't know if I said any of these things. When I ask Clement if I did, he says he can't remember. He was very worried: I couldn't keep anything down, not even water; the doctor said there was a real danger of my becoming dehydrated. He said he was too worried about all that to listen to anything I might have said.

Is this the truth? I think that it must be.

I smelled of sweat and vomit. I slept for a while. When I woke up he was still there. I lifted up my arms to him. We began to kiss. It was part of my illness. We kissed with our mouths closed. We were very quiet. We didn't move at all. After a while, I shifted in the bed so he could lie beside me. He was holding me. I heard words spoken in a strange, male voice, words I had seen on the windows of the Oak Street Congregational Church, which I had gone to as a child. *I am the resurrection and the life.* Then I realized they were really there. A narrow sign on the white wall. It might have said: "No Smoking," or "Checkout Time 10 A.M." or maybe "In Case of Fire." But it said, I AM THE RESURRECTION AND THE LIFE. And I believed it.

I believed he was bringing me back to life in faith. But not in God. Exactly not in God. In appetite.

He didn't know what to touch. I had to take his hand and put it on my breast. He groaned; I thought he was in pain. He was in pain. He'd never done anything like it before. For years he'd dreamed of it. It was the end of something. Touching my breast, he was putting something to death. His groan was the death cry of a twenty-year struggle, vows, a way of life, a way of knowing who he was. Touching my breast, he no longer knew who he was.

We could have stopped. I asked if he wanted to stop: I told him that it was fine, that we could stop. We could pretend that nothing happened.

"I couldn't pretend," he said. "I want to be in love with you."

When I think of what he said, those words, and I often do think of it, I'm sometimes alarmed. And perhaps even hurt. And more in love with him than ever. Every time I hear him saying, "I couldn't pretend."

He can't. He can't dissemble. He can't pretend himself in the semblance of anything other than what he is.

But that's not true anymore. Now he does it all the time. He pretends to be keeping his vows. When people, like the salesman in the men's shop, call him my husband, he pretends. He pretends to me that being my lover doesn't fill him with terrible guilt. He knows that he pretends. And yet he says he doesn't want things to change.

I try not to hear the last part of what he said to me that first day in the white room with the black cross on the wall above the sign that said, I AM THE RESURRECTION AND THE LIFE. "I want to be in love with you." It tells me something that I know but try to hide. He wanted somebody. It was time. I came along. It could have been somebody else.

I wonder if I have ever been myself for him. Or only the right time and place, the right place to be after Our Mother of Sorrows turned into Shalom Shelter. Or if he has ever been himself for me, rather than the man who had no other women, the man who would not compare me, couldn't even try, no matter what. The blankness on which I could write a new history—my own, only rewritten—his, which I would help to write. I don't know who we are to each other.

But I know that I don't want somebody else. Not after I've had him. He came to me pure, untainted by the images and pretexts of a bad age. He came to me full of belief and hopefulness that what we were doing was not only good but of enormous importance. There was no need for him to take revenge. I was the body he had dreamed of. He was grateful, he still is grateful, and surprised, that I give him access to my body. This body which I have not loved, middle-aged now, this body with its small breasts that have just begun to flatten out, a bit like empty satchels, the pattern of broken veins on thighs and calves, its sex that's lost its prized tightness, its elasticity: no longer springing back like a well-devised toy in the shape of fruit or flower. This body losing every day its power to charm, its trick of starting up desire.

His is to me the one desirable body, known, knowing, yearned-for, troubling, arousing, safe.

It's a strange thing, a strange adventure in a way, to love a body. In spite of anything, because of nothing. To approach another animal: two animals meeting in a cave, sweaty, covered with dark, damp, matted hair, rank with the other's smells, but the smell is your signal and your code: this one is mine. I love his smells. As I have loved the smells, dirty and clean, of my two children, the yeasty, sweaty hair, the soil accreting to the flesh after hours of wholehearted play, the milky breath of the first morning kisses. And now with Clement, I lie back, my neck stretched out as if I knew I could be killed—but I won't, no blow will fall there on that exposed neck, only kisses—and our mouths will travel, for we know that too, the taste. And then the quiet times of grooming or of tending. "Let me wash your hair." "Your shoulders are so tense." And sleep. Holding, moving apart from. Waking. "There you are." Waking perhaps to penetration. The surprise. "There you are. And here I am with you." *With*. The beautiful and rare word. *With*.

His body is the site where I am freed and brought to life. When he touches me between the legs a light strikes and travels up in darkness. He enters me and there is no place that I need to go, nothing further I need to be or strive for. To wish to be where and what you are. To wish for nothing further. Not to be alone.

And not to be compared to anyone who went before you. There is no one. You are only you.

I think he may compare me to other women now. The women at the shelter, younger, freer, more courageous or more victimized. More beautiful. At this moment, he may be comparing me to the woman I will lose him to.

Both Boniface and I suspect he'll leave me, and Boniface knows that if Clement leaves me, Clement will leave him too. In some ways, Boniface has very little left, and yet, of the two of us, he will be more able to bear the loss.

The room in St. Gervaise where Boniface now lives, the room he rarely leaves, except to be wheeled into the dining room for meals, or upstairs to the recreation room for parties, or out onto the roof for barbecues the first and third Tuesdays in June, July, and August, this room is similar to the room that Clement and I don't leave when we are lovers. The same blue color of the walls. The same white curtains on the windows. The same finitude of possibility: the limited, repeated moves. The body being filled or emptied, tended and caressed. The body with its small expected repertoire. So necessary. In the case of Clement and myself, surprising: we cry out. In Boniface's case, ordinary, unsurprising: I am kept alive.

He can't sit up by himself. When the tremors are bad, he can't feed himself, but he probably won't die soon. The other people there, most of them old, don't notice that he slobbers, that his tongue lolls and his eyes roll in his head on bad days, that he forgets the words of a sentence he's just begun. They don't know that he's less than seventy, younger than them all. They call him "Father." They ask him to bless them. I ask him what that means.

"To them," he says, "it means: 'I keep you from evil,' but to me, only 'You're not alone.' "

Old women bring up the torments of their youth, old men who can't hold in their hands a chicken wing or a section of an orange, weep for their brutalities. Because of who they think he is.

He says, "I'm among the unbearably unwell, and when we're together, we make something new. A new world. No one is well here. No one will ever be again. And yet we go on living. It's interesting to me, since I'm one of them. Completely indescribable. A worm and no man. Yet we're living, we're living lives. There's no shame here. Shame is local. All of us are ruined, so there's no shame. Some basic body parts don't work. So what? To lose your urine used to be the worst shame for all of us. When Clement was taking care of me I thought it would be better to die if I was a person who lost his urine. Now I see how foolish that is. Imagine killing yourself because of urine? What's urine, after all? Nothing lethal, something that can pretty easily be cleaned up. It's not nuclear waste," Boniface says, laughing—I don't know what to do when he laughs like that. "Just think, sweetheart"—he calls me sweetheart—"of the difference between urine and nuclear waste."

He goes into a trope, the trope of a theoretician: the tremendously successful preacher. Now it's not a trope on hellfire or the boundlessness of divine love, it's a trope on the difference between nuclear waste and urine. He enjoys this sort of thing. I can get a glimpse when he's like that of the pleasure he took in his sermons: yoking two unlike beasts, two unrelated ideas, so they would do his work. Leading the faithful, the slow stragglers, to the high place of his vision: windswept, empty. And the dazzling hint below, the size, perhaps, of a small dinner plate, of ice-green sea. Salvation, truth, so tantalizing, so unreachable. He would lead them there. It was within his power. He would use his power, then move on. To some new audience, another parish with another view.

"Now nuclear waste could look like water, colorless, it might not smell. Yet it could mean the deaths of thousands, or the ruination of many lives. And yet what we fear, what we would die for, isn't the lethal thing, but the shaming one. We're so afraid of the bad body smells. There were so many things I couldn't do in my life, things I believed were important, things I castigated myself for not being able to do because I feared bad bodily smells. I wanted to be a missionary; I wanted to work among the poor. But when I got near the poor, I couldn't speak to them, because of their smell. I've learned things, being here. Which is one reason I don't want to die. Here we're not ashamed. Many of us lose our urine. Some of us shit on the floor. And yet we don't want to die. We want to live, here in this place from which we've banished shame."

Boniface lets the nurses put cheerful hats on him: red berets or boaters. He goes to the events they plan: bingo or arts and crafts. He sings "When Irish Eyes Are Smiling" and "O Sole Mio" or "La Cucaracha," anything the others sing. He pastes felt and sand-paper to cardboard in what he is told are interesting shapes. He'll never leave; he'll never be other than he is, or what he was, as Clement will never be what he was before he knew me.

If Clement leaves me and goes off with another woman, she'll blame Boniface for all the wasted years of Clement's priesthood. They won't bring the new baby in to see him. I will always see him. We'll always want to be thinking, talking about Clement. Wherever he'll be, whatever he'll become without us.

Right now he's the person we both need him to be. As he has always been: of use. My lover. Boniface's youth, and his belief.

Clement has never in his life not been of use. He has never been on his own.

Boniface is happy among the unbearably unwell. If Clement never came to see him again, he could bear it. Even with so little, even though Clement is the most important thing in his life, he would bear it better than I. I who live and move around the world, the city, with my job, my children, and my healthy body. It would be worse for me. I'd have to re-place myself. Place or replace myself in some way I can no longer imagine. In the cold light of a night without him, on the white frozen path of life without him, among strange birds and unfathomable animals who cry out and signal that they mean me harm, or else remind me that I am one of them and there is no way back. I know that's ridiculous. It won't be that bad. It's just that I won't recognize myself. Boniface will recognize himself. His body has been ruined but it hasn't been transformed. Who would I be now without my transformation?

This will be surprising to you. I'm in Paris now with Clement. We've been here a week. We're leaving tonight.

He wanted to take me to Paris for a week. These last two years have been the first time he's had money. The diocese pays him a salary, which the order says he can keep: he's responsible for his own support. He doesn't know how to spend money. He has very few wants. He lives in the shelter and cooks his food there. He buys very few clothes. He rents the studio apartment and he bought the furniture, but it didn't come to much. One day he said, "I want to take you to Paris. I want to pay for everything."

Usually, we share expenses. Usually, I insist upon it. But I wanted to go along with him, with this pleasant, perhaps adolescent dream, whatever it was: a man taking a woman to Paris for a week and paying for it all.

He so rarely looks completely happy, but he looked that way when I agreed to his plan. When I said, "Of course, take me to Paris."

I want to tell you about Paris from the point of view of a woman who is with a man who pays for the whole thing, although she doesn't believe this is right or just. From the point of view of a woman with a man who has his own money for the first time at the age of forty-five, a man who's never been anywhere before, out of the country for the first time in his life. From the point of view of a woman who is happy. Who's spent the day looking at beautiful things, has eaten and made love happily for hours into the night and slept in the arms of a man she loves and who believes for now that he loves her.

I'm not going to describe Paris, except to tell you this. Clement likes all the tourist places. He insisted that we go to them. He was right to insist. We were very happy doing things I'd have been ashamed to do if I were with anyone else. We went to the top of the Eiffel Tower; we took a boat ride down the Seine. The city of Paris by night, so remarked upon, shone with exhilaration. Looking down from that great, hopeful, mechanical height, our bodies glowed as if we'd just come from a too-cold ocean. Our boat along the Seine was called the *Juliet Greco*; all the boats were named after cabaret singers. We leaned back on our blue canvas pillows. An accordion played for us, world-weary, tolerant; the river breezes stroked our skin and cooled it; we'd open our eyes from time to time and watch the faces of the buildings with their angels and their iron balustrades.

He wanted to go to Versailles; I didn't, but I went along with him. When we got there, the lines for the château were impossibly long, so I persuaded him that we should limit ourselves to the gardens. It was nearly noon when we arrived; we lunched near the canal: goat cheese and baguettes. And for dessert, apricots we paid too much for, blushing, swelling like the faces of smiling girls. I remember feeling grateful for the pleasure of the food: it made me feel religious for a moment. What merciful hand had lowered and spilled out those blushing apricots, that challenging and pungent cheese, the crisply neutral bread? We walked the long formal paths, around the dead fountains which did not splash playfully for us, it being only Thursday. The fountains splash playfully only one Sunday of the month.

It had rained most of the morning and the bluish grass was slightly wet. There were only a few people. It was easy to be apart from them, to leave large spaces between us and the other human beings who were walking where so many of the famous dead had walked, thinking perhaps so differently from us that we might find their thoughts unrecognizable. The gray sky brimmed with moisture; under the opalescent clouds the weak sun, pale as a moon, dropped its cool light. We walked on the dirt or gravel paths past statues separated from each other by precisely measured gaps. Full-bodied, mature, noble or divine, symbolic or historical: the press of experience gave them weight. Each full curve of upper arm or thigh witnessed an innocence lost so far back, so thoroughly, it was beside the point. Impossible to imagine any of these figures with a childhood. There was a statue of a god who was a shepherd or a hunter. He kept a pet deer, tame and beloved of the other gods, garlanded by them with fresh flowers each day. One day the shepherd or the hunter shot his bow and killed the deer with a careless arrow. He wept for all eternity.

I thought about eternity, timelessness, life without end, because Clement still has faith in it. But his faith is different from that of the Versailles architects. Those gardeners, designers, the sculptors who with all their work seem to be making a pact with death, holding up a model for death, suggesting that there's a way that death can have its mastery. The dead will be alone, removed and uncommunicative, like those statues. There will be no movement: that will be given up. But their frozen postures will be spared decay and ravage; their loneliness will cause them neither to rebel nor to despair, nor to lose their sense of who they are. Hell will not be in flame nor heaven musical. There will be neither word nor flesh. But there will be elaboration, space.

I always feel that these apparently stoic and serene planners of great monumental works were really rather frantic. Holding a blueprint up to death, suggesting this: "Now I have thought of everything. Do the one thing you must do: take away motion, breath. Nothing else. Everything else must be as I have planned it."

The eternity that Clement sees is substanceless and humble. No heroic poses, only restfulness. I think this is only possible because he hasn't yet been disappointed in the flesh. Simplicity is only possible before disappointment, or as in Boniface's case, when you've given up forever your belief in your power to get your way.

I wouldn't mind the Versailles gardeners' blueprint for eternity. Clement's belief would be fine with me too. But I don't believe in eternity. I don't believe in anything that has no end. I read once in a magazine that some physicists think that there are in the universe huge walls of emptiness, or bubbles of vacuity, tens of millions of light years in diameter. This comes so close to my ideas of eternity that I was terrified. I could easily see myself, I have always been able to, spinning and spinning through millions of light years of emptiness, the others I have loved spinning millions of light years away in their own emptinesses, none of us with anything to recognize, anything to attach to, nothing to stop any of us, no reason to go one way or the other, one place or the other, since there is no place or placement and no stopping, only emptiness and motion, senseless motion, hurtling toward nothing, to and with no end. How, then, could I dream of eternity, since what I can't see or even hope for is the face at the end of motion, the embracing arms? I know Clement and Boniface believe those arms will be there to receive them. They believe they will remain forever in a paradise of lodgment and eternal rest. *Eternal rest grant unto them O Lord and let perpetual light shine upon them*. This is their prayer for the dead. But it was never mine.

What I wanted was not to describe Paris, but to tell you what happened there. To tell two stories, one that Clement told me, one that we read in a guidebook.

It's May now. We chose this time to come to Paris because we hoped we'd get here before the tourists. But we've come in a bad week: most of the days are taken up by a holiday called *point*. A combination of patriotic and religious observances: a day honoring the war dead, followed by the Feast of the Ascension. Clement asked if I minded if he went to Mass. And would I like to go to Mass beside him? Those were his words, "beside me." Not with. Or not only with. I couldn't possibly say no.

I went with him into St. Germain des Pres. I kept thinking: people have been coming here for hundreds of years. Each of them had a life, and they all died. As I looked at Clement I was thinking that I didn't want the two of us to die. That death was separation, the end of knowing the person. The end of the refreshing renewal of new, daily sight. That whoever is left behind is bereft. This can't be denied or passed over: the dead abandon us. We are less than ourselves without them, wounded, wandering, no longer whole.

I looked at the priests on the altar vested so archaically in white. I was afraid to ask Clement: Have you ever looked like this? Would I have had to look at you as I look at them? I was afraid to ask because I knew the answer: yes, of course.

In the church, he was perfectly at home and he seemed happy. Neither of us understood the French of the service, but he knew when to kneel and sit and stand. I did what he did, I copied him except when he went up to take Communion. I didn't ask him: How can you take Communion when your life with me puts you in a state of sin? I knew the answer: Boniface explained that he and Clement had come to an understanding that his life with me was not a sin. Boniface told Clement that, and he believed him. I don't know if I would have, if I did.

As I sat in the pew and watched him in the line with the others, I felt terribly alone. I wanted to run away, into the city streets with all the other ones more like myself, unbelieving, worried, unattached. I guess this was when I began feeling tearful. Clement understood right away. When he came back to the pew, he held my hand. He held it while he prayed. What was I doing while he prayed? Not praying. Grieving. Having my hand held by him when he was somewhere else, somewhere I'd never been and had no wish to go.

When we got outside he wanted to tell me the story of the Ascension. I suppose I knew it but I said I didn't, not at all. I knew he wanted to tell me this story that he liked. He was very happy, very full of hope, telling me this story, as if I were a child, a whole circle of children, sitting near him, needing to be near the reassurance of his body. Or was he preaching a sermon, something he had had to do, but had always done badly, he said. Boniface agreed: Clement was a disaster in the pulpit.

Who was he when he was saying these words to me? Who was he saying them as? And to whom?

"Jesus had risen from the dead. So He was back on earth, but in what He would have called a glorified state. He could be seen and felt even, but not at first. He even ate, but He didn't have a body. That body had died. He was light on the earth.

"He came back to prepare the apostles to be ready to live without Him. Then it was time to go away, He'd done enough, they knew what they had to do, they had to know they could do it themselves."

"I'm not telling this right," he said. "I'm not getting you to feel it. Everything was very light, they were so glad, they felt they had another chance. I'm not telling it right."

"You are," I said.

"And anyway, He took them out to a high place and told them He's going and they shouldn't be afraid. And then He ascended out of their sight. I keep wondering what that was like, if they kept looking at the soles of His feet from underneath. Then He said, 'I'm going first to prepare things for you.'

"And then there was emptiness. And then this strange man, dressed in white, said to them. 'Don't look up in the clouds, it's not in the clouds what you're looking for, what you have to do, it's on the earth.' 'Feed my lambs,' He said to them, I mean Jesus. Another time. And then they were very alone, they feared they couldn't do it without Him."

He was right, he told the story very badly, he was no good at telling stories. You couldn't listen for the story, just the occasional remarkable sentence, something about emptiness, something about looking up at the soles of Jesus's feet. It always seemed to happen with Clement: the badness of the storytelling left spaces you could fill in so in the end you saw more, understood more, than you would have from somebody who'd told it well.

I saw how he'd based his life on stories like this one. He'd given every character a face, a body, and he'd lived by them. What did he live by now? My body, not weightless, my body that could be touched, not light, but weighted down. Was I weighing him down? Should I disappear? He seemed so happy, holding my hand in the little park outside St. Germain des Pres, next to the statue of Apollinaire, a poet he never would have heard of. I wanted to say: "You were better off before you met me. I'm not as good as what you broke away from so that you could feel you were an ordinary man."

He began kissing me right there in the park. We were teenagers, passionately kissing in the open air. I guess it was another thing he'd never done.

"Let's see some sights," he said. "This is wonderful. I'm having a wonderful time."

When he was happy like this, so happy to be living the life he felt he'd missed, I was afraid for him. It seemed dangerous, like when my children were running too fast, playing too hard. One of those nights when I'd be watching them, it was getting late, the sky was turning royal blue, the first stars began appearing, and I could see them, running, laughing, and I was afraid. But I couldn't stop them, and I couldn't stop Clement when he got like this. Sometimes he just gets tired from these states, and I don't know what happens or where he goes. Far away from me, anyway. He did it often when we were first having sex; he'd be so happy, then I could feel him wander someplace to heal himself, like a sick animal, as if it all had been too much.

He was smiling and his eyes were wide. His skin was young and beautiful, his color full of health. He took out the guidebook. "Now I'm going to read you something about this street we're on. The rue Jacob.

"This woman lived here, Marguerite de Valois. Chère Margot, she was called. The book says, 'She knew love at eleven.' "

He shivers. "Eleven."

I knew what he was thinking about. He was thinking, as I was, of the children at the shelter who'd "known love at eleven." And how little he can do for them. Wounded, embittered, brash, frightened or depressed. Love wasn't the only thing they'd known from their mother's boyfriends or their fathers, or the thirteen-, fourteen-year-old boys who made them feel for once they might be worth something. By now, even Clement knows how to recognize another kind, who feels, already at eleven, "I've got this thing and it can get me what I want." The terrible sexual bravado of ruined children.

"She was the sister of two kings, the wife of one," he went on reading. "It says she led a debauched life. I wonder what they mean. But now she's fifty-two, bald and fat. She snips the blond locks of her pages to make her own wigs. She wears a belt around her waist with amulets containing the hearts of her dead lovers.

She has a twenty-year-old lover, but he gets too old for her, so she takes an eighteen-year-old lover, a carpenter. The twenty-year-old gets jealous and stabs the eighteen-year-old right in front of her. He dies. She demands that the twenty-year-old be strangled with her garters, right then and there in her sight."

He's just finished the story. I'm walking fast. I feel afraid. I want to say: "I've just heard two stories, one about a man with no body, who could not be touched, and one about a woman who made two men die. I have more in common with the second. That is more the world I represent. You should leave me. Go back to the clean weightless world, where the men wait and pray and look up at the clouds and then are spoken to by angels. Feed your lambs. I've taken too much from you. I've wanted you beside me, your hand on me, your mouth, your body wrapped around mine, your goodness and your clarity, your kindness and your need to comfort. I've taken too much from you. Go back to the other world, or else to one of the Marias (I've always called them the Marias to myself), whose hungers have nothing to do with death or age, who want you just to keep them safe, who make you laugh, whose younger bodies would move more lightly beneath yours, who are not in collusion with a man who also loves you and may also have stolen your life."

"Wait," he says. I'm walking very fast.

"I want to tell you this," he says. "I'll never leave you."

This is where we are right now. We won't be here for long. We'll take the Air France bus to Orly. Then we'll be on the plane. Then it will be starting to be over. The next day we'll be back at work. He'll be seeing the Marias, one of the Marias. Next year he may be married to her, buying a house. He may be taking her to Paris, where she never will have been. She may be pregnant. It may be his child, it may not. He may be in disgrace, breaking his vows to marry, and losing his job, so maybe he'll be broke. But maybe he'll be happy. Maybe he'll feel that after all this time he's part of life.

He holds me in his arms here on the street, the rue Jacob in Paris. "I'll never leave you," he says again. I believe him. But I don't know for how long.

LIVING AT
HOME

For Helen Miranda Wilson

I've lived with Lauro for five years, and I still admire him. He doesn't seem to be afraid of death.

He travels to the death spots of the world, the trouble spots. He's a journalist, and covers revolution. I'm a doctor; I work with autistic children. He seems happy with me for a while, but only as a place to come back to. For some time, I won't feel his restlessness. Once it was eleven weeks.

Our house is in the heart of London. On a radio he has, we can pick up broadcasts from all over the world. I know his restlessness is back when I hear him fiddling with the radio, trying to pick up some remote station. I hear crackling and static, buzzing, whirring, then a distant English voice, and words it takes a moment for my mind to place: Burundi, Kampala, and the names of leaders I've never heard of, recently shot, soon to be deposed. I know he'll be on the phone soon with his editor. His voice is happy planning a new, dangerous trip.

Lauro is Italian. My family are German Jews. Unlike Lauro, I was born in England. We stayed here till I was four, then left for America. My father was a gastroenterologist; he took a position at an American university and for ten years we lived in Columbia,

Missouri. Or we didn't live there; we were too unhappy to understand where we were. In the overlarge modern house, where our English furniture was dwarfed like the chairs in *Alice in Wonderland,* my mother wandered, wringing her hands, unable to comprehend the space. I locked myself in my room with its plaid curtains and painted sills, or rode my bicycle through miles of new construction, shocked by the gashes of red soil cut to make the new superhighway that unfolded, foot by foot, before my eyes. After ten years, my father rejoined his old partner in London. How happy my mother was in the house they bought in Richmond, placing her possessions in the right relation to each other, finding her furniture again proportional and adequate and safe. I'd made no friends in America, yet I'd lost the knack of speaking like an English girl, so I had a bad time settling in. I still haven't quite got the knack of English speech. Sometimes I use an American word for something, sometimes the English. My language always places me as somebody without a place. Like the children I work with, I cannot trust the English tongue.

Lauro loves English, especially English poetry, but he doesn't always understand the words. It doesn't bother him not to understand. He asks me for help. Holding a book of Auden, Byron, or George Herbert in his hand, he presents himself to me as the humble foreigner. The stranger needing help. He assumes I am not a stranger. I understand why he is so successful, why his stories give so perfectly the flavor of the country where he is. I imagine him in the bush, in a Land Rover strafed by bullets, asking for help with his canteen. Brave, fearless, as the bullets sing over his head, but quite unable to remove the cap of his canteen. Driving at top speed through an ambush but unable to get his flashlight to work. Everyone helps him. Then they tell him, "I have a son at home, six months, a strapping boy." Then they allow him into the secret meetings; they lead him to the hidden camp. He says, "The most important thing in my work is to have a strong stomach. You must always eat what they offer you. Then they will like you. Otherwise, if you don't eat what they give you, they will never trust you. Sometimes, this if very difficult."

At home, he is a vegetarian.

Both my parents and their families left Germany in 1935, before it was too late. My parents were newly married and they brought to England many of their wedding gifts and other personal mementoes and effects. Domestic treasures: little boxes, spoons, cream jugs, pen sets and inkstands, ornately framed photographs, decanters, figurines. My mother spent the days of her young marriage serving these objects with a deep sense of her own inferiority to them. In America, she tended them as if they were asthmatics forced to live in an uncongenial climate: anxiously her eye fell on them or her fingers touched them, always alert for signs of strain. When we went back to England, her attentions became mixed with gratitude; she couldn't do enough for them to repay them for their constancy, their valor, their refusal to give in. I understand this, I have always understood. She was serving her youth, her past, her dreams of home, her sense that it was possible for some things to outlast horror. Nevertheless, it drove me wild. I liked my mother, but her way of living among the objects of her life could only wreck my peace.

I'm telling you this so you'll understand why, although I'm far from irresponsible, I've left so many men, and why with Lauro I have been so happy.

My history with men didn't begin abnormally, you mustn't think that. It began in the usual way. A marriage to a *copain*. We were students. It was 1967. I remember we wore identical corduroys, black turtlenecks, rough cardigans. We didn't wash enough. My mother suggested that both my husband and I smelled bad, and as we were both studying medicine it might turn into a professional impediment. We had a child when I was in my second year of medicine; it was difficult, but not impossible. I quickly lost interest in cleaning and cooking, except the mushy foods I prepared for the baby, a son, whom I adored. When I began working in the hospital, my son was three years old. The flat was really grotty then. Porridge would congeal in lumps on the sitting room floor. The colorful pillows from Pakistan began to split and spill their innards on the brown Danish settee. I never cared. I enrolled my son in Suzuki violin and had my mother teach him German.

I fell in love with someone else, another doctor in the hospital. He was older than I and married, too. Quickly, he left his wife; I wasn't sure if it was for me. I left my husband. It was sad, we'd been young together, but it worked out; he took our son on week-ends. I married the older doctor; we moved to a larger flat. I grew flowering plants from seeds. I painted the walls light blue and put up curtains of two colors: aquamarine and yellow-gold. We had a son. I began specializing in psychiatry, working in the school where I'm now the head. My secret with the children is that I can sit silently in a room with them for hours, occasionally performing simple gestures. People interpret this as sanctity, poetry, or self-ablation. That isn't the case. I like the quiet. I understand what it is these children fear. When Lauro came to watch me work, he cried. He asked if he could write about it: my work, the children. "You're the real hero," he said. "I only pretend to be the hero.

I told him not to come again, and that he couldn't write about us.

My third husband wasn't a doctor. He didn't do much of anything. He was a cheerful, cocky boy, half Russian. I liked the way he smoked a cigarette: holding his cigarette in one side of his mouth, gripping the astrakhan collar of his winter coat, he believed completely in his power to charm. He played an old, very large accordion that had belonged to his grandfather. My sons loved it; they loved him, and he spent hours playing with them each day, teaching them things: how to build edifices out of toothpicks, how to construct a raft without a single nail. He wanted to live in the country; I drove into the school where I am medical director only three times a week. They allowed me to do this. They were terrified of losing me.

We made jam from the pears and apples off the trees around the property. We had a window seat and a huge fireplace in the kitchen. We sat in front of it on wooden benches, drinking tea. On weekends, when the children went to their fathers, we would stay in bed whole afternoons. It was a dark house, on account of all those trees.

I think I kept leaving men because I got so tired of the places where we lived together. Where they lived so seriously, so steadfastly, sitting on the furniture, using the crockery and silverware as if it were eternal, as if they could rest, because at least those things would never change. The men would begin to be angry at me for taking no interest. "How can you take no interest?" they would say. It wasn't just that I felt out of love with the men. It was that I could only go on loving them if I hadn't yet grown tired of the place.

When I know Lauro is getting restless, I comb the newspapers for trouble spots, trying to outguess him. This week there are riots in Tibet. Once more they are fighting over sacred places. I don't think this will interest him; he doesn't like religious wars. But there has also been an attempted coup in Sao Tome, an island off West Africa. Forces loyal to the Marxist government captured thirty-eight of the forty insurgents as they tried to overrun the police headquarters near the capital, Sao Tome. Only forty insurgents in all. The other two, not captured, were killed on the spot.

As a doctor, I look for the sites of medical disaster. Today I read about meningitis in the Sudan. The paper says: "Meningitis normally strikes the Sudan every summer, but this year it began a month earlier than usual because of unseasonably high temperatures. The temperature today was 111 degrees Fahrenheit."

When Lauro is happy with me, I never read the newspaper. He doesn't understand this, and I know it shocks him, so sometimes I sit with him at breakfast and pretend to read. But I'm not reading; I'm watching him read.

My children, who are twenty-one and seventeen, think habitation is a joke; they are long-legged, loose, they run through the world from here to there, kissing me, their mother, as they pass through. Pass by where I am at that time, in a room they are moving through on their way from somewhere to somewhere else. Cambridge. Havana. The home of some girl and her parents for the weekend or for lunch. Between me and my sons there is a bond of gold. Truthfulness and light. Words that are never false in the mouth. At the school, I sit in silence, watching for the slightest gesture that would indicate to me that the child believes he or she exists. At home, with my long-legged boys, words fly, bright disks of language spinning through the air, our pleasure in each other's company. They don't stay for long; they live out in the world. When they come home, I fill the fridge and the cupboards with childish, easy foods: bread, butter, yogurt, marmite. Tins of rice pudding. Soup. They never sit for a meal or for the whole of it. They shove the seventh piece of bread and marmite into their mouths, jump up, bring their dishes into my tiny kitchen, kiss me on the head, and go out to the world.

They don't like Lauro as much as they liked my third husband, who was a kind of brother to them, whose new wife and babies have become their sister and their nephew and their niece. These children have become my grandchildren; I indulge them with expensive gifts. But my sons understand my choosing Lauro, they always understand. Each of them shares the other's biological father as a kind of mythic background force. The air is thick for them with the historical male presence.

Do I deceive myself that my leaving those husbands, breaking up those homes (broken homes: you see a house split open, torn up, like a mouthful of jagged teeth), do I deceive myself when I say I believe they didn't suffer? I don't believe they suffered. They seem happy in their lives, my older son at Cambridge, studying philosophy, my younger son in Cuba now, cutting sugarcane beside heroes, he writes home to say. Lauro believes this son is naïve in his enthusiasm, but he doesn't tell him. I didn't have to ask him not to say this to my son. Lauro's tact is part of his wonderful generosity. Always, he has seen more than anybody else, but he's careful not to leave people with the impression that they're provincial, naïve, self-indulgent. He doesn't believe it, in any case. He likes almost everyone. He loves being out in company. Until suddenly, I'll see him pout. He'll turn on me his face of childish blame. "We're never alone," he says, accusing, as if it weren't he who said yes to the invitations, or invited people in. He'll turn to me with a petulance I'm sure he has no use for on his travels. "Why are we never alone, just here, the two of us, at home?" Then I phone and lie and cancel dates, and he is happy. He lays me down on the bed. He takes my shoes off, he massages my feet, my hands, my temples. As if I were the one who had been petulant. As if I were the one who wanted to stay home. "You're tired, you work too hard," he says, rubbing my shoulders. He believes it. He is seized with a longing to care for me, to make my life more pleasant, easier, until he goes away again.

I wonder where he'll go next. I hope it won't be Africa. The meningitis, early this hot year in the Sudan. Malaria: pancontinental. AIDS. He won't take pills to prevent malaria. He says he likes the onset of malaria. In just that moment when the fever strikes he feels great joy. He says he always thinks of me happily then; I don't know why, I've never asked him. I did ask him about how he feels afterward, after the seizures take hold. He shrugged. "This is terrible, you are so tired, you think you cannot fight, you have no will to fight, it's just easier to die." Then why not take the pills? He shrugged again, as if I were being purposely difficult. "People take medicine. They don't eat this, they don't eat that, they die. I don't take medicine, eat everything, and I don't die."

Once, I checked his passport. I wanted to see if he had filled in my name as the person to be notified in case of an emergency. I was worried that he'd forgotten and hadn't crossed out his ex-wife's name.

But her name wasn't there, it was mine. So if he dies, I'll be the first to know.

I should tell you about this house. A modern flat. We painted the walls white. The rugs, Lauro brought back from Mexico: black, gray, and white stripes, geometric shapes. The settee is gray; I had the chairs covered in gray sailcloth. The tables are modern, Italian, shining white. Our kitchen gleams with white conveniences. We have a woman in to clean, so even when Lauro is away, the kitchen gleams. Although when he isn't home, I never go into the kitchen. Never. Not even to make a cup of tea. Everything that goes into my mouth when he's away I eat or drink outside the house.

Lauro is shorter than I by five inches. He is slight in my arms like an Asian boy. His skin is always dry and fragrant, as if he'd just bathed in the sea and lain out in the sun. Lying on top of me, he is no weight at all. How easily I breathe beneath him. I never want him to leave the warm inside of my body, where he finds his way so tactfully, so purposefully, where he seems so at home.

I never want him to go away.

I'm always afraid of his dying.

I'm afraid of the pictures I make of his dying, of his actual death, and of learning the news of his death.

If he would promise me he wouldn't die away from me, in one of the bad death spots of the world, I wouldn't mind his going.

I like this house. I like my white bed and the window and the hard, light, modern objects all around. I have never grown tired of this house.

I wouldn't mind his leaving if he could promise me that he'd come back.

Of course he can't promise and of course I'd never ask.

Sometimes I wonder if I'd have lived differently with a daughter.

How would you house a daughter, knowing how you yourself were housed, and how unsatisfactory it was for you? How much, in the end, you hated it?

My mother insisted upon certain things, but she mustn't have insisted too hard, with too much threat of punishment, not enough anyway, because I didn't do what she wanted in the house, not with any regularity, or long enough to please her, and certainly not after I left home.

If I'd had a daughter, I might have tried and failed to do what my mother did. I might have felt that I had to keep one consistent, tidy shelter going for her, in the same way I would have felt I had to take her to the gynecologist to see about contraception.

And supposing she'd been tidy on her own? Suppose she'd been one of those girls with pretty ways. Sitting, sewing dreamily at a low chair by the window, looking out at the damp garden, hatching plans. "When I have my own house." What would she mean by that? When my sons were sitting looking out the window, I never thought they were reproaching me about the house. At least I didn't have to worry about that.

When you worry about the body of a daughter, it's the future that you think's at stake. Even if you've left behind the whole idea of chastity, even if you imagine you're beyond that, it's hard to give up the idea of the girl as vessel. Her body will contain the race. Every injury can have an implication, secretly harbored, revealed only years hence. What would you have to build, to plan, to purchase, to maintain, in order to keep this vessel from harm? Also, to keep her from the curse of not being able to keep house. Keep house. Keep the house from what? For what? The future?

The future and girls' bodies. I thought of this connection first in relation to the children at the school. How else could we explain menstruation to them, except in terms of a future? So we mentioned the future to them, as if we believed the future we described for them weren't empty and a lie. We created a series of pictures; we pasted sanitary towels to pieces of cardboard; we colored the crotches of underpants bright red and reddish brown. We knew everything we said was a lie. They will not be permitted to have children. One of us will step in.

For the children I treat, the idea of the future is one of the hardest things. They speak only in the present tense, so sometimes it's difficult to know when in time the thing they are speaking about happened. Not believing in the future, they often find it difficult to express desire. When you ask them what they want, they may answer with any word at all. Today, when we asked a little boy what he wanted to eat, he answered, "Pandemonium."

Yet we had to speak to these girls as if they understood the idea of a future that would not exist. So that the present wouldn't terrify them. This bloodiness from nowhere, this breaking through. All the wastage: fluid, plasma, eggs. We don't say to them. "Don't worry, we'll see to it that you're barren." Certain words terrify me: I'd rather not hear them coming from my mouth, entering the air, which after all I have to breathe again and would prefer not to have filled by terror. The terrible emptiness of the word *barren*. A dry pebble in a huge rusted bin, silent, unliving, jostled accidentally by who knows what in the dark windy plain where it lies hidden by the overgrown stalks, brown grasses, and dead leaves. *Barren:* the aftermath of an evisceration, the inhuman blank. A word we don't use for a man or boy. The word *sterile* holds nothing like the same terror. *Infertile:* just an accident, an oversight, a small, inessential minus, a mistake. There is nothing curable or scientific that the word *barren* suggests. *Barren* is ancient, irreversible: a curse, a fate.

But I suppose fate always hangs over the body of a girl. Which is why, not having daughters, I've been able to care less about the future. Able to care almost nothing for a house and to be happiest with a man who leaves it all the time, leaves its safety, so that he can be in danger. So that he can be sure he's alive.

You may be wondering—since we're so different and we do such different things—how Lauro and I met. It was as you might suppose: through friends, at a dinner party. Who knows what drew us to each other? Not looks. Neither of us is unusual-looking, although I guess we're both thought attractive. But it wasn't that. Nor do I remember what we talked about. It must have been a lunch party, not a dinner party, because we went out walking together afterward, up and down the streets, talking. I was tremendously excited. I wanted to be in bed with him. I didn't know if he was married: I hoped we wouldn't have to go to a hotel. At the same time, I loved walking with him, and I didn't particularly want to stop that, even to go to bed with him. It was winter, February, not too cold. Good weather for walking. He noticed everything on the streets. But I talked a lot too. I can't remember what I talked about: my work, my sons, my mother? I think I made him laugh talking about my mother's house.

We walked so fast we both began to sweat beneath our coats. I kept having to fight the impulse to throw my coat on the grass of St. James Park. I could imagine my black coat with its gray silk lining there on the green grass. I could see myself walking away from it. In my mind, I walked with an amazing ease beside Lauro. Beside him and without my coat. But in the end, I convinced myself it would be mad to throw my coat down. It was a good coat and I liked it. Yet I've always regretted not doing it. I think about that coat, its wool back warm against the dampish grass, its silk belly shining up against the sky. I often wish I'd done it, but it isn't the sort of thing I do. It's the sort of thing Lauro does, I must have known that, even at first. Was I trying to become more like him? I wish sometimes I had his courage and his faith. His speed. But really I don't want to be like him. Too many things I'm good at, things I'm used to being good at, come to me because of my limitations, which I'm also used to, which I can't imagine now will change. Lauro thinks anything can change.

Because I didn't throw my coat down on the grass, because he didn't think of doing it with his, we were hot and thirsty and we stopped for drinks. This made us both more amorous. But we didn't go to bed. Not that day. I was still married, living in the country. I had to drive myself back home.

And perhaps I was thinking: not again. Not another mistake.

For a while, I thought I could both be with Lauro and be married in the country to the Russian. I couldn't, though, because I wanted to be inhabiting the same space with Lauro day by day. I couldn't give up the idea of that.

I was right not to. He makes me feel, walking beside him, or lying in bed, that he is opening up life. I've always felt that we all live so much of our lives as if we were in a sealed jar, the lid tight, looking out. Things tap on the outside—branches, fingers—but not hard enough. If they tapped too hard, there would be breakage and that mustn't be. That's the damage that must be kept back. The walls of the jar must not split or fracture. They must remain whole.

The children whom I treat would know very well what I'm talking about, but they're always afraid of the fragility of the jar's walls; they think that anything can break them, and there's no way they can prevent it. But what I wanted for myself was for an opening to occur in response to some heat or gradual pressure of the contents. Like the uterine, the vaginal walls, when a woman gives birth. Or that round bone, the cervix. Something opens up. You could say there was a rupture, but a timely one.

And this is what I've always wanted: that the contents of the jar press up against the walls, or some heat causes it to expand. There will be a rupture in the sealed glass walls. Fragmentation. Room for entrances and exits. That's what I've always wanted, and what Lauro makes me feel. As if he put his mouth against the walls of the glass jar, and the heat of his breath, the shape of his mouth, caused opening, enlargement. Causes it again and again. Something pours out: it can be anger, or desire, wisdom, foolishness. Something moves. Something isn't the way it was.

I couldn't give that up. I didn't want to.

But for years I'd kept the jar well sealed. I had always thought I knew who I would be at some point in the future.

When I worry about plans, Lauro says, "Why not let the earth take a couple of turns."

As if he can hear it. The silent whirring in the cold, pure dark.

When we first met, he told me we couldn't make love in his house, his house was ugly. For months we went to hotels. I began to suspect that he lived with a woman. Finally, I insisted that he take me to his flat.

It wasn't ugly, but it was the home of a very young man, a young man with no money, whose furniture, all of whose possessions, were given to him by someone else. In fact, Lauro had bought them. The pictures were unframed, stuck to the wall with tacks. The furniture was repaired with tape. He said that when he was married, he'd put a lot of time and effort into his house, and then lost it all, so he was reluctant to do it again. I've never believed that, and the longer I'm with him, the more I know I'm right not to. It's just that buying things for the house himself would have bored him, and he never does anything that bores him. He simply doesn't: like an adolescent boy.

Nevertheless, we were very happy in his flat. By "his flat" I mean his bedroom, we never went into the other rooms. His sheets were blue-gray and made the room seem peaceful.

When we moved in together, we decided to spend a lot of money and a lot of time buying things for the house. Sometimes at night, I walk around here, turning on the lights and saying to myself, "You're happy here," and wondering if it's because everything is so new and expensive.

When he goes away, I save his dirty shirts so I can have his smell. I save the pillowcase he slept on the night before he left. Peasant, animal, he calls me, pretending to be amused. But I can tell that he's embarrassed. He would never do the same for me.

When he's away, and I'm at home, I'm not unhappy. If I'm ever away (it isn't often) when he's home, he says that nothing works, it's a terrible house, you have to be a genius or a scientist to understand the way things work in it. When we're in the flat together, he does everything himself, he never asks me about anything, he understands everything, and I can't imagine he would live any differently alone.

I don't know what it is that he imagines about me. I don't think he spends any time speculating about the way I live.

This is a great difference between us. He says of himself: I like to get in the car and drive it, see where it will take me. I don't care to know what makes the engine work. You are always with your head inside the works.

Because of this, I've had the courage to say quite wild things to him, things I'm not sure are true but that I'd like to try out saying, sentences whose words I'd like to hear ring in the air.

I say: "It's possible we're not really alive."

He says: "No, it's not."

I say: "Do you have any idea what it means to be human?"

He says, "I do what I can."

Lying in his arms after sex, I say, "Everything I've just done is the part of me that's not my mother. As if I were a negative number whose name is Not My Mother."

He says, "Your mother has some very wonderful qualities."

Once he said that people thought of me as very steady, but that in fact I was very unsteady, I tipped and that was why it was exciting to live with me.

I said, "It's exciting to live with you because you arrange for the walls of the jar to cave in partially and for the jar to be filled with roots and stems."

He said, "Since when have you become a gardener?" I don't think he knew what I was talking about, but he didn't ask me to explain. Instead he said, "Most people think of gardens as very safe places, but in fact I have been in some that are quite dangerous." He told me a story about men hiding in gardens, crouching behind statuary, behind hedges. "Armed and dangerous," he said. I didn't know whether the story was true. Often I don't. I never care.

Perhaps Lauro's wrong about me, thinking I need to know so much. My work with the children is possible because I know very little, except that there's not much that can be done. People say to me, "How do you do it, get up in the morning knowing what you'll see that day? Knowing you can't make these children really well."

I tell them that I like the work because it interests me, because I can no longer take for granted what it means to be human, because there are many ways of being human, because the people I work with understand this, because elation is possible in our work. We're elated at what might seem a tiny thing: a child learns to turn on a light switch, a child stops running around a room when you talk to him and looks you in the eye. Because each day I see pain, courage, heroic efforts: simply to shape a life. As if we could say what a life is. As opposed to a nonlife. A not-life.

I know what people think when they ask me: "How can you do your work?" They think "You can't cure them, why do it?" I say to them, "If a child came to you with diabetes or arthritis, would you refuse to treat him because you couldn't cure him?"

I've learned to give up the twin ideas of cure and blame. I've learned that most blame is useless, but that we love it because without it we're left with something worse: not knowing why. I've learned this from the children and their parents, linked, each in his or her circle, often unable to reach out. They've taught me the cruelty of blame. For years, authorities blamed autism on parents who wished so violently for their children not to exist that the children, out of love, tried to simulate nonexistence. But I've seen the same symptoms, the same behavior from children whose parents have sat patiently for hours with their children, parents who've devoted their lives to getting their children to speak a single word, and from children whose parents tried to fry them in a pan on the cooker, or put them in the dustbin with the previous night's rubbish as a lesson. Where, given these pieces of evidence, is there room for blame?

To the parents, I try to suggest explanations for their children's lives, which I speak of in terms of luck or genes. It's better that way. Great change is beside the point for most of the children, hopeless. I suggest to the parents that they should get help shouldering the tragic burden of their children, who cannot give them the futures for which children stand. I believe in the possibility of help with these burdens from someone outside. If I can't give them hope for much change for their children, I can try to give them hope that somewhere there is help for them. At least to feel less alone.

The children are always alone. They may feel too alone, or not alone enough to suit them, but aloneness is what life is about for them. So they feel the ordinary human anxiety, the despair, that each of us is alone, but they also feel an outrage that the sameness and order they need to feel safe is in danger if they're not sufficiently alone. They obsessively create borders: between one thing and another, between themselves and the world. They create edifices or machines to separate themselves from the world. One child would speak only inside a construction of cardboard, wires, tins; one would sleep only in a house he'd made for himself from newspapers and boxes. They can't predict, so they are safe only in sameness. They are so far from an experience of time that only space and its emptiness remains.

And yet there are things that can make their lives better. One child would eat only if she was plugging up her ears and nostrils —she could only feel good, she said, if the holes that let bad things in were closed up. She was helped to eat, first with a therapist plugging her ears for her, finally without having to plug herself at all. A boy who believed he was being run by a machine called Valvus, and so would not go anywhere unless he was connected to wires, was able to free himself, with our encouragement, of his constructed tyrant and see that he still lived.

We can teach them to memorize gestures and responses. Humans get much that they need through responding and engendering response, but for the children whom I treat, this is almost impossible. For many of them, at first, a smile is indistinguishable from a grimace: Why should they return a smile with a smile, when those parted lips, those visible teeth could mean either kindness or a will to do harm? And yet to get what the world can give, you must return a smile with a smile and protect yourself from the grimacing stranger. We teach the children the difference between a smile and a grimace, by hundreds of simulations, thousands of repetitions.

The children don't understand their place in the world, so relatedness is difficult. We give them scripts for relatedness: If someone says this thing, we tell them, then you must say this. I remember one of them being very angry when he was taken to a play. "How can they give someone money for that," he said, outraged at the actors. "It's just a lot of people making believe they're somebody else and getting paid for it." I understood that he was angry because they were getting paid for what he had to do to live.

They live in fear. We can make them less afraid of things. They come to us full of terrors we would never have thought of: of candles, of fruit, of cats, of televisions, of pianos. We can teach them that there are some things they need not fear.

Of course I feel frustration and despair. Even when we're doing something, it's very little. We can't give these children a full life. Something—some broken chromosome, some missing mineral—limits them to a life we're always tempted to describe in terms of the lives of animals. We say that they can rage, but not mourn, feel terror but not pity; they may have appetite but not affections. But I don't stay in despair long. Because the school is a place where these children are simply who they are. Living differently. Being human differently. Their progress has nothing to do with the rest of humankind. So if a child learns the difference between a smile and a grimace, if a child can ride a bus or play a game on a computer, there is joy for all of us. Real joy.

The children's parents and the staff believe I know things; they simply don't believe me when I tell them how little I know.

Lauro can live with knowing very little. He can go into a foreign country, unable to decipher the alphabet, unable to recognize the spices that create the taste in the food, not knowing where he'll sleep or if he'll be killed. The next day he knows more. Soon he feels there's a great deal he knows. I love him for this. I could never go to a country where I couldn't make sense of the alphabet. I love him because of his fluidity, so unlike the sick children who move wildly or are inert, who can't move in relation to other bodies, who bang up against other people or who hurt themselves on furniture and walls they slam against, or who stand too far apart, who think that they're part of the floor, or that the window is a mouth to eat them. They move too little or too much; they waste movement or they fear it. Lauro moves through the world as if movement were his reason to be alive. Then he stops. When he sleeps, he sleeps like a restful animal. He knows that his skin contains him; he knows that he can move and move and always be himself. The children don't know that; it's one reason they're so afraid. The world is full of things that Lauro doesn't fear or question, which is why he is, for me, the place of rest.

I've said Lauro isn't afraid of death, but in surprising, almost shocking ways, sometimes he is. So you see, as much as two people think they know one another, there is very little they can say about one another and be confident it's true. I've seen this brave man, this death-defier, fall to pieces when quite minor things go wrong. This man who travels to the death spots of the world trembled in the taxi on the way to see the dentist, his good friend and admirer.

One afternoon, the dentist told him he would have to have a tooth pulled the next day. When Lauro told me, I asked him if he wanted me to come along.

By way of response, he asked me if I knew where his will was kept.

I said, no I didn't know where it was kept. My will, he said, is in the tin box in the bottom drawer of my dresser.

I deliberately didn't look.

"Are you afraid about your teeth?" I asked.

He shrugged and lifted his hands, palms to the ceiling. He said, "I have a premonition."

"Let me go with you tomorrow."

"I don't like you to see me weak." And then: "I might look terrible. Suppose he disfigures me, this dentist."

"You can cover your mouth with a handkerchief," I said.

He turned over and settled in for sleep. "We'll see how I feel in the morning. If you wake up, maybe we'll go together."

I didn't sleep at all. I tried to imagine myself after Lauro's death. It wasn't difficult. I saw myself doing the ordinary tasks, but stopping, standing in the middle of the room, letting my hands hang empty at my sides. I knew that if he died I would go on living, that not for a moment would I consider suicide. Knowing that I wasn't suicidal, I saw that, to me, everyone is more or less replaceable; no death would in itself cause me to seek my own, and this made me dislike myself. I was beginning to steer firmly toward self-loathing; then I remembered he was only having a tooth pulled.

It began raining at four o'clock. By six, when he awoke, the air was full of thunder, in the grip of an exciting storm. I like thunder in the morning; it signals for me a true break, possibilities, as if we all stood on the brink of something better. I asked Lauro if he wanted me to go to the dentist with him. Yes, he said, he'd like me to come. I asked if he minded if I went in blue jeans. He said he didn't care, that I should please myself, but I saw that he did care and that I'd made a mistake. At that point, though, to change my plans would only have signaled to him that I thought the event had great import, the very opposite of what I'd tried to do. Of what, in fact, I believed.

He sat hunched beside me in the taxi, silent and removed; I held his hand. The dentist asked him if he wanted me beside him. No, he said, he wanted me to go away in case he cried out; he didn't want me to hear that. I said I'd go and get some breakfast. Downstairs in the dentist's building, there was a poisonous-looking café, but the human warmth and ordinary liveliness attracted me.

By the time I came back, Lauro was in the waiting room. The job was done, he looked no different, except for his lip, swollen by novocaine. I expected that he would be jokey and ebullient with relief, but he was quiet, and in the cab he looked out the window and didn't say a word. He got straight into bed when he came home. I fixed the pillows for him, and kissed his forehead.

"I didn't tell you that my uncle died having a tooth taken out," he said. "Right in the dentist's chair, a heart attack."

"You're all right now," I said. "I'll make you soup, and for later some custard. Close your eyes."

"You're good to me," he said.

I cut the vegetables to make the soup, thinking about his will. I didn't want to look at it.

Another time he had to have minor surgery, an old injury to his knee, torn cartilage. Originally he'd got it playing ball, and it bothered him from time to time. But he'd hurt it again, running for a bus, and the trouble didn't go away. The surgeon said there was nothing for it; it had to be operated on. He didn't sleep for three nights. I told him facts: medical fact after medical fact. I told him how interesting the procedure would be if he could only visualize it. I showed him his patella and told him they would lift it up and go inside it with a periscopelike instrument to look about. "It's fascinating, inside your knee," I told him. "It looks like an undersea world."

"Must you tell me these things?" he asked angrily. He demanded to be put out for the operation.

I told him he had nothing to fear, but he feared anyway: nothing I could say came close to penetrating all that fear. There was nothing I could do for him; he believed he was going to die. From an operation on his knee! He was burrowing into a darkness where he could be undisturbed and unresisting, as if death, finding him resistant, would be punitive and make things worse. I tried to tell him they were going to repair a cartilage, which was something like a snapped rubber band. He didn't listen; he was getting ready for his death.

As he was wheeled down the hall in hospital, he raised his hand and looked back at me tragically, as if he were boarding a train with other soldiers going to war. The First World War, the one where the innocent and literary boys went off so stoically to their doom. I raised my hand in response, but I wanted to say, "For God's sake, you'll be fine in a day or so. You'll be as good as new." But I didn't, I knew it wouldn't help, the best thing I could do was let him go off to the thought that he was going to his death, but that I would keep his memory fresh.

Of course, I wondered what had happened to the man who dodged bullets and lay feverish and dehydrated in a hut, with no one paying attention to him, in places where death would have been commonplace, so commonplace they might have let him die, it would have been too much trouble to fight. What was there about civilization, hygiene, comfort, and attentiveness that weakened him so? Were there two men, the man who traveled and the man who stayed at home, two who didn't communicate, shared nothing but a bodily appearance? Which was the one who lived with me, who came into my bed and ate the food in the fridge, who bathed in the same tub I did and used the towels that were laundered with mine? But who left? Who always had to be leaving? The children whom I treat have trouble understanding the idea of what makes up a person, a person consistently recognizable, consistently the same. The odd thing, to me, is how wholeheartedly the rest of us pretend to understand.

In a small room on the hospital floor where he would come after the operation, I was reading the newspaper, waiting for him to be brought up. I heard my name called, and I was alarmed; I didn't think anybody knew me here, and I felt guilty. Lauro had referred to me as his wife; the doctors and nurses called me by his name, and I hadn't corrected them. I've never changed my name, not one of the three times I've been married. I've gone through my whole life with only the one name. This wouldn't be remarkable in a man, but in a woman, it isn't nothing. Because of this I felt that, in allowing Lauro's name to be attached to me, however briefly, I'd transgressed, and I was waiting for an accusation or a blow, like any inexperienced thief. At the same time, I felt resentful and ridiculous that I'd allowed them to call me by his name, as if I were pretending to be an invalid, with a fake bandage or a fake limp.

So when my real name was called out, I was startled. Ready to defend myself. The person who'd said my name wasn't anyone I knew. Then she said her name. She was Lauro's ex-wife.

They had, according to him, not been happy. They'd parted bitterly. There'd been unpleasantness about money; they vilified each other to their friends. And yet, I thought, she seems to be a perfectly nice woman. Good-looking. To tell you the truth, that was my first thought: that she was better-looking than I. I was sure that if he met both of us at a party today, knowing neither of us, he'd move toward her first.

She works at the hospital; she's a research geneticist, rather well known. A friend had told her Lauro was here. She had thought she'd just drop by.

We chatted for a little while. As if we could be friends. In other circumstances, we could have been. I understood why he had chosen her, for her quick movements, her intelligent, bright eyes. And of course, in a way they belonged together. I was tempted to suggest that they get back together: both Turinese, small, Christian, the same age. I thought they should be together because of the way they would look on the street. Not like Lauro and me. I'm younger, taller, English, but a Jew. I always think people can tell that, but I might be wrong. In taking up with me, Lauro had taken on my displacement. Or my lack of place. With someone like him, he could have been placed, recognizable, and so approved of on the street.

"I'm sure he ignored this knee thing until there was no alternative," she said, angrily. I heard his vowel sounds in hers.

"It's the same way with those moles of his," she said. "He was always convinced they were cancerous, but he would never have had them checked. It would have been so easy to have them checked, but he never did it."

I thought of the endless times we talked about his moles, and how angry I'd been that he'd never seen a doctor about them. Angry in the same way she was.

As I stood chatting with her, I was thinking, You and I know the same body. What did this make me feel? Kinship and competition. I wanted to both take her in and drive her out, to assert my ascendancy beyond question, for all time.

It happened that we were both involved in the antinuclear movement and had political friends in common. We'd probably marched in the same demonstrations, held signs in the same freezing air, sent food and money and clothes to Greenham Common, perhaps we'd been there at the same time.

I wanted to say to her: Isn't it strange, we both know the sounds he makes when he comes?

I wanted to treat her as a friend, but there were things that got in the way. She'd hurt him; how could I forgive that? Also she'd borne his child, as I had not, and never would. I was pained by the old image of them, a matched pair, a young married couple, new parents, hopeful, appropriately so, in a way that he and I had never been. I wanted to feel like a friend, to include her in the circle of our life, not to be dreadful as I'd seen other people be. I was perfectly able to be friends with the new wives of my other husbands. But I couldn't be with her, because I knew he didn't want it.

I knew that even the mention of her name agitated Lauro. I wanted to protect him from seeing her beside me when he came out of the anesthetic. I didn't want to appear to be banishing her, but, for his sake, I felt I had to.

Was it for his sake or my own?

I said, as humorously as I could, "I think the two of us at his bedside is more than he can handle in his state. It's sort of like a bad movie, don't you think?"

She laughed, and said that she would leave, but that I should tell him she'd been by.

He was wheeled back to his room. He opened his eyes briefly and smiled, thanked me and went back to sleep.

I was happy, sitting beside him, reading, looking up at him, watching him sleep. He was all mine. I thought of everything I knew about his body: the different smells, the different textures of hair on his arms, chest, head, the pubic hair that I had known so closely. Even as his ex-wife had. He shifted in the bed and the sheets became dislodged. I saw his cock and balls. I was so glad to see them! They were so familiar, and they looked so fresh, so lively, compared to his face, old and deathly after the operation. I wished I could touch them, but I knew how touch can disturb a person still recovering from anesthesia, so I held back. I was glad to look at them, though.

I knew that what I felt for him would go on, that it was centered in our bodies, that it couldn't end without assault to both of us. So you could call that marriage.

He woke up and said, "When I thought I was dying, and I was thinking it would be easy to give up and die, I began to think of having sex with you. So you can say the idea of you kept me alive."

I was touched and amused by his use of the words, "have sex," as if we never had, only talked to other people about the possibility. But I also wanted to tell him: There was no chance you were going to die. The whole thing was very minor.

Yet people have died under anesthesia. I began to be worried that he was sleeping too long, that his color was bad. Sometimes I believe his superstitions, he describes them so convincingly.

He was still sleeping when I had to leave. I went home and looked at his will. I'm the executor, the lawyer had been after me to read over it for years, but I'd always put it off. But now I felt I must. As I held the pages at first, I was afraid of surprises: hidden children, aliases, debts of honor needing to be paid.

But there were no surprises. He's leaving everything to his son, and, if his son predeceases him, his mother.

My will is almost identical. Neither of us mentions the other in a will. But our sons, our mothers, we are provident for them.

I haven't really said enough about my mother, considering what a part she plays in all this. By "all this" I guess I mean how I have shaped my life.

Four years after my father died, my mother sold the house where they had lived for twenty years. The house they'd crossed the ocean to buy, a purchase they'd made for themselves—it obviously wasn't a house for me, I'd be leaving for university soon, they knew. It was a house about my mother's ideas of living in a house, about her governance, a house about its garden, about the dark wet grass, the low casement windows with their inconvenient hasps. My mother spent her days tending this house with no sense that this was inferior employment. Once or twice, I came upon her in the afternoon, sitting in one of her flowering chairs, her feet up, her ankles still attractive in the brown leather low-heeled shoes she wore around the house, dreamily conducting a radio orchestra playing Schubert or Mendelssohn. But it was very rare that I saw her sitting down.

My father was as nearly invisible as anyone I've known, so I don't know what the house was to him; I have no sense of his occupying space. Strange that his work should have been with bodies; gastronomical disorders were his specialty. And what could be more physical? His conversations with patients must have included sentences about what they ate, their habits of elimination. Yet he himself hardly ate, and he chain-smoked in the toilet, so there was never any sense of him as an eliminator, only as a smoker having happened to stop by the toilet to have a cigarette. Perhaps my mother needed such a massive house, a house full of nineteenth-century implications, to press my father down into the earth. She might have been afraid of his disappearing altogether. As a child, I dreamed that I followed him up a sand dune. It was an arduous climb. I lagged behind him and eventually lost all trace of him because he'd left no footprints when he walked.

My mother enjoyed widowhood. For the first time in her life, she discovered girlfriends, widows too, who took the train together for the theater, or lectures at museums. They traveled once to Brussels for a van der Weyden show. For all the years my father was alive, my mother had never done anything like this. I wonder whether it was true of the other women as well. Four years she lived like that, and then she moved into a flat. It hurt her that I didn't want her furniture. "What will I do with all of them?" she asked mournfully, thinking of the pieces individually, as if they were children. She decided to put them in storage, in case one day I might change my mind, or in case the boys might want them. I nearly laughed, imagining the boys wanting that heavy furniture, the ruination of what might have been between them and their grandmother. "Don't put your feet up on the settee. Sit carefully on that chair, it's a treasure." My sons who own nothing that can't be put into a rucksack. But she may have been right. Who knows whom they might marry, or what they may one day become.

My father left my mother well off. She bought a flat in an eighteenth-century house that had been cut into five pieces for simpler modern life. It was in Pimlico, right near the Tate. She and her girlfriends liked that. She lived on the third floor. But in the flat itself was a staircase; you reached the bedrooms by climbing it. I thought that inconvenient for her, but it seemed to bring her peace. The sitting room and kitchen were below. She climbed up not only to her bedroom, but to what she called her study. What could she have been studying? I wondered at the time, unkindly. She sewed there and listened to the radio. In her last year of living there, she watched more television, which she kept hidden in a cabinet, like the equipment for a private vice.

It was Lauro who noticed the disintegration of the flat. Small signs: coffee stains on the stove near the burners. Spots on the bathroom mirror. Fruit in a bowl, about to go rotten, giving a sickish smell to the whole room. You'd lift a peach to find it liquefied, a dark puddle at the bottom of the Spode dish.

"You must tell her that she needs help," he said to me. "I would tell her, but that would be for her an insult, a sexual insult. Like I was telling her that as a woman she was no good."

Lauro was right; she responded to my suggestion as if I'd accused her of losing her virtue. It was a bad position for me. We'd never been close. For me to point out all the details of her failure would have been to turn myself surveillant: the police she'd left Germany to get away from: searching, turning things over, going through things, leaving, but coming back, so that you felt you weren't safe.

I let it go. I watched the household fall to pieces. Then the moment came when it had gone too far and I had to intervene. No one knows the details of what I did. I didn't do it in a good way. Perhaps the way I did it was the worst. I hated every minute of it. Each individual action started in my mind fantasies of flight so extreme that I would see myself running, carrying a torch, dressed in an Olympic athlete's shorts and satin top. Crowds cheered me, I was spurred on to greater speed, nothing could stop my brilliant run. But I never did run, I stayed where I was, doing whatever task I'd come to do, on my knees before the fridge or scraping congealed custard from pudding bowls, soaking dishes in steaming water to dissolve grease that had solidified like steel, pulling carcasses of chickens from plates, holding the stinking meat as far as I could to tip it into the bin, closing the metal top and running to the sink, praying the meat smell on my hands wouldn't make me sick.

I should have done one thing or the other. I should have kept after things so these scandals had never occurred in the first place, or I should have accepted it as a normal event in the course of life, an effect of aging. I wouldn't have felt shame, for example, had my mother grown deaf or developed cataracts. I should have thought of her failings in that light. But I didn't. I couldn't. Shame covered me like a bucketful of filthy water spilled from a window I walked beneath.

I knew enough to know I had a choice. Many choices. I could have been firm with her and hired a stranger, even a series of them, to contend with the neglected house. To bathe her and to wash her hair. She stopped doing that too. In the end, she was unpleasant to be around. She who had been so fastidious. She'd hurt her women friends by refusing to see them. Once, one of them came by without ringing first, but she never came back again.

Lauro wasn't upset by my mother. The only time she came out of her stupor was when he stopped by for tea or to bring her a takeaway meal from the Indian restaurant down the street.

At those times, I could say, "You have to wash your hair, dear. Lauro's coming. And bathe carefully; you want to look your best." How can I describe to you my outrage, my remorse that I should have to speak like that. My mother! My fastidious mother!

Nothing I had learned in any part of my life was of help to me. I spent large portions of the day thinking about washing my mother's hair. I would be sitting with one of the children, doing the work that I have done for years, whose most important aspect is attention, and I couldn't think of Jacky, who sits and rocks and says, over and over, the names of kings. I couldn't visit with Theresa, watching her put stones in a straight line, or with Rene from Cambodia, who spends the day drawing circles in the sand with a stick, or Philippa who is obsessionally afraid of the idea of razors in water. I couldn't listen to the staff's complaint about the cleaning women, or to one of the therapist's ideas for a new treatment. None of them engaged my mind. I was supposed to be the camera that moved as they moved and recorded what they did, made a coherence out of incoherence, the one whose responses they could trust. It's crucial that the children have my full attention, essential that the staff believe I'm utterly behind them in their difficult work. Who knows what I may have missed, what crucial thing, thinking about my mother's hair?

Her hair that used to be her pride. "It has a natural wave," she used to say, as if it were an achievement. "It's too bad yours is more difficult." I knew she didn't mean it. She would have had a wholly different life with a daughter whose hair had a natural wave.

She'd always kept her hair short. Each week she visited the hairdresser. When she moved out of Richmond into Pimlico, she found a new hairdresser, a girl named Jasmine who talked about her boyfriends. "Terrible character," my mother would say, but I could tell she liked her. Then it stopped. The visits to the hairdressers just stopped. How did it happen? I don't know. I reproach myself for not having paid more attention. It was Lauro who read the signs.

My mother used to say: "I can't stand the feel of hair on my neck." She would bend her head in an exaggerated gesture, thrash it back and forth as if even the imagination of hair on her neck were torture. "I don't know how you stand all that hair," she said to me. I've always kept my hair long, usually pulled back with a clip, sometimes on the top of my head. "So much more appropriate," my mother always said when I wore it pinned up. In the sixties, when my fringe grazed my eyebrows, my mother was always coming up to me and pushing my hair out of my eyes with her fingers. It was not a tender gesture.

When she neglected her hair, it flattened against her head. She lost her natural wave. She'd go to a hairdresser if I took her, but not back to Jasmine. Then she began having a series of falls and resisted leaving the house. Part of her unpleasant bodily smell, a distinctive part, emanated from her unwashed hair. When I reminded her to bathe she always did, and I would notice that the next time I came and for a little while afterward her smell was less unpleasant.

It's impossible to speak this way without sounding brutal, I know. The smell of an old body is the smell of death. It pervades and endures. You see no end to it. This is what the children in the school think life is: pervasive unbreakable extension. As a physician, I know that old women who have borne children often have trouble controlling the flow of their urine. You would think this knowledge would have made me less horrified by my mother's state. It never did. Knowledge never touches panic, and my mother's smell made me panic.

Although she bathed when I reminded her, she refused to wash her hair. "I feel a draft," she'd say, although the day was stifling. Or: "They've forecast rain. I heard it on the radio." I bought her an electric dryer. "You'll avoid a chill if you use this," I told her. She said it made her arms tired holding the dryer above her head. "Of course if you did it, that would be all right," she said. Only then did I realize that she was asking me to wash her hair.

I kept waiting for some miracle, some deliverance, some change, unforeseeable, untraceable to any natural cause, anything that might intervene so I wouldn't have to wash her hair, so that would not be my fate. But then I had to do it. The flesh of her shoulders was shockingly buoyant. She had the shoulders of a girl, and then, with no warning or transition, the tired upper arms, the sag and droop of age. The straps of her brassiere, pink and yellowish from neglect, dug into her shoulders. I wanted to tell her that she needed new brassieres, but I knew she'd resist the suggestion, and it would be another task for me—to convince her, then to buy them—so I said nothing.

It was hard to get a lather on her hair. She hadn't washed it for so long. It wasn't like washing my children's hair, the joyous soapy times, their slick flesh shiny and desirable, the peaks of shampoo —"a crown, Mummy, look, feathers!" I used to linger over washing my children's hair. With my mother, I did it as quickly as I could. With her hair wet, even clean, she looked skinned, mutilated. I was never the kind of girl who gave time to her hair, who played at style or, deadly earnest, stood in front of a mirror, curling, teasing, feathering, as if death, or, what was to her the same thing, a life of unmarriedness, were at stake. My mother would have liked a daughter like that; she herself stood in front of the mirror, loving her reflection, giving her hair reassuring pats to praise it, running her fingers through it, fluffing it up, then frowning at herself, as if to undo the punishment she feared would follow on her own self-love. I used to watch her in front of the mirror, and know how different we were. Now I had to stand behind her as she looked in the mirror and I styled her hair. I did a good job, although I'd never done anything like it before. My mother thanked me. I wanted to hurl the hairbrush through the window. I wanted to throw the bottles of shampoo, break every object in the house, hear the noise of glass shattering. I wanted to run out to the street, scream at everyone. Ethicists, social engineers, trendy philosophers discussing the abject. I wanted to say: "Not one of you knows anything. Everything is about my mother's hair."

Instead, I went home and turned on Lauro. I told him he didn't know a thing about the world, that he lived in it as a visitor, the world was a hotel for him and he was always skipping out before the clerk made up the bill. What is it like to live as you live? I said, distorting my face to pain him further.

He got himself ready for bed. He lay down on the bed and turned his back to me.

"You have said about me what I always fear," he said.

He didn't try to defend himself. That night, I thought of leaving him and living with my mother.

Of course, I didn't do anything like that, but in that bad time with my mother, I seemed always to be angry at Lauro. When he'd go away and I had to see her without him, I was always writing him angry letters that I didn't send. Here's one of them:

Why are men always attended to? Except perhaps when the woman is an invalid or the man guilty about his sexual inadequacy. No, even then. To be inattentive for a woman is to declare herself unwomanly. "She pays no attention to him." The woman guilty of that description must be ritually cleansed or stoned, she's outside the realm of the desirable. Except as the transgressor. This is a powerful way to be: the unmoved mover. I imagine a woman who files her nails while a man caresses her breasts, who reads a magazine while his mouth is on her. Who cannot be made to pay attention.

It was a good thing I didn't send that one. Yet I've kept it. This must mean something, but I don't know what. I've kept all the angry letters I wrote during that period. Here's another one:

Every man with whom I've been involved for any length of time has told me in detail about at least one of his former lovers. The men begin by talking about their "feelings." By "feelings" they mean pain. They may even think that by talking this way, they're talking like women, the way women talk to each other, but eventually they become quite specific about the bodies of other women. This always happens. Sometimes they speak about her sexual mannerisms as well.

Do I mean to say that they talk about their pain only to be able to mention the bodies of other women? To describe these other women under the assumption that they aren't being prurient or tasteless? Finally to put a woman's body at the center of a story, as they've always dreamed? And whom do they imagine listening to the story, the story with another woman's body at the center. Who, if not a woman, listening, bodiless, except for the all-important organ, open to them and them alone: her cunt? Why no, her listening ear.

I wrote that one, I remember, because one night after I'd come home from a long evening of tending my mother's mess, I was tormented thinking of a story Lauro had told me about a woman he'd loved, who didn't love him, whose breasts were so beautiful her doctor had told her it was an honor to examine them. She didn't love Lauro; she used him for sex; with men she valued, she pretended she was still a virgin. His friends said: "What's she doing with a marrow squash like you?" In Italy, all insults are based on food. Except the ones that are based on the female sex. Even Lauro's mother thought this beautiful girl was too good for him.

That night I couldn't sleep. I got up and wrote the letter. I decided I'd never have sex with him again. I couldn't because nothing I was capable of doing or being would make me as prized as that girl, whom he hadn't seen for thirty years. I was terrified of meeting her one day; at the same time I wished that I could see her so that I could know what was what.

I tried to imagine a woman who could listen to the story of the girl and the doctor calmly, with interest. She would be a woman with no fears about her own desirability. I couldn't imagine her.

All that time, when I was so angry, such a bitch, Lauro never got angry in return. He always forgave me, he never defended himself; he never accused me even when I felt I deserved to be accused. It was a bad time, and he was very good to me. Perhaps he wouldn't have put up with it for much longer. But then things changed, and my mother had to go into a home.

She fell and broke her hip. She was unable to drag herself to the phone; she was downstairs, where she'd refused to have an extension put in ("I do my telephoning in my study—it's where my records are, my bills, right there in case a problem with a tradesman should come up"). She banged on the floor until the woman in the downstairs flat responded, shouting through the keyhole, then getting the police to break in the door. My mother was terribly ashamed. Even I, arriving half an hour later, when she was decently covered with blankets, waiting for the ambulance, felt shame. Shame made me silent. I was like a stone. I could hardly open my mouth to reassure her or to comfort her. I'm here, I wanted to say to her, isn't that enough? Don't ask me for more. She asked for Lauro.

When I think of Lauro, two pictures come to my mind immediately. The first is the top of his head when he's making love to me. His thick, silvery hair. I always focus on it when I'm concentrating most on my own pleasure, so I know it in a way I know nothing else. In the other picture, he is sitting on the floor beside my mother, who lies there covered with blankets. He holds her hand as if they are children playing at waiting for an ambulance, instead of modern people, trapped, caught between the cracks of faulty bureaucratic structures.

That day, the day that we were waiting for the ambulance, I left the two of them on the living room floor and went into the kitchen. My mother's tea things were still in the sink. The sugar had hardened in the bottom of her cup. I let hot water run into it and watched the sugar melt. I lost track of what I was doing, hypnotized by the prospects of the immediate future, trying to make sense of my own response to my mother's fall. I responded in stages. First I was frightened, shocked into immediate action. Then I was thrilled. The smooth plane of my problems with my mother had been broken up. Something had happened; something would change. I wasn't doomed to an eternity of cleaning out her fridge, washing her hair. She could go somewhere; someone else would have to care for her. I could empty out her house. Then I was angry at her: She shouldn't have chosen a flat with a staircase; she should have moved the telephone. I wanted to leave her where she was: She ought to pay for her bad judgment. Why should I pay?

Letting the water run into the cup, I wondered how I had become like this, capable of these thoughts. In reparation, I tenderly dried her teacup, taking a fresh towel from the drawer. At home I never dry the dishes; even before we had a dishwasher I didn't dry them. My tea towels are all grotty; sometimes I use them to wipe spills from the floor. But that day, in my mother's kitchen, I carefully dried her cup, running my finger around the gold rim as if to give it pleasure. To reward it for its fidelity, its silence, with a gesture conducive to female joy.

The ambulance took her to hospital. She stayed there for a month, then they arranged for a nursing home. Her days don't bear thinking of.

I know she's fed and cared for; they even see to it that her hair is styled. Cut short, above her ears, not a style she would have chosen, but not a horror. She has no concentration. She can't finish a book or sit still for a symphony on the radio. The cultured people in the home, who at first recognized her as one of them, have now given up inviting her to play chess or read their interesting books or magazines. She doesn't talk to anyone. She is the favorite of no nurse or attendant. I would have to say she sits all day and thinks. What does she think about? Her furniture, unused in the forlorn darkness? My father, whom she seems never to have mourned? Me or my sons? Her own impending death? I don't know if she thinks about any of these things.

She doesn't talk to me. She talks to Lauro. He visits her and holds her hand and tells her what he saw in the street that day. Only with Lauro can she concentrate. Only with him do her eyes seemed moored. She even laughs with him. When my sons go to visit her, and they try, they do try to engage her, it's as if she's only waiting for them to be gone. She keeps looking over her shoulder, as if someone she mildly fears may be in the vicinity.

I said to her once, "Try and find something you're interested in. Something you like."

She answered me, looking at me, as she rarely does, as if she knew I was really there. She said, "You have to understand. I don't like anything."

Then Lauro came in. He'd brought her hazelnut chocolates. He told her about a man playing a trumpet in Hyde Park. I could see that she was happy.

I wanted to take him away from her. I wanted to bring him home to the place where we live, where she doesn't live. I wanted us to be in bed, and afterward, to be walking around the house. Quietly, as if we had all the time in the world. I was afraid she'd drain the life out of him. And I needed his life.

Because it's not so easy, just living a life. Going through my mother's decline simply widened the scope of what I'd guessed at all along, what I seemed to be born knowing, but what working with the children in the school made even clearer: the extreme difficulty in managing the details of ordinary life. Things that are, for most of us, unimaginable not to do are in fact quite easy not to do or to stop doing. It isn't hard to slip out of the circle of the acceptable. Suppose for example, one has accumulated—as nearly all of us have—the possessions of a bourgeois lifetime: clothes that become unfashionable or partially worn out, saucepans with broken handles, books whose information has become obsolete, faded bedding, chipped crockery. And then supposing one day all of it is simply too defeating. The process of coping with leftover food. Of disposing with what's gone bad. Remembering to put the milk back in the fridge before it spoils. Understanding what to do with the clot of butter, the size of a penny, still left on a dish, not thrown away because of thrift but too disgusting to eat. To be unable, one day, to think what to do with the fat at the bottom of the pan after you've grilled a chop. To find the purchase of buttons and thread beyond your grasp. What do you do? Allow disaster to accumulate and literally breed, or walk out of the door with nothing, headed nowhere, leaving it all behind, setting a match to it, perhaps, therefore unable to go back because of shame, and more important, downright criminality? Is there a moment before the habits have given way when you can feel the torpor as a luxury? Or a moment, perhaps in the afternoon when the sun is strong, when it's a pleasure to have no address? But the moment would change into something horrible. At some point it would. To live a continuous life a person needs to be in relation to the world of objects. Why does everyone assume this is an easy thing, an accomplishment not worthy of praise? In the blink of an eye, we can be overtaken by or else abandoned by the things we live among.

The children I work with know about all this. Or is *know* a misleading word? What is it that we might say, and consider ourselves sensible, that they know?

They don't know who they are. But that's too abstract. I want to tell you things that won't seem like metaphors or seem generally applicable to the whole of the human race. They don't know what it means to be one person rather than another person. They don't know where they end and someone else begins. They don't know what to eat. They don't know how to eat. How can I explain what food is for them? As I sit in my white kitchen, with the shiny white machines that look as if they were intended for life on the moon —a cold exacting life—all of them existing for a specialized response: chopping, mixing, heating, liquefying, freezing, how can I tell you what is the truth for these children, that they don't believe that food goes into their mouths to please them, fill them, or keep them alive?

Food terrifies them.

Often they refuse to close their mouths. Or they don't want the food to touch their teeth. They are afraid of biting.

They remind me every day how difficult it is to keep alive. The minimum for existence requires an attention we wouldn't agree to if we understood its scope. The process of growth, elimination, and decay goes on with these children, as it does with any other animal, but they want no part of it. Too inert even to become suicides, they nevertheless cannot stop the lively cells. This liveliness creates an unfathomable problem of care. Their teeth decay, for example. Then you must explain the dentist, and the pain he causes for their eventual good, to children who see no difference between time and space.

Lauro thinks this is the kind of thing I do, but that's not the truth, it's his romance about me. I used to do more of it; now I spend a great deal of my time watching, supervising, conciliating, correcting. I'm not the one who sits with them for hours in the bathroom, who allows them to defecate in the tub and play with their feces mixed with water, rejoicing in their doing this since it shows some contact with the world.

I saw a therapist do this: I spoke to her about it and we mutually agreed on its appropriateness as a treatment. When you're with the children, when you understand how it is that they live, you know they don't live like other people, but you can see as well the completeness of the circle in which they endlessly rotate, and why they go on with their rotation: It is their place. When I'm researching the children's language, for example, and taking down their obsessively repeated expressions or strange syntaxes, I always find a logic and I can reassure them easily that where they are is fine, what sense they make is fine for me and for them. I can meet them in their closed circle; sometimes I'm lulled by their skills or their hypnotic repetitions, frightened even of leaving the new closed circle I've begun to inhabit with them. But more and more now, I'm removed from direct contact with the children. At the distance I am from them now, I rarely remember that their way once struck me as good, as good as our way, simply another way. I see the parents' anguish and when I'm with the parents I realize there is no other way. Only the world's.

How could I tell the parents, burdened with their own lives, trying to cope with the siblings of the disturbed child, that the child's playing with his or her shit in the bath, pouring it over his head, is a good sign in the process of the differentiation of the self from the nonself, and that they should encourage this at home? How can I tell them how extraordinary it is, their child's uncanny ability to locate herself in relation to a moving object, when their hearts, their ordinary father's and mother's hearts, are seized up in fear because the child won't move away from the swing another child is on, when they can see, in their mind's eye, the bloody gash when the swing hits the blank, rapt forehead of their child?

I made a list of the drawings one of the children did, because in writing down the titles for my research, I was struck by their beauty. This was the list:

a sheet torn into a road
a sheet torn into two rows of teeth

a boundary
a boundary turning a corner
design with two centers
design with a white hole
man as a tube
the electric papoose
the nest tree

I remember spending a whole evening in my office, copying the list of titles again and again, as if it were a poem. When I went home I showed it to Lauro. Then I was ashamed. He didn't find it beautiful, he found it frightening or sad, and I thought: Of course. If I were their parents I would always be ashamed.

But what I must do in my job is not join the children in the place they were, but make a place for the child where there is no shame, a place they can enter from where they are, and yet know it is a place different both from the larger world that they have left in despair and the one they inhabit now in their extreme aloneness, a place where we do not only meet the child in his or her desolation and accept that desolation, but a place from which there is a possibility of making a go of it. Even starting from "down there," where they are. They must know there is or can be a place where they are not alone, where they can move, where they can know that movement need not leave them bereft, that this place is a place to which they can return, alive, the same, accompanied.

I feel so often the similarity between the children and "ourselves." Whoever we are. So often the children feel uncertainty that the parts of their body belong together; they have a fear of fragmentation, a terror, literal for them, that the one thing called a body will fly apart and scatter all over the world. Isn't this perhaps why "we" take such care, lavish such attention, insist we cannot live without our houses, which we think will keep us all of a piece, intact?

Or maybe some people never doubt that they're intact. Like Lauro. I asked Lauro if he ever had trouble believing all the parts of his body belonged to one unified whole. He put down his book for a moment, then he said, "This is not a trouble I have had. I have had many troubles, love of mine, but this one, no."

I think he thought I was talking about the children, that I, like him, had never had that trouble, and I let him think that. But that night I felt closer to the children than to him.

I guess maybe some people don't find it so difficult to live an ordinary life. When I think of Lauro's mother, I'm sure she doesn't find it difficult, that no matter what happened to her, there are things she would always do.

I only met her three years after Lauro and I were living together. In fact, it must have been a year before Lauro said a word about his family. I never pressed him. I made for myself a picture of a family from the press clips about him. Like many people, perhaps most everyone who'd met him in England, I formed my first image of him from interviews. I imagined a large, expansive family, Naples or Calabria, the expansiveness of his family an occasion, perhaps, for his need for travel. I imagined a small white stucco house with a red roof, a kitchen garden heavy with tomatoes, tile floors on which his mother walked in backless, toeless, leather slippers—pink or blue with gold heels or gold lines across the arch—endlessly shouting, endlessly producing food for her family who also endlessly shouted and endlessly consumed the food she was producing.

The truth was nothing like that at all. And in fact, he'd suggested nothing of the kind in any of the interviews. It was simply that his warmth and quickness, his enthusiasm, his attention to children, his habit of pressing food or money on near strangers, gave us Northerners an outline we were only too happy to fill in erroneously.

He's from Turin, which, as any Italian will tell you, is hardly Italian at all. Quite near the Alps and French in its layout, the efficient industrial capital, the source of modern wealth. His mother was very slow-moving, very quiet, I don't think she ever cooked. Of course she had lived in only one place all her life, unlike my mother, who had been uprooted twice; perhaps my mother moved so quickly and so angrily around the house because she was afraid at any minute she'd be asked to leave it.

Lauro and I had been living together for three years when I went to Turin with him for his sister's wedding. He said we simply had to go, in a blustering unpleasant tone I'd never heard him use. He kept that tone from the moment he told me we were leaving to the moment he put me on the train in Turin. I was going back to London; he was on his way to Somalia. But I'll speak about that later.

His sister, not the one who was getting married, met us at the station. She was a small, thin, fashionable woman; she hardly met my eye; she and her brother seemed to see no reason to embrace; he carried his bags and she refused to listen when I told her I could carry my own. I had no Italian; she took advantage by speaking rapidly to her brother in Piedmontese. She drove down the Corso Vittorio Emmanuele furiously, vengefully, and stopped the car in front of their building with a harsh jolt.

Lauro began smoking heavily the moment he set foot in Italy. At home, he never smokes. He lit a cigarette waiting for the lift. The courtyard of the building contained business establishments, a furniture showroom, a hair salon for both women and men. At the end of the courtyard, what should have been a wall or a vista opening out to a garden, was a large window of painted glass.

The lift was small, made of glass and wrought iron, and the smoke from Lauro's cigarette, in addition to all our luggage, made us feel suffocated. Lauro and his sister began to fight about the smoke. Then the lift stopped, and the second we alighted, a huge wooden door opened. Lauro's mother walked into the corridor.

She must have been waiting behind the door, but she would never acknowledge that. I know what she was feeling, having sons myself. I know that fearful, expectant waiting on the other side of the door. You can't let the son know how hard it's been for you, just waiting for the sight of him. It's impossible that he will ever desire a glimpse of you as you desire a glimpse of him. All the songs in all the languages are lies. The choked refrains, sobs for the absent mother. There are no songs of choked loneliness in the mother's voice. And rightly so. The concept is too disturbing in its truthfulness for all of us, best left as a secret or a joke.

But of course what I know is different from what Lauro's mother was experiencing because so much of my life has been lived outside the house and all the important hours of her life were spent behind that heavy door.

I can hardly even imagine such a life. I've often tried. With women who stay at home, with my own mother and the mothers of my sons' friends—often people I've liked very much, more than I've liked many of my colleagues—I've tried to imagine how they live in relation to those houses they hardly ever leave, that they direct their labor toward, that they think so many thoughts of in the course of a day. I simply can't. I begin by trying to imagine the house, going through it room by room, seeing myself with a broom, a mop, a scissors for cutting the dead leaves off the potted plants. But by the time I have walked, in my imagination, from the bedroom to the sitting room, I can only see myself sitting in one of the comfortable chairs, my face in my hands, weeping. Saying to someone, in tones of anguished accusation: "How have you done these things to me?" Or hearing the door open and realizing that I have sat in the chair for hours, in a stupor, the mop on the floor beside my feet, the bottom of its soft head shamelessly facing the ceiling.

I can more easily imagine satisfaction in the closed life of the

children whom I treat—their endlessly repeated numbers, patterns
followed obsessively—than I can imagine happiness in caring for
a house. And yet so many of these women, women whom I gen-
uinely like—seem happy. Seem to have reached an understanding
of the world that makes them not only admirable but pleasant to
be with.

When we got out of the lift, Lauro allowed himself to be embraced by his mother. Many deceptions were involved. He was
pretending to himself that he only allowed himself to be embraced,
that he had no desire for her to embrace him; he believed that in
this subterfuge he was single, thoroughgoing, and independent of
her. And he believed that she fell for his performance as the gratifying son. In fact, he was happy to see her face after so long, and
sad to part from her, but not even for ten minutes could he be a
devoted son without feeling rebellious and distracted. She understood very well what he was doing, and that he had to be away
from her to feel he breathed air as a man.

I'm trying to tell you what I admire about Lauro's mother, all
the things it wasn't difficult for her to do. There were very few
things she found impossible. I think it was because of the way she
lived in the rooms in which she had lived for so many years.

I'm not sure what she did all day. Of course she didn't do any
of the housework. A very young-looking girl named Rosita (she
wasn't entirely Italian) wandered about with a mop, looking se-
pulchral in a pink overall.

The flat had a lot of important-looking objects that required
attention and specialized care. This was not unlike my mother's
house, but my mother's objects seemed more domesticated, therefore more fragile, as if each one were a pet requiring her tender
personal ministrations to maintain its state of animal contentment.
Lauro's mother's relationship to her possessions was much more
businesslike. I can't imagine her ever holding a duster. She scru-

tinized her objects; they existed for her eye and her eye was exacting; you could imagine that if one day she judged that one of her things didn't come up to the mark, she would ruthlessly, silently get rid of it. I imagined a back room of that cavernous flat full of shunned objects, banished for having failed her. I can't imagine my mother giving any of her things away, or replacing them, except if they broke, in which case she would mourn them. Lauro's mother's attitude about her things was such that if she no longer had room for them, she wouldn't be involved in shame. She'd hire someone else; or she'd sell them all up. She would simply do it, understanding it had to be done, in the same spirit in which she accepted her husband's infidelities.

I wondered what she'd done during the war, how she'd lived. She'd been a young woman, and Turin had been badly hit. What had happened to her objects then? What had it done to her to see those houses, so solid, so suggestive of imperishability, reduced to rubble, rafters, furniture exposed like a sexual crime. Had she been Fascist or anti-Fascist? It was impossible to connect politics with her; she seemed so fixed and impervious to any kind of public change. Yet Turin had been the center of the Resistance. Her brothers had been killed. All over the city you could see plaques in honor of the Resistance dead, with small vases of fresh flowers still faithfully placed in front of them.

Had she placed flowers? Where? And for whom? You could never ask her that; you couldn't imagine her speaking about herself. If you had asked her what she really felt about something, she'd have looked at you strangely, as if you'd asked a question about chemistry, or bridge building, or law, some field of enterprise she couldn't be expected, with her history and education, to know about. Some field belonging to her husband and her son.

I never met Lauro's father; he'd died when Lauro was at university. I wonder whether Lauro would have been able to take up the life he has—so irregular, unstable, open—if his father had lived longer. I only know about Lauro's father from what his sister tells me, and from the small pieces Lauro parcels out to me from time to time. He was a large man with a brush of steel-gray hair. He bellowed orders to the servants. He respected his house and the idea of family, although he was rarely at home and kept a mistress. He habitually talked quite loudly, according to Lauro's sister Marina, the one Lauro was fond of, for whose wedding we had come to Turin. The house was always ringing with his shouting, Marina said, with his prejudices, his enthusiasms, his ideas, which, she said, because he wasn't intellectual, were like a rude bumptious child he'd brought into the household for the holidays.

When I thought of Lauro's childhood, I imagined dark heavy furniture, high walls, stone floors which gave the flat the acoustics so congenial to the father's thundering, so perfectly designed to make it frightening for the children. I could see the entrance of the large, loud father through the door, and the strategy each child created in response to that thundering. A battle plan, a plan for life! Lauro invented his talent for escape. Cati became cynical, and Marina, the youngest, who suffered most, withdrew into her room and put her fingers in her ears, creating fantasies in which she avenged the oppressed everywhere. Now she defends the homeless; even elegant Turin has its homeless, sleeping on summer nights outside the railroad station, hunkering down against its thick, civic-minded nineteenth-century walls.

I'm sure Lauro's mother didn't need to invent a strategy; the father's thundering was just something else that she went on in spite of. She was happy in her marriage. Everyone agrees they were devoted to each other. Sometimes he would come home at lunch-time to discuss a business problem with her. She never said any-thing: nodded and smiled, agreed with everything he said wholeheartedly, agreeing with exactly the opposite position she would agree to ten minutes later when he did an about-face. He would make his decision, he would noisily kiss her and tell her how intelligent she was, that everyone knew women were more intelligent than men. Would he then take her into the bedroom, undress out of his heavy suit, close the shutters for an afternoon of slow-moving marital love? It doesn't matter. You see what I mean: she was happy in her marriage. It both prepared and didn't prepare her for life with a son like Lauro, but what it did do, thoroughly, was eliminate any habit of expressing what it was she really thought.

She was by no means a weak woman, and when I say she didn't express herself, I don't mean to imply she was without character or lacked personal force. She was really rather imposing with her imperial head, slightly oversize for her body, the thick gray hair, impressively, expensively cut, the large light eyes, the strong fingers with their competent-looking nails, polished a shade of reddish brown that made you unable entirely to forget the idea of blood. In fact, many people were afraid of her, particularly younger women—what a trial she must have been for her young son's girlfriends. She's much larger than Lauro—he's the smallest in the family, which must have been sexually disorienting for those girl-friends, even the ones most blindingly in love. I wondered if she had been larger than her husband. If so, I'm sure she kept it from him, that he'd died not knowing it, that she'd done something to keep him from knowing that he was a laughingstock on the street, that she'd lied to him about both their heights, and that he'd believed her, that she'd made up her mind that it didn't matter the first time she met him, and so for the rest of time it didn't matter.

I liked being with Lauro's mother, and I hope she knew it, because all the time I was in the house with her and Lauro, I had to make it seem as though I understood she was a dangerous and clever enemy, who lived only to entrap him so that he would never leave the flat, the family, the city of his birth. But I knew she'd long ago given up hope of keeping him near her, so that she'd even forgotten it was something she'd once wanted. That was what was remarkable about her; she was enormously adaptable, and yet she gave you the sense that she had always been the same. Lauro didn't understand that this was why it was so easy for him to leave her, because he knew that whenever he came back to her she would be the same person in the same place.

He's not like that. From the time we left London to the time he put me on the train in Turin he was at least three different people, none of them having anything to do with one another. He was the Lauro I lived with when we were at home in our flat, then he was the petulant son and brother, then at the railroad station, he became another person I didn't know, but one that I had read about.

In the car driving to the station, he was sullen and ready for a fight. To break the tension, I remarked that the trees on the Corso Vittorio Emmanuele, where the railroad station is, were leafier and planted more closely together than the trees on the streets off to the right. Lauro made a clucking noise and turned from me to look out his window. His sister Cati and their mother sat silent. I was glad to be going home.

He bought me ridiculous things to take on the train. Chocolates I would never eat, glossy magazines that I would never read. The train was late; he spent the time looking at shoes in a shop window. Trying to be tactful, Lauro's mother and sister stayed in the car, but that was worse for me; I was concerned that they were uncomfortable there, hot. I suggested that he leave so they could be on their way home, but he made that clucking noise again and said, "It's the least they can do."

A fight erupted on the platform. A group of Senegalese (I had seen some of them on the streets selling disposable lighters) were

violently arguing with the police. They had with them a huge number of large cardboard boxes tied up with string. The police were
telling them they couldn't take their boxes on the train. Violence
was in the air. The passengers already on the train were hanging
out the window; I feared that soon there would be racial slurs.
Lauro sprang into action; his sullenness, his truculence, his torpor
were all gone. He was speaking to the Senegalese in their language;
he was passing out cigarettes. To the policemen, I heard him men-
tioning family names and addresses. I was lost in the welter of two
unknown languages; in one, I could pick out occasional words, the
other baffled me entirely. Then some kind of agreement seemed
to be reached. The Senegalese were giving Lauro names of relatives
he must look up. He pointed to me in the train, introducing me
to everyone as his wife. He told everyone that we were about to
be parted for three months, I could understand that: "*Mia moglie
. . . tre mesi.*" And then he said something about dying a little, I
assume from the way the policemen were nodding their heads that
he was saying it was like dying a little to leave me. The Senegalese
got on the train, the train started up, and everyone clapped. Lauro
was blowing kisses to me, his eyes shining with tears.

But who was the man blowing kisses to me? The same as the one
who could barely be civil to his mother? The same as the one who
lives beside me, who sleeps beside me, who takes me in his arms
so readily, and with such ease, who assures me that I mustn't believe
a thing he says in interviews, that I must understand the game of
interviews, how untruthful they are? I tell him I understand the
game, but I don't really, it frightens me. What happens to language
frightens me, and what happens to truthfulness when words seem
to signify the opposite of what is intended, when what seems to
be candor is an elaborate screen to keep people from what really

is the case. It's disturbing that the Lauro of the interviews is no one I've ever met, but it's even more disturbing when he speaks of me—referring to me as his "companion." I don't recognize myself. I have to ask myself (after all, it's a possibility) whether he's telling the truth to the interviewers and keeping his real self from me. I have to ask myself this because in ordinary life no one asks the bold sorts of questions interviewers ask. Who of us would ask someone, even the person beside whom we live, this kind of question: "What does death mean to you? Why have you risked your life so many times? Why do you go to places in which it is so easy to die?"

No one could ask these questions of the person they live beside because the answers would be too unbearable to live with. But interviewers ask these things all the time. These strangers, these professional intruders. When they ask him about death, he talks about adventure. And about his curiosity. When asked about death he talks about geography. About the nature of the globe. He says he's driven by a combination of stupidity, greed, vanity, and a passion not to be left out of things. "I'm really a child," he says. "I've never had to face many things I dreaded about growing up. Above all, I don't have to go to an office every day, wearing a suit."

Here are some things he's said to interviewers. "I will begin with the year of my birth, which explains a lot: 1932. When my home city [he doesn't mention it by name] was bombed most heavily, I was ten. I lived in a state of shamed excitement. I had so disliked the life of childhood. I felt constantly like a prisoner. I suffered from asthma, but I felt like the walls of the flat, of my school, were giving me that feeling of suffocation. Then suddenly the walls were gone. The bombs destroyed the walls. My mother was distracted, two of her brothers had died in the hills, so she didn't notice me out every day, walking around in the rubble. I am ashamed to say that I was happy. People had died, and I knew that, but that wasn't what I saw. What I saw didn't frighten me. It seemed full of possibilities. When I walked into the bombed site of my *liceo* and saw the desks upended and the books scattered, I felt elation. It proved to me that oppression was an illusion, force could change it, you weren't doomed to secret tyrannies behind doors, protected by walls, those daily cruelties to which middle-class children were subjected as a matter of course. Of course the tyrants who were doing the bombing were infinitely worse than our parents and the schoolmasters, but that was not real to me. I saw that the silences I'd lived in weren't inevitable: you could talk to your neighbors with spirit, you could say what you felt, you could give each other things, you could work together. They were terrible times and we suffered, but for me as a child they were hopeful times. The Fascists were defeated, then the Nazis. When the city was rebuilt and life went on as before, I was less happy. That's why I like being in situations of revolution; it reminds me of those days when people were believing things could change. When you didn't have to submit to the closed circle, endlessly repeating itself. I like the openness of the bombed city. I've never felt as comfortable in places that are truly impermeable, truly built."

"You still believe in revolution?"

"*Believe* is the wrong word. Of course I've seen disasters, but also revolutions in the name of justice where progress was made. But it's not a matter of belief. It's a matter of interest. I'm always interested in the moment of change. What makes a revolution at a particular time. For example, in Ethiopia, a revolution came about because of an increase in the price of petrol. But the price of petrol had been increasing for some time. Why suddenly a revolution?"

"Do you ever feel like a parasite? You never write about your own culture; you interpret the culture of the Third World, but you are a person of the First World."

"Yes, I worry. But if I see things, should I not speak of them?

I speak of them because they interest me. Not from a distance, judging harshly. I speak from my own feeling of being alive there. I feel truly alive only there. Why? Because the things I find difficult about life don't come up there. The things I find trivial and deadening don't exist. Also, I can move freely without constriction, from place to place. Even when I'm being followed by secret police I feel I can move more quickly than in Europe. This is an old colonialist story, you say. I don't think I am colonialist. Of course I take things from the place: a subject. I colonize the subject matter. But would silence be better? I don't know. Perhaps not. At least there is the perhaps. Most of the time that is enough. To be able to say: perhaps not. One day I may no longer be let into these places. Then there will be no more perhaps, only 'definitely no.'

"But we must understand that most of the world is the Third World, the future is theirs, and I am hopeful. Because I do not feel so much "they." Terrible things are these: diseases, famine. But perhaps not so terrible as in the past. In any case, it is of no sense hiding in our closed houses pretending the Third World is a knot of diseased children. The world is theirs. Our closed doors, our careful houses, are the houses of the past. We don't know the future. It isn't ours."

"And all this doesn't worry you? The chaos? The atrocities?"
"I replace worry with interest. It interests me very much. Sometimes I am horrified. But always interested."

"What has it been like to be near death?"
"A calm comes over you. You say: 'This is the end of it.' But of what? And that is the thing that you can never know. How to answer that question. The end of what? To try to answer that question is to sink into a hopeless swamp. So I don't ask it, most of the time, until I'm in a situation where it seems to answer itself.

The end of what is, you say to yourself. The end of all you know. In a dangerous situation, you have no time to mourn. In a lingering illness, you feel mournful. But for all my experiences, I have not yet died. So I don't really know what it is to face death, because something has always come between me and death. I have always been glad to know that I will have the chance for more life."

Reading these interviews, often thousands of miles away from him, what can I make of the words? Nothing, he says, they mean nothing. "If I were an actor, saying words in a play, you wouldn't try to connect them to the rest of my life. It's a play that I put on for them. I give them what they want."

I believe him, mostly. But I don't understand why he speaks to these interviewers at all when what is required is such false speech. I think of the children I work with, so frightened of each word, sometimes believing literally that words are bullets, that something can come out of their mouths that will kill. Or so terrified that the word might not fit the object that they mean to name, or so incredulous at the possibility of being understood, that they hold on to each word as if it were their last cent, their last bit of food. They send words out into the world with the same terror they experience while shitting. Sometimes they endanger their lives with this false, disastrous economy. This faulty valuation of what comes from the inside—words, shit. They could die of their false economies.

But Lauro's false economy opens him up to life, and opens life up for other people. Sitting on their chintz settees in Stoke-on-Trent, allowing their eyes to rest on their striped wallpaper in Clapham, the English hear Lauro's voice. It charms them; it's not one of theirs, not English. But its differentness presents no danger. He presents them with the world they fear, the world of their nightmares and their poison thoughts, and says: It is not the thing you fear, but something different.

But whose is this mouth, speaking these false words? To what body is this mouth connected? Is it the body of the man who lies beside me, who enters me, whose anger, whose fatigue I know so well? This person who tells strangers all over England that he has no home and that he is only free and happy in the kind of country I have never visited? This person who approaches death and doesn't try to keep away from it? Who deliberately walks down roads on which it is quite easy to die?

I'd like him to stay alive for me. Not that I couldn't live without him. But I would like to be the fixed point in the world marking the difference between life and death. What I would like to be for him, most, perhaps, is this: the thing at stake.

And so, you must be wondering, since Lauro can be so many people, how could I assume that he would be faithful to one person, me?

I tell myself no, that I can't expect it, he is who he is, a healthy and attractive man, away from me a great deal of the time.

But usually I believe he is.

I read descriptions of women in his articles. One he described as a "silent blonde, calm, with misty carnal eyes." Once he spent a long time on the description of the metal belts worn by the bar girls of Kampala. I had to ask myself: How did he know so much about those belts? Had he had one of those girls? A number of them? And what exactly did he mean by "carnal"? How much time did he spend looking into those misty eyes?

Nevertheless, I usually believe he's faithful. Because I believe I'm the woman he wants. Before Lauro, I felt that men were with me because of their own lack of faith in their ability to get a woman they would consider a prize. A woman they really wanted: more beautiful, simpler, more domestic. I don't feel that about Lauro.

I know that he knows how to look, that he could look for the woman he wanted, and make her his. Of course I can't quite believe his picture of me: it's too flattering. He forgets—unless he's experiencing the full brunt of my insults, my bad temper, my injustice to him, my perverse desire to hold a grudge—how difficult I am. He ignores my inability to let go of a grievance because I'm afraid that without my grievances I'd disintegrate. I understand the children and their incomprehensible rituals, because in my refusal to forgive, in my repeating and repeating the details of an offense against me, I am comprehensible to myself. He thinks I'm a model of patience and compassion. It disturbs me that he thinks this; it's so close to what I want to be and know I'm not that it seems dangerous.

But what is it that I fear? Perhaps some day some person, speaking harshly in the cold voice of real truth, will say to me, "You may fool him. But I know what you really are."

Still, I seem to believe I'm the woman he wants. I believe that without each other we are missing something vital to us both. I believe simply that.

Perhaps, you will say, that isn't very much. Perhaps. But in our desire for each other, there's a mutual humility, as if so many years of belief in desire had been fatiguing, and, having seen ourselves drawn into a series of passionate mistakes, there's an aspect of surprise in our constant need for each other. Surprise that there should be so much between us physically. A beguilement at realizing the extent to which our life in bed together is a simple fuel that causes the rest of our life to operate. To have lived through years of sex, and to have come to this: that a touch of the hand, the glimpse of the back of a neck, a shoulder, entering another person's body, being entered by another person, that all this can still make us feel so much. We're like people who have seen an earthquake, and who now sit back to watch, from the porch of the house they have built from windfall lumber, a fertile valley spread out before them like a lap.

And the humility comes as well from this: We could once again be living through only a part of life, something we may later call a mistake. Even the modesty of what Lauro and I expect from one another is no safeguard against that.

A friend of mine, a woman of my age who's been married and divorced twice and has a young child, told me about meeting another friend in France. They were speaking about a famous woman, now in her sixties, in ill health and close to death. "She lived for love," my friend's friend said of the dying woman.

My friend said she began to laugh. Because the idea of living for love, which had once seemed so desirable, so descriptive of herself, seemed like a joke. We wondered how we would be described by people younger than ourselves if we lived to be old and they were trying to learn something from the way we'd lived our lives.

Given the modesty of our claim on one another, why would anything that I've said about Lauro and me rule out a quick fuck with a bar girl, a tryst with a somnolent colonial wife while waiting out the boring hours before deliverance in some besieged town? A friendly romp with a young colleague in the spirit of comradeship and danger shared?

Perhaps because I know he's no longer young, no longer thinks of himself as young. Boredom, the desire for contact, a flash of ordinary lust are no longer enough to overcome the difficulties of one of us having sex with someone else. To be with someone else would be to displace ourselves. Neither of us wants that: to find ourselves in a new sexual place. Ten years ago, either of us might have. But not now.

This may all be nonsense. A ridiculous dodge I dignify with the name "instinct" to mask or displace fear.

I asked him once, fearing his anger, but fearing my own death more (I have my sons), to have himself tested for AIDS, if there were any reason to think there was a need. If he won't even take malaria drugs, why would I assume that he would use a condom with a prostitute, or a lazy blonde too indolent to fully open her eyes, much less track down pharmaceuticals in a ruined city? I felt I had to ask.

He was outraged. The head of a Mediterranean family. He began pulling at his thick hair. "How could you think this of me? Would you think I have no respect for you? Would you think I have no respect for all this?" He pointed all around him. He began picking up objects, turning them over, putting them vehemently down. "Would you think I have no respect for our home?"

I was very surprised at this part of his reaction. It would never have occurred to me that there was a connection between these two things: his loyalty to my body and the furniture. The paintings on the walls.

Because I so often feel there are large parts of him I don't understand, I thought it would be helpful to meet some of the friends he knew before he came to England. As I was thinking in this way, an old friend of his wrote and asked us to visit him and his wife in Canada.

They are both painters. Thirty-five years ago Lauro met the man, Jerry, while he was traveling as a student. Jerry shaved his head and smoked marijuana: a daring thing in 1955, particularly in the eyes of a twenty-three-year-old Italian. They shared a room in a house on a Spanish island, now a seaside paradise for the rich, but then a place where peasants lived and nothing happened. Once, at a party we went to, someone who'd also lived there, but a bit earlier, told Lauro there was a whorehouse on the island where he'd spent all of his time. Lauro was astonished; he'd never known about it. When we talked about it later, Lauro wondered whether the whorehouse had disappeared by the time he got there or whether he and his friends simply hadn't discovered it. He wondered if he would have gone if he'd known about it. I don't know whether he wishes he'd gone or not. Of course I know: Everyone always wishes they'd had more sex.

On the island, Lauro's friend Jerry had a nervous breakdown. He recovered and went to Germany where he married a fifteen-year-old German girl. They ran away, trailed by police. He took her back to Canada, where he was from. They moved onto an island off British Columbia, living in a log house with no electricity where they spent their days fishing, building the house, bringing in water from the well. And working on their paintings. They were, they are, serious painters. They have two children who have thrived. Of course her parents forgave them.

Lauro hears from Jerry about once a year. They get on the phone and talk like American beatniks. "How's it going, man?" he says to his friend on the telephone. Becoming another person I don't know.

On the plane over, a fourteen-hour trip, I decided to imagine what Jerry and Ulrike were like. Six hours into the flight, I decided I didn't want to meet them. Unlike Lauro, I usually don't like anyone too different from myself. I judge people harshly. Lauro thinks I don't because of my work with the children and my easy relations with my ex-husbands, because I often lend people money and allow them to spend the night when they seem to be in distress. But I set myself apart from other people; I don't become one with them, as Lauro does. Which is why I understand the children I work with and their inability to connect. Lauro is frightened by this aspect of them.

I imagined a large couple in rough clothes, taciturn and superior about their austere life. I knew Lauro would finish up by giving them a lot of money; I tried to reckon how it would occur. "The pump broke down," I could hear them saying to him, or "I hurt my back last winter and can't afford to see a specialist." When we got off the plane, I barked at Lauro when he couldn't find the baggage carousel. He kissed me and said I must be tired. We took a bus ride to a ferry that went to the island. I was silent and sullen, but he didn't seem to notice. He was in love with the mountains and the accents of the passengers, the shape of the road signs and the cakes in plastic packets from the machines in the bus station.

No one can be unhappy on a boat. The idea of prospects, of remaking a life, is unavoidable on water, and I put my head on Lauro's shoulder, liking the feeling of the wind and the rather dirty smell of his hair, which he should really have washed in London.

Lauro hadn't seen Ulrike in thirty years; Jerry in twenty-five. I was afraid they wouldn't recognize each other and that it would be embarrassing. But then, a man as large as I expected, handsome in a European way, bounded up the gangplank, embraced Lauro, and then took our bags. He embraced me too, but since I didn't know how to receive his embrace, I could tell that I disappointed him. Leaning on the car, a woman stood smoking a hand-rolled cigarette. She had dyed red hair and was dressed like a teenager in rose and peacock-blue stretch pants. Her sandals strapped all the way up her calves.

The men sat in the front seat and we sat in the backseat. They talked and laughed and called each other "man." They were loud and happy. We were quiet and unhappy. She told me her children were visiting their grandparents in Germany. So we would be all alone. This made us both feel desperate.

The log house was beautiful. One wall was nearly all window: the lake was like a lawn before the house. The mountain seemed reachable from the front room. There was a piano with sheet music by Bach and Schubert; you could tell that the music was actually played. On the wall were her paintings, which weren't what I expected.

Because she lived in nature, I expected her to paint it, and I was prepared to be embarrassed by the paintings. But what she painted was the opposite of nature. Her paintings were allegorical. They were about ideas and people. When landscape entered, it was a background for a story, like the unreal cities glimpsed out of the window in a Renaissance painting. But even the unreal landscapes Ulrike painted were nothing like the place she lived, the place she had always lived as a married woman. As someone not the child of the family house. Her characters were placed in middle-European fields and meadows, gentle, fertile tracts of land suggesting centuries of cultivation. In these cultivated fields stood women, tall and thin with sharply outlined hair, dark slashes of mouths, no eyes. In one painting, a woman held a knife to her breast, in the other hand she held a bunch of roses, which were bleeding. The painting was called *Romance*. In another, three men, identical-looking, dressed as gauchos, knelt before a naked woman, supplicating. This one was called *Infidelity*. In another, a woman sat peeling potatoes at a kitchen table. A man, his back to her, stacked wood. On the floor by his feet was a bloody axe. On the far wall: a large clock. This painting was called *Marriage*.

I told her I admired the paintings. She seemed pleased. We didn't talk much, although we liked each other. She did several things which in fact I liked very much. Each morning she played the piano, usually Bach. She never offered us food, but allowed us to understand that we were free to help ourselves. The men cooked noisy, sloppy evening meals, arguing, drinking whiskey as they cooked. We sat and looked into the dark lake; the moonlight fell straight down on it as if deposited from somewhere: some repository, warehouse, safe. The loons called out. Ulrike could hardly keep awake through dinner; we both went to bed early, and I know that we both read. The men talked politics, washed the dishes, and drank.

Lauro and I made love every morning, strenuous athletic love. I could tell he was feeling young, he was young, he was in Spain with Jerry. There was no place for him to imagine going.

I can no longer remember having sex with any other man. Everything about sex now is connected to Lauro. I can only locate his body as the source of arousal, pleasure, satisfaction. I know I've had sex with other men but I can't remember what it was like. I can remember rooms, but when I try to remember the bodies of other men in these rooms, I can't. It's always Lauro's body I call up.

One morning Ulrike did something else I liked. I realized to my horror that I'd left my diaphragm on the edge of the bathroom sink after washing it out. When I went back to get it, I found Ulrike had laid a towel on top of it, casually, carelessly, as if it had been dropped from a helicopter. I wanted to thank her, but how could I? What would I say?

That wasn't the only time language failed me on that holiday. I was walking on the island, and I came face to face with a moose. I was distressed by the intrusion of this large, stupid animal, who wouldn't move, but stood blinking and immobile in my way. There was nothing I could do to make him move. No sound, no action of my body or my arms would count for anything. I was completely frozen. And I didn't want to move from him, turn around, walk off the path into the trees. Physically, I could have done that. But I had a terrible need not to. A desire I could in no way have contravened, not to save myself but to be saved. All I wanted was for some human to appear, anyone, and make the animal turn around. I wanted him taken away, as the violent, the insane are taken away. I knew he wasn't dangerous. But I wanted him taken away. I wanted to see the back of him, his tail, the rear view of his head, the horns from the back. If I could have shot him, I might have, but for what? I would certainly have shot him if I'd had a gun. It's a good thing I didn't. He was a harmless animal and I might have shot myself as well. But no, that's not right, I wouldn't have shot him or myself. I didn't want to initiate action. I wanted to be a beneficiary. I wanted some assurance that the things in life that are random, senseless, immobile, impervious would be taken away, not because of anything I did, but because someone was there to do it.

Of course no one was there, and after a while I turned and walked back to the house.

On the ferry back to the mainland, I wondered how the piano got to the island. How Ulrike made her wishes for a piano known. Did she simply say, one morning, for example, "I want a piano in the house." Did he say, "Impossible, we live on an island," and then back down, afraid of her? Or did he say, "Of course," immediately, wanting to please her, wanting to keep her happy, beside him in the house.

I think he knows she doesn't like the house or the place where they are living. She said, "I can't paint forests or mountains or lakes." She said, "This place here isn't home. It's something else. You'd have to call it something else, I don't know what."

They've been living there for twenty years. He loves the house.

She didn't come to the ferry with us. As we drove away, I imagined I heard her playing the piano.

I knew that she'd like to leave that house, but that she's not like me and that she'll never do it.

I went on that holiday hoping to learn something about Lauro and myself. I learned nothing about us, except how different we were from other people. I learned again how no one else's life can teach us much about our own.

I wonder how we ever learn anything. Sometimes I think it's a trick or a miracle that we know anything at all. The problem: that we're often compelled by our positions to act on this knowledge we only think we have.

This is true both for my work and for Lauro's. Damage or acts of heroism, murder or crippling or rescues unbelievable in the light of day, are all results of partial knowledge.

I think of the woman who trained me. I love her, but I believe her to be wrong. She's really English, as I am not. She trained as a physician before the war, unusual for a woman, but she didn't think of it as unusual, she always thought of herself as ordinary, although she's anything but ordinary—sometimes extraordinary, sometimes merely odd. Her father was a clergyman; as a child she had a collection of beetles. Her mother presided over the church altar; Harvest Festival was her crowning glory. Lydia seemed to spend her childhood with books and animals rather than people; she married a scientist and produced two children to whom she paid very little attention. "It was remarkable they didn't fall into the river and kill themselves," I've heard her say. They didn't, of course. Her son became a scientist like his father and her daughter is in Kenya, teaching native children. They both live well, if not introspectively. If you asked them if they were close to her, or even if she was a good or a bad mother, they'd look at you in bewilderment, as so many English people do when you ask them anything like that.

In her work with disturbed children she was remarkable. She seemed to understand what they were unable to say, to piece together from the smallest clues a coherent and correct expression of desire, terror, rage. She was strict with them. She was able not to give them what they demanded when she felt they were manipulating her. Even sick children, victimized as they are by illness that tyrannizes them, can be tyrants, she used to say. Certain things in her position didn't anguish her, as they do me. She wasn't tempted, as I am, by the hazy children about whom it is unclear whether their illness is exacerbated by a low intelligence. She felt no qualms about taking only the most hopeful cases. Briskly, she would close the door on the hopes of the parents of a child whose condition was difficult to diagnose. "Nothing good can happen from a muddle." She was sure of that. What was astonishing to me was that she always seemed sure of what a muddle was.

I learned from her; I put myself in the position to learn from her. And I wasn't wrong to. I don't know how I learned what I learned, because, although she claimed to have a method, if you followed her method, which many of my colleagues tried to do, you didn't get her results. The results, if you followed her method, were very bad. Her method was rigid, but her rigidity was helpful to her because of the flexibility of her intuition. Her intuition, of course, came from the place in herself that was like the children; she could easily see herself in them, as I could.

She knew we were both like that. Although she never said anything; she never would have spoken words that might sound intimate or praising. Her refusal to praise pained me for years; at the same time I suffered from my colleagues' jealousy about what seemed to them her obvious favoritism of me. She liked my going from man to man: I think she imagined I was doing it for sex. She liked my sons; when they went through difficult patches, she assured me they'd get through it. When they were rude to me in front of her, she pretended not to notice, but told me later that in the long run I would see their rudeness (which mortified me) as a good thing. Her own daughter had disappointed her. She'd never been involved with a man, and went to Kenya almost as if she'd been several generations older. Lydia never said anything to me, but I knew we made a place for one another because of our disappointment with the mother, daughter, we'd been given.

She was bitterly angry with me when I began to disagree with her about the causes of the children's illness. I believed that she'd been harmful telling the parents the illness was the result of something they'd done. Her merciful understanding of their pain, her forgiveness of them, made it worse: they felt they couldn't turn against her. Turning against her would have been one more proof of their human deficiency.

We didn't speak at all in the first years of her retirement. When I heard she was ill, I visited her. I brought Lauro with me to break the ice. He told her about the various parts of the world where he'd lived. He explained the part of Kenya where her daughter worked, and comforted her by allowing her to imagine that the daughter lived a fascinating life. He told her about the meals he'd eaten there, meetings he'd attended, funerals he'd observed, families he'd come to know. I didn't need to say anything. Then he left us, pretending he needed to be somewhere—somewhere important, somewhere related to his work, but he had no place to go, he knew he had made a place for us to be together and he left us to it.

She looked at me with her fanatic's blue eyes. "Even if you're right you won't be able to help the children if you've no firm ground. If you can't explain things, you're left with nothing but a muddle."

I told her I had some firm ground, limited and conditional, but there nevertheless. It was this: Some ways of treating the children, many of which I'd learned from her, seemed to work, for reasons I could partially understand. I couldn't understand broken chromosomes, or trace minerals, or brain viruses present from the time of birth. But, I told her, the DNA people couldn't understand the brain-virus people either. So it was all a muddle, even for the ones who thought they had the answer. I said I thought I was helping some of the children by applying some of the new linguistic research. I talked about that.

"I helped some of them too, you know," she said.

"Of course, you helped hundreds of them, quite marvelously," I said.

I didn't suggest to her that her need for a system, an explanation, had caused grief and trouble, because in some cases it had also done good.

And she was dying. I wanted to hold her hand, to reassure her that she had done well in the world, done well by the children. And to reassure her that we were in the same game.

"Tell me about the brain-wave fellows, what they say," she asked me.

I tried to explain, but the more I told her, the more I was aware that I didn't know enough. I said I didn't want to appear to know more than I did.

"Perhaps that's what one hopes for," she said, lying back on the pillows in the bed she'd slept in every night for fifty years.

I didn't know if she really meant that or if she didn't want to die feeling separate from me. She didn't die, but she's lost her reason. She's strapped to her bed and raves when she's not sedated. She doesn't know where she is and she recognizes no one.

Maybe I spend so much time looking at Lauro because I'm trying to recognize him. His face is so mobile that it's sometimes hard to keep track of what he looks like. On our walls there are many photographs of him; there are no photographs of the places he's been. Sometimes, when he's gone and I haven't heard his voice or been near his body, this alarms me. All those replications of his face! I never know who took the photographs. Professionals, I guess.

He says he doesn't like to have pictures of places, particularly places where important events are happening, because the camera becomes a substitute for looking and remembering. Similarly, he won't use a tape recorder. I believe in my eyes and ears, he says.

Why, then, these framed images of himself? Does he, too, have trouble placing himself, recognizing himself? Does he look at them when I'm not around, when he's alone here? Does he wander from the young man of twenty in Addis Ababa, to the thin fellow in his thirties who stands beside a tribal chief? Does he say, this is my youth, my life? Does he praise himself: How handsome I have always been, how interesting my life is! Is he remarking to himself how surprising it is, after all this danger, that he should be in this safe, settled flat, among these photographs? Does he look on them with simple gratitude, touching them primitively, thanking someone for his deliverance? Or does he use them as a spur when he's beginning to get too settled or afraid to go to some dangerous, uncomfortable place?

There is no picture of me anywhere in the flat. I wouldn't dream of placing in what I would call my home, where I was living every day, a picture of myself. It would indicate to me either that I'd forgotten what I looked like or that I cared so much about how I looked that I couldn't bear being without the sight of myself. Or that I wasn't sure I'd been alive in the past in a place other than the place where I was living.

I sometimes fear that Lauro's afraid he's not the person who had all that past. That this body, which he seems all this time to have been continuously inhabiting, is not continuous but something he could lose track of. Or perhaps I have a greater fear, that he loves his own countenance, his own existence, so much that he wants to demonstrate to others just how valuable his past, his bodily existence are.

And yet he is more modest than the other men I've known, as if he thought corporeality itself were an affliction that required tact.

He knocks if I'm in the bathroom. I've never seen him on the toilet. If he needs to be sick, he closes the bathroom door and runs the water, and stays in there a long time, opening the door only when he can walk out and pretend that nothing happened inside.

I don't know what his body means to him. I know he must give up this modesty when he's living somewhere else, in terrible conditions, living in a way that's exactly the opposite of how he lives in this house.

He takes no pleasure in grooming. Sometimes I have to tell him that it's time to wash his hair. He doesn't wear deodorant, so he often gives off an unfresh, adolescent smell. But it's not unpleasant, nor does his hair look bad when it's dirty. He always walks in the world desirable, contained, moving quickly to some definite and interesting place. Unlike my poor mother, whose failure to groom herself propelled her out of the web of civilization into the world of the segregated old.

Now that my children are grown and I've had to change my relation to their bodies, his is the body in the world dearest to me. The body which is part of my life, a factor in my life like my own health.

It always pleases me to watch him. Sometimes I put the seat down on the toilet and sit there chatting to him while he shaves. I hold a mug of tea in my hand; I cross my legs; we have a conversation about people or about the world, but really I'm there for the pleasure of looking at him, his bare chest and broad back whose muscles move with the motions of his shaving, his legs, covered with exactly the amount and texture of dark hair that I prefer.

Sometimes we make love for hours. In these long times, when

I feel I'm on a sea voyage traveling to some distant place whose name I've never heard, moving slowly, speeding up, then silent, then delivering messages or receiving them—that code—I understand that this is the last body I will know in this way. I couldn't be interested in another body again, having known Lauro's as I have, so well, so thoroughly, and having been so well known by him. So that if he should die it would mark the end of a certain part of my bodily life too.

I'll probably die not knowing many things. I don't accompany Lauro on his travels, because there are certain things I never want to see. Mutilated children, death by starvation, shootings that are thought of as commonplace. I don't want goods shoved under my nose by people urging me to buy shirts saying FLORIDA STATE COLLEGE or I LOVE MICHAEL JACKSON; or baskets that they claim are made by natives in the bush. I don't want to wait in a hotel room listening on a radio for the outbreak of war. I'm afraid of having to flee gunshot. And of course of rape.

I've kept myself from a lot. All sorts of sex involving pain and danger. I've lived my life to keep back degradation, which I know is a part of common life. Anonymous coupling in dark corners, waking beside a stranger realizing that you have, not knowing how, become a criminal. There's a great deal of life I don't know about. Lauro knows about it, and I wonder sometimes, as we pull the white and gray striped duvet up around our naked shoulders, if he thinks of that part of life when he's in bed with me.

Yet I think I know my children in a way he knows no one, certainly not his own son.

Once I was lying in bed with him and I read this in a book that had been given to me by my best friend: "Having had a child, could a woman then speak of another love?"

I was almost sure that the woman who wrote this hadn't had a child. I'm not even sure if a woman loves differently after she's had a child. How would we know? Not enough women have done it and spoken about it afterward. We don't know much yet about how women might really be, if they felt they could be however they liked.

When I see my sons' girlfriends, I'm hopeful, because they seem so much more adventurous than my friends and I. They're not afraid of travel. The idea of their mother's house doesn't sit on them, pressing them to acquiescence or self-banishment, both cruel.

But what will happen to them when they have children? Will it be what happened to us? The inevitable dilution (sometimes delicious, desirable) of the content of one's attention? The almost irresistible pressure to conform? And to be still?

What will happen to the children of moving mothers? How will these children have their baths or learn to read?

Perhaps they will be hopeful children, generous children. Perhaps the older ones will teach the younger. Perhaps their mothers will seem to them to shine, desirable in the moving distance, as our mothers were not. As only fathers were. Some fathers, coming back occasionally from the distance, only wounded their children with the longing, the romance, the hunger that could not be fed. Certainly not by the mother, offering the nourishing, warm, constant food. Not in the still rooms where the children felt that they were trapped. What would it be like to be a mother who believed she moved freely in the world?

I could still have a child. Last year, in fact, I became pregnant. I was forty-four; Lauro was fifty-six. Not for a minute did we consider having the child, but we were sad, and perhaps not so good to each other. Maybe because in saying no to the birth of a child we were admitting that we had come to the end of youth, or we were admitting the end of possibility for a certain way of life, casting our lot with others like ourselves, saying that life was difficult, perhaps too difficult, and there were things we could or would no longer do.

At first, I was incredulous, so I didn't say anything to anybody. We hadn't been careless. Pure accident, my gynecologist, a close friend, said. Too bad you had to be the one. I allowed him to be paternal, to pat my hand in that comforting way people like me don't allow, to make all the arrangements for me, to jump me to the head of the queue. (A Socialist, I normally wouldn't have allowed it, but this time I did.) I phoned Lauro in Uganda to tell him, although he was due home the next day.

How can I describe the things we felt, the mix of shame (had we wanted this to happen?) and pride (we were, after all, still young, here was the proof). The peculiar strength of our sadness, the strength of knowing we were of one mind and we would go through something without wavering. Lauro's son is thirty; they are comrades. Once a year, perhaps, they see each other. They are bumptious together, like twin bull calves. Sandro works for television in Rome and he comes to London with girls who smoke a lot and carry camcorders, thin girls with short streaked hair, white T-shirts, men's shoes and black jeans. It occurred to me to ask Lauro the obvious question: Are there other children of yours in the world, besides Sandro? The obvious, the banal difference between us: I know the fate of the children I engendered; Lauro couldn't possibly know. But did I want to hear him say that? No, which is why I didn't ask him. I didn't want to be so separated from him in the meaning of what we had to go through, so reminded that there are points at which our lives so completely diverge. I knew I'd been involved in the creation of only two other human beings, my sons, and that there wouldn't be a third. And I didn't mourn that. What I mourned was the fact that life wasn't like a simple, rich story, with a cast of characters who exited and entered, and children trailing along, being brought up somehow. I mourned the truth that we couldn't be the people who we were and properly bring up a baby, that we couldn't even think of ourselves that way without giving up too much.

When Lauro got home, I let myself cry in his arms like a girl. It was a pleasure, I felt no responsibility to hold myself back, to stop myself as I normally would; I knew I had a right to tears. It was as if he and I had the same disease, only I was the sicker; no one could call me weak. He said, "For a minute, today, in the plane, I thought perhaps we could have the baby. I thought, a baby is a blessing, a fruit of our love, a proof of it, perhaps it would be a girl. And then immediately I knew I was wrong, that I'm always away, that I could die at any time, I couldn't be myself without putting myself in this position. I don't know how I could live, how I would recognize myself if I had to stay in one place and think about protecting my life, if you weren't someone I knew I could leave in a minute, and come back to in a minute, so that I could be where something was happening in the world."

I wondered what his love meant for me if it included putting me constantly in jeopardy of bereavement. Do you owe it to the one you love to try and keep yourself from death?

We were close to each other in those days, almost as if we'd had the child. I set the date for the abortion. Everyone connected with it called it "the procedure," and I was grateful for their false language, it protected me, as the invented language of the children whom I care for protects them.

Three days before I was to go into hospital, news came over the radio of a coup in an African country he'd been writing about for some time. He said, "What day are you going into hospital? It doesn't matter, of course, only it would make things difficult if I missed the one important thing."

I picked up a piece of sculpture an Italian friend of Lauro's had made: an egg shape, or a woman's head, or a wave solidified, or merely a stone eroded by a natural process. I'd never liked the piece but I was happy to have the weight of it in the house. It must have weighed ten pounds. I held it above my head, in my two hands, and threw it at Lauro like a shot put. It could have wounded him badly, but it landed on the carpet inches from his feet, making a dull, unsatisfying noise, of course not breaking.

"Don't bother coming with me, then," I said. "I don't want you coming. Go off and I'll deal with it."

He was immediately ashamed.

"How have I said that? It's my fear for you that made me talk like that, my nervousness, you know how I get when I think you're sick or something, of course I didn't mean it, I'll be with you, I would never not. You must forgive me, you simply must."

But I didn't want to forgive him. I knew that if I didn't forgive him and told people why, everyone would take my part. In those minutes, life without him seemed desirable, easy, even. I imagined at last living by myself, letting myself in the door after the abortion, resting alone on the bed, going out to a movie with friends. I went over all the times he'd been selfish and neglectful and I decided to leave him.

That night, I moved my body far from him in bed. I rehearsed the words I would say to him; I went over the scenes in which we would split the possessions; I told him I thought I should keep the flat since he was so rarely there. I thought of how I would tell my mother, and worked out what I would write to his mother, thinking I would have to, after all. I imagined running into him in ten years, and asking him polite questions about the course his life had taken. Then I looked at his head on the pillow, his naked shoulders, the muscles of his upper arm. I knew I wouldn't leave him. Because I knew that nothing, no righteousness of blame, no justice, is as true as the fact that without him my life is smaller. I never believed before that forgiveness, which is a discipline for me, unnatural to me, was something I would work at to gain only imperfect love.

What's the relationship between forgiveness and desire? Or, more accurately, between forgiveness and satisfied desire? Desire that is satisfied again and again, and rises up, again and again, and is as repeatedly satisfied. Satisfied desire. Is it as simple as that, that I stay with Lauro, that I allow him imperfections and transgressions I never allowed in my other husbands, because of this desire that returns and that he satisfies, because of his desire that I cause to return, that I cause to be satisfied? Some inexhaustible capital that is drawn on and drawn on and is not diminished or used up? Is it some joke of friction? Why should it be that of all men's bodies this body calls forth my hunger and my expertise, my loyalty and my attention, my tenderness, my impulses at once voracious and custodial, my plain wish to rest? Is it for this that I forgive him and will go on, perhaps foolishly, like other foolish women in history, because without him my life is less abundant and I do not want a less abundant life?

He came with me to the clinic and he waited like a father for the news of a birth. When the abortion was over, before I saw him, before I would let him see me, I wept tears that were involuntary. Tears like sweat. The doctor, my friend, dried my tears. I was so moved by the literalness of his gesture that I cried more.

When we came home, I didn't cry. Lauro put me to bed, he bought me all the foods I like—figs, and olives, Stilton cheese, French bread—he held me while I slept off the drug. All that time he was awake. What were you doing while I slept? I asked him. Thinking, he said. I didn't ask him about what.

We watched funny movies on the video. We didn't talk about what had happened. It was another thing that we could go on from, like offense, reparation, resolution, error, loss. Something had happened to us that would change us, and it was difficult to know what it all meant. What did it mean that life was begun and ended, that we didn't suffer much or cause much suffering, that we went on, that what we did was right, that we can wound each other in some ways neither of us would have predicted, and yet go on. Mated, but in the way of our age, partial. That we are people to whom many events happen, events open to interpretation, events which in other ages would seal one's fate. That because we can interpret things, we do. That we are different from any people who, when we were young, we thought of resembling.

I don't know how to judge whether or not I've been a good mother: it seems a useless process, a question all of whose answers are bad. I sometimes wonder if I'm wrong about my children, when I say they haven't suffered from my leaving their fathers. If they'd been daughters, would they have railed at me, accusing me, turning from me with bitter words? Or taken drugs, eating or starving themselves to death to show me what I'd done?

I love my sons so much, so easily. From the beginning, they were courtly to me. As babies, their first acts were acts of praise. Lavishly, they took my milk, as if in tribute. They seemed to me born good. Nothing in them was there to thwart me. When they spoke to me about their grief, it was to include me, not to blame. Sometimes they were quite rude, often for years, but I believed they would grow out of it. They did.

There were times I knew they were in trouble. Smoking marijuana. Failing in school. Having their hearts broken by perfectly nice girls or girls who were dreadful (I'd have put knives to those girls' throats for causing my sons pain). Whole years of lying on filthy sheets and refusing to bathe, with secret caches of beer tins hidden under dirty clothes. The younger leaving school at sixteen to travel with a backpack for a year. I woke up every night convinced he was dead on some *Autobahn,* some *autostrada,* or in some forest, picked up by a maniac and hacked to bits.

They suffered, and now they're grown. They kept their suffering from me. Perhaps this was because I am a woman, and this made it necessary that they think of themselves as men. Or perhaps, unlike what I am for the children I treat, I was not the fixed point for them, not still enough to place and speak to, with the difficult words requiring so much mutual attention.

I left their fathers, and there were uprootings. New houses, temporary houses, transitional periods in the homes of friends. Times when they couldn't fully unpack their things or find what it was they were looking for. Then their anger would flare up, but they themselves would tamp it quickly. Did they do that because they were afraid that I was grieving, having left a man?

I was distressed and regretful, but I didn't grieve. I left because I needed to be in a new place.

But perhaps they didn't need to. Perhaps what they needed was one place. One place to start out from in the morning, to return to after school or at the end of holidays. Rooms that are dear because they've held your infancy and been the shell in which you could mature. Protecting you from the world.

I didn't want them protected from the world. I wanted them to live in it.

But where in the world did I want them to live? And how? What place did I allow them to name as their own?

I heard once about an Irish monk who lived in the sixth century. He'd been involved in land disputes and caused the deaths of many men. In his guilt, he felt he must create a penance for himself. The severest possible. He chose not flagellation, nor starvation, nor mutilation. He decided that the worst punishment would be self-exile; never again to see his home. He set sail, and did not return.

This is not the modern story. We go from place to place. For some in the world the place they arrive is unimaginably different from the place they left. Even from what they might have seen at home on television or in newspapers. A Sudanese in Cambridge once told me how hard it had been for him to come to England. He told me I wouldn't be able to guess what the hard things were. "Imagine having to ride the underground," he said. "We are afraid to go under the ground. We had never gone under the ground. We didn't know how to use the telephone. Even to ask for help. We would get lost. Once someone in my family rode the underground for fourteen hours, unable to find his way out."

The pathos of displacement is something I've never known. No place has ever been so dear to me that leaving it would make me suffer.

So how could I have given placement to my sons?

My mother left Germany, the German tongue, mourning for the rest of her life the house in the country where the clouds were whiter than anywhere else and the water from the spring more pure. Germany was the white clouds, not Hitler's troopers, to her; I couldn't ever quite understand that. My father simply shut the door between his past life and the first new one in England; then he shut it again to go to America; he must have felt that death was only one last shutting of one last door.

Did my sons hide from me their sorrow at the way I'd made them live? Were they exiles from the early dream of home?

What could exile mean to me? Exile from what place?

Should Lauro or my children die, I would feel exile. From those bodies. Then I would be cut off. Oh, I would have memories, but what are they? I need to reach out and grasp, not empty air, but the solidity of those I love. The people I love go away and they come back and I pretend to understand this. If I leave one of the children I treat to go on holiday, they really don't understand. They panic or they grieve. They don't believe that I'll be back. That the same body will walk in the door in a month, tan from the sea, bringing them a shell or rock for their collection.

Why should they believe it?

Would it be better for me, wiser, to attach myself to land or houses?

Would I be different if I could? More hopeful? Less afraid? If there were one place I could think of as my own, the one desired and desirable place? Would it have been better for my sons? It's no use to speculate on this; it never could have happened.

I know that I have never desired a place because I never dream of places unless I'm there. People do, they dream of quite specific places all the time. A friend at work told me about a dream she'd had.

"It was morning in the dream," she said. "The air was very light blue. It was misty. Houses were just visible in the mist. There was a shining road, but not a highway. Not a scary road, the way some roads can be. Little by little the houses began to show themselves through the mist, and finally I could see smoke from the chimneys. Gradually, I could see water. A silver band, a narrow one, small river, a stream. I woke and said to my husband, 'I've just dreamed of Zagreb.' 'But you've never been to Zagreb,' he said. 'I know,' I said, 'but that was the name of the place. I was very happy there.'"

What does it mean to be happy in a place? To know the birds' names, and the sound of water bubbling in the ditches, to pine for a place, to sicken when you're apart from it? It means having had a particular kind of childhood, having had the confidence to wander in a place, the confidence as well as the freedom, having been alone as a child, and silent but not frightened, feeling neither persecution nor reproach. Possibly having a house in the place but not necessarily. The place can be a refuge from the house or the house just an extension of the place, as the trunk extends down to a lap.

The house can be the part of the place where the rough dirt is bathed away and the cleanliness of nightfall is provided after hard exertion.

I never had a childhood like that; how could I give my children one? Lauro never had it either. We're always surprised when we're happy in a place, we always like new places, since as children we imagined places we had never been. We attached geographies to printed names or names picked up illicitly from adult conversations. We pored over faded maps, or maps with the old names of places, useless for real navigation. We looked at photographs of people we could recognize as kin, standing in landscapes unlike anything we had imagined or in the doorways of buildings whose function we couldn't guess. We were there in the places whose goodness came precisely from the fact that we could not have known them in our lives.

I'm always afraid in new places, even though I like them. I even like the fear, it means I'm taking things in, the fear creates a transparency. Lauro isn't afraid, but he takes in more than I. I grow transparent, he becomes an insect with a huge eye and a thousand feelers. Moving quickly. Not afraid.

New places make me tired. When I sleep in a new place, I dream of what I saw when I was walking and I love the dreams, as if they were part of the trip. Lauro never sleeps much when we're in a new place: he never wants to rest. I like to rest in strange rooms; I say to him, "Go on without me." I'm happy resting in the strange harsh sheets without him; he comes back and wakes me, he gets into the harsh sheets beside me, and I love him more than ever when I whisper, "Tell me everything you saw."

Lauro never remembers his dreams. "I know it was a happy dream," he'll say. "You were in it, but I don't know where we were." Or he'll say, "It was a bad dream, I was frightened, I don't know of what."

I usually sleep longer and more deeply than Lauro. He always wakes before me. Sometimes he's up several times at night. He's never bad-tempered on waking. I am often frightened or reluctant, leaving the place where I was happy, the place of sleep, the only place where I know that I could live a complete and simple life.

But sometimes after he's traveled, Lauro only wants to sleep. I find this frightening and dangerous. I lose patience with him many times on the days he spends asleep. He says this is because I don't understand immobility, the need for immobility, the hunger for paralysis. He says I live the way I swim. He doesn't like the way I swim, too far out, he says, in water that's too cold. When I swim he paces back and forth on the shore waiting for me with a towel. I like this very much.

I am happy swimming, swimming far out for a long time. I particularly like swimming without my clothes. Lauro never swims without his clothes. He worries when I'm swimming naked, although he likes to see me walking out of the water naked and he likes to dry my naked body and chafe the cold flesh.

In water I am perhaps most female, spacious and buoyant simultaneously, the space inside me like an openness to chance, I'm missing nothing, I could contain anything, the emptiness is in itself desirable, and if my breasts bob, who is it for but me, no one can see them, they are for no eye, or mouth, they are for my pleasure only. When I nursed my sons, I would often fall into a dreamy swoon; they would sigh in contentment, these full boys of mine, and I would sigh with them, wanting to go nowhere.

Lauro is wrong when he says I don't understand immobility. I understand it all too well. I fear it even as the children I care for do: what guarantee is there that movement will ever start again once it is given up? It's one reason I'm unkind to Lauro when he's ill. I depend upon his vitality so that I can feel alive. He doesn't understand how much I need him for this, as I used to need my sons, as a pledge of physical faith. As a model I can follow any time I need to, which I often do, more than he knows. I often need to be pulled from the torpors where I sink, like the children whom I treat, into a state of unaliveness. He doesn't know I'm in these states because often when I'm in one I appear to be engaged in some task, absorbed in it, and beyond thought. He even finds me rather sexy then, in my need to be searched out. But he could never find me; I would always be too far away if I allowed myself to sink down. And it is so easy to sink down. Into the bluish light where nothing is distinguished or distinguishable, where boundaries are swallowed up, borders once, for all, erased, and nobody knows how. Only habit pulls us back.

Perhaps women are really doing that all the time when they seem to be performing household tasks: hiding their states of death absorption, death fear, death similitude. Perhaps that's what household tasks are for. The craftsmanship of the habitual.

"You don't deserve to live in a house," one of my husbands said to me once, in a domestic rage. I wasn't hurt by this. I understood that there was something right in what he said.

He said it because he didn't believe in the possibility that one day I might not live in a house, a building, some place with four walls. Therefore it didn't frighten him. But it frightened me, because I've often imagined myself homeless. All women do, or many. They see themselves wandering, holding everything they own in a bag, sleeping against the warm sides of buildings in the freezing night. It is apparently a more common fear than the fear of rape.

I don't desire places, but I need a place to live in. It's not only because I don't like the extremes of heat and cold that I'm interested in shelter. If only it were that. It would be so much easier. But I like a place where I can read and listen to music. In the flat beside us, there's a man who plays the violin. He's old now, but occasionally in the evening he gives lessons. There must be a piano in the flat. When a lesson is about to start, he plays three notes on it, the same three, I don't know which, I'm not musical like that. Then the student begins to play the violin.

At other times, a sound will come to me, the voice of my other neighbor down the road. I can never identify the song or the words she's singing. It's why they seem so precious to me, pure sound, devoid of information, unattached and floating. Most often she practices early in the evening, and I'm happy sitting with my lights off, watching the lit squares of the neighbors' windows, all of them lit in the same way, evenly, and the dark blue air that falls on the bars of the neighbors' gates until they are obscure and it's no longer obvious what I'm watching and I think it's possible I may not be alive. Or I'm not sure.

This is the sort of thing I need a house for. To remind me, or to reassure me, I'm not sure which. I don't know: Do other people need to be reminded, reassured that they are still in life? The border seems so permeable to me; and it would be too easy to fall asleep at one's post. The children whom I treat know this; they fear it. I believe that they are right to fear. I don't know how many other people who are not called ill believe it, or if they have experiences that blur the line of unaliveness as mine sometimes do.

There was the time, for instance, when I was on the beach and a fog came up. It covered the ocean and the sand so everything was strange. Everyone was a stranger; people spoke to each other but not to me. I could hear their voices, but only at a distance; they were indistinct. All of them speaking to each other, communicating with each other, quite apart from me. I was unknown to any of them, and perhaps, though I couldn't tell, invisible to them. All the categories were confusing; the confusion, though, was pleasant. Two white women played with and cared for a black girl child. I imagined the women were lovers. I imagined asking them if I could be with them, live with them, the three of us together, caring for the child, putting her to bed, then getting into bed ourselves, fondling each other, stroking each other, opening the lips of each other's sex.

A boy who had long hair, long as a girl's, sat with his back to me. I couldn't see his face. He hadn't taken his black clothes off; he was fully dressed in trousers and a long-sleeved shirt. He lay down with his girlfriend, and they kissed, like that, in front of everyone. I imagined she was Polish, Yugoslavian; she took off the top of her bathing suit revealing small breasts with dark nipples he'd made hard.

I didn't know where I was, who anybody was, where they came from, how they might behave. I thought it was possible I might be among the dead, and I didn't care, I was quite happy to be with them. Then I began to miss my sons: I wanted to be with them if there was anyone to be with. I wanted to be with Lauro. For my sons' sake and for Lauro's, I made myself get into the ocean, do something ordinary, take a swim, to make this strange state go away. But even the cold water and the strokes that moved me through it didn't convince me that I wasn't dead. And I thought how easy it would be to be swept out beyond even these strangers. And to what? That grayness. That whitish light.

Yet I was happy. I was happy getting out of the water, I was happy as I walked up the beach. I saw what looked like a white rainbow. An arc of whiteness penetrating, no, superimposing itself over the fog. Hints of color at the top, but the bottom solid white.

Is that a rainbow or just light? I heard somebody ask someone else.

Just light, someone answered.

I like these kinds of confusion, but Lauro doesn't. Which is why I know he won't like being dead without me, or even the moment of death, and I'd be angry that he died, that he was far away from me experiencing nothing that would please or interest him, nothing that did him any good.

If Lauro died, I'd leave the flat and move into a small room which would soon become depressing. I would spend more and more time at the school; I'd begin going to movies. I would see my friends at restaurants. In twenty years, when I'd no longer feel the need to work regularly, I'd spend a lot of time traveling. I would arrive at my sons' doorsteps carrying interesting gifts and washable clothes in a small brightly colored bag, suitable for stowing under the seats or in the overhead bins of airplanes. I'd rarely come back to the place I lived. Objects would take on the corruption of disuse.

Yet it would be sad to be living where the sound of those three notes, or of the voice in the evening air, were no longer something I'd be able to think of as part of my life.

It's always possible I'll die before Lauro. I don't believe it, but it's possible, and when I think of it I'm not afraid. I don't know whether or not death is a pleasurable state. I mean the first moment of death, the foggy vision, that sojourn in the tunnel. Whether the sight itself is so arresting as to obliterate all of life as we knew it when we were alive, or whether in the middle of the whiteness or the shadow or the brilliant, clear, drenched air, there is regret. Whether we miss the people we have left behind, simply miss them, and that the missing gets in the way of what we see, and we fight what we see and only want to get back, like Eurydice or Lot's wife, but there is no going back, that place is where you are, it is the only place.

I worry about Lauro, alone, without me in that place.

I am lying beside him now. The air is silver, it is almost dawn. It is neither night nor morning. The moon has not yet grown invisible. But very soon he'll be awake. And then, I don't know what will happen.

THE REST OF
LIFE

For R.S.

*T*hree people are in a first-class compartment on a train traveling from Milan to Turin. An old woman, a young woman, a young man. The young man is the old woman's son; the young woman will marry the young man when they return to America in two weeks. The old woman is small with pale skin and dark eyes; the young man is tall and muscular, his hair is curly, he has large strong teeth and green eyes that proclaim his artless health. The young woman doesn't lean against the dusty blue-black corduroy of the compartment seats. She is holding a bottle of mineral water and three plastic cups; she offers water to her lover and his mother. Her lover accepts; his mother shakes her head and smiles, leaning back and closing her eyes. She seems tired.

The young woman's father is the son of an Igbo chief; in 1969 the family fled for their lives, through the Nigerian bush, arriving finally in Queens, New York. Forty-one years before that, in 1928, the old woman left Turin, the city of her birth, because it was believed that she had caused the death of a young man. She and the young man, in love with poetry and the Romantic Age, had made a suicide pact. He was sixteen, she was fifteen. At the last moment, she changed her mind, and he didn't. He died and she remained alive. She was sent to family in America. The last time she was on an Italian train, she was fleeing shame. No one in America knows this story. Her husband never knew it. Her son doesn't know it. He thinks he's taking her back home—a gift— so that she won't die without imparting her precious memories. He believes she has neglected to pass them on through the forgetful tendency, the careless and negating wave, the casual erasures of the modern world. He wants her past. He has no idea what it contains and no sense of the effort she has made to keep it in the sanctuary of its shadows.

"This must bring back a lot, Mama," he says.

She looks out the window of the train. Through the window: her childhood trees: poplars, cypresses, furled in upon themselves like rolled umbrellas.

Bring back from where? And to what?

She's always surprised at how free people feel to speak of memory. They imagine it a liquid, mobile, a stream that flows in one direction only. They speak of it as though they could return to something navigable, something they can enter any time at will. No sense for them that the small, fragile boat in which they find themselves will fail to protect them. No possibility for them of the wrecked craft, the splinters and the skeleton hurled up. Memory: the cataract, the overwhelming flood. And the freezing power of horror, of shock, when memory stops dead and nothing moves on the gray, windless plain, the place of stone, blind stone, and you inhabit it because you must, it is the only place, you must choose it or death by drowning.

Only those who haven't known the sight of horror think of memory as amiable, nutritive. Why wouldn't they try to bid it back, as you'd turn the leaves of an old photo album, charmed by the discolorations, the tender fadings, the sweet displacements of old-style dresses, the archaic shoes? But what if you turned the page to find the stinking dead, unburied, not sealed off and incorporeal, but rotting: rot that takes away the breath? Death by drowning. Death by suffocation. Better a hundred times the frozen life, the half life, where the forms of the dead flicker, faceless and perhaps unrecognizable, perhaps indistinguishable, not themselves but standing for each other in the blessed neutrality of the annihilating dead.

I will not see your face. I cannot.

She is thinking of her father's face. She has borne three children, she has lain in the arms of two men. She has come near death. Yet nothing has ever been so beautiful, so desirable, so important as her father's face. I am the beloved and the beloved is mine. Nothing I can do is wrong.

But she had done wrong. From the moment she met Leo, she began a life of wrongdoing. Even before he touched her, talking to him began the wrong way she would live her life. It had never been right again.

She is seventy-eight years old. She is riding on a train from Milan to Turin. *Milano a Torino.* She hasn't been back in sixty-three years. No one she knew from then is still alive. She's going back to please her son and his girlfriend. They never knew what she ran away from. She hopes that she'll leave Italy without their knowing. If this happens, it will have been a successful trip.

Why did she agree to go at all? Because, although she is still healthy, she knows there won't be much more of life. What does she hope to find, to see? What she hopes is that there will be nothing to be seen, that everything has disappeared, or been covered over by the incrustation of subsequent life, buried so thoroughly that it will not rise up, even at the moment of her own death, to accuse her.

My father's face.

He is at the top of the hill, wearing a straw hat. His face is half in shadow, yet I know he's smiling. He always smiles when he sees me. Is this his face or the face of a photograph? Do I remember anything that is his face? Is it the love he bore me that I miss, or the face that stands for everything I'll never have again. I hear the word girl *in his voice: I know it's his voice, not a copy of his voice, because his voice was never replicated. His voice says "Girl." I am safe. I am beyond questions of safety.*

I am walking with my father. I take his hand. He has no rings, neither do I. We walk down the hill. The sun casts the harsh mountain in purple shadow. The sun is mixed in color like a bloody egg. I am with my father. We will eat something, then take the train. I will never be happier.

"Are you happy, Mama?" asks her son, patting her kneecap tenderly as if it were fragile, which perhaps it is. "We want you to be happy, Katherine and I."

She smiles falsely; she is very weary. "I am happy, thank you," she says. She is thinking: No one but I knows what it is to be happy. No one had the father that I had.

She looks out the window. She sees that there are not so many trees as there were when she rode on this train before. The land has shockingly changed. It is a different land, and this relieves her. She can say without untruth: *The place I left was a different place.*

That day, the mountain was an accusing curtain shut against her; pushing itself out of the scalding blue of the late August sky. She remembers the mountain, the sky. Then a blankness. And after a minute, bobbing up like the head of a swimmer only pretending to be drowned, something else. She remembers now that she was menstruating on that day. As she climbed the hill, instructing her legs to pull her up, her body pulled itself constantly downward. She knows she must not be pulled down. She must climb like him. She can't tell him, but she will have to tell him. They are lovers. She is fifteen, he is sixteen, they are here, climbing up this hill to do something no one she knows has done. No one she knows would think of doing it. But he has thought of it, and anything he thinks of he can do.

Does he like being her lover? Does it make him happy? When they're finished, she always wants to say to him: "Are you happy?" but that's the kind of thing that annoys him.

Are you happy in my body, that I let you see me, go inside of me, do what it is you do there? You say you know how not to make a baby, but I don't believe you. I don't tell you that I don't believe. What will we do if you have a baby? What would that mean—to have made something in that way? Poetry, from the verb to make. We are, we believe, both poets.

But I'm bleeding so you haven't made a baby. Perhaps you do know what you say you know.

I would do anything in the whole world for you.

Ask me anything.

I am very young, but I would give you anything. You are superior and you have chosen me. What would I be if you hadn't? And who? The person who I was? What girl was that? Someone I no longer know whom you would now refuse to recognize? The one my father speaks to, not knowing she isn't there.

My father. My father. My father who even now is waiting for me in our quiet house. He may be in the garden which at night is perfumed so strongly that our eyes close (we can't help it) the moment we walk out of doors. My father who teaches science at the university. There are things he's taught me you will never know. He studies insects.

My father knows so much! But the new girl I am, whom you have made come into being, he does not know her. I think he never will. Who does he speak to in the morning? Good morning, my darling, my shining light. I don't know who she is, that one he speaks to, only that she's no longer here.

"That young bull calf needs his horns cut." It frightened her to hear her father talk like that. She didn't want to think of him as someone who had those kinds of thoughts. She could imagine her father with a shears, coming toward Leo, and on the top of Leo's head what she had seen on the tops of the heads of calves in the countryside: two bloody stumps that festered and filled with flies. She would have to put ointment on the stumps and scrape the bloody sores; the dead flies would mix with blood and hairs on the point of her knife.

Later, when Leo was dead, she dreamed of her father running from him, blood dripping from the shears. Leo was bleeding between his legs. The blood filled up his pants, and then the blood turned to roses. And her father laughed and laughed. "My calf's producing veal," he said, through his laughter.

She knows now that Leo didn't know how not to get her pregnant. She thinks of how he was afterward, after he pulled out from her and wiped himself with his handkerchief, and then put his face between her breasts, sobbing, saying he was sorry, he was sorry, she must make him promise never to do it again. She must promise she will never leave him; in the whole world there is no one who cares a damn about him, who has ever cared a damn about him. He is lying beside her, their clothes are mostly off, her breasts are naked, wet from his tears. She can't bear to think of his believing no one has loved him. She can't bear his thinking of himself as a child so lonely, so forlorn, with no one to dry his tears. So she says the words that are bursting inside her mouth. Her skirt is beside her on the ground. "What about your father and mother?" she says. "What about your grandmother?"

He stands up and looks at her with hatred. "You must be the stupidest person who ever lived."

He spoke to her like that, yet they were lovers. Carlo and Katherine are lovers. This proves to her how little words can do, how little they can describe. How foolish even to think for a moment that what she had with Leo resembled in any way what it is they have. Words are too pliant, too elastic. It's another reason why she hasn't spoken. How can she trust words to tell her story so that it would be anything like the truth?

It need not be said that Carlo and Katherine will sleep in the same room in the hotel. Will they ever have a child? Paola doesn't care. She's had enough grandchildren, all strangers to her. Perhaps this child wouldn't be a stranger. She likes Katherine. She's glad her husband's dead; he would have said things about Carlo marrying someone of another race that would have made Katherine feel terrible.

Is she glad her husband's dead? There are times she thinks that anyone could die, and it wouldn't mean anything to her.

She wonders what she thought death was. Back then, before her first death. Her mother had died of pneumonia when she was two years old, but she has no memory of it: she never felt it had happened to *her*. Leo's death had happened to her; it had separated her life into two parts: before the death, after the death. What had she thought death was before, when she was thinking of dying with him? This is a question she hasn't asked herself. Not once in sixty-three years.

She was fifteen years old, not as unhappy as she pretended to herself she was. Unhappiness was a fruit she plucked, something she could consume and make a part of her: an orange or a pomegranate. Dark seeds of unhappiness she could spit out. He'd never seen anyone die, but he told her death was beautiful. No one he had ever known had died.

When he thought about death, was he thinking mainly of his mourners? His repentant parents? The teachers who had given him a bad time? The girls who didn't pay attention? Did he imagine that in death he could choose one of those confident girls with their sharp hair like tufts, their white ski outfits, the toes of their shoes like daggers and the heels that went clip clip on the pavement as they ran from one person who wanted only them to someone else who couldn't do without them? She believed that in death he would find someone he preferred to her. One of those girls he always talked about: courageous, unafraid. In death she would be more alone.

In death, she would see him through a fog, witty and prized. Dead, he wouldn't look back at her or apologize. He wouldn't even stop to say: "Thank you for coming with me, into death, but I'm sure you see I must go ahead without you." She imagined herself in death well mannered and ignored. The other dead would concentrate on him.

Her father had no use for him. Yet she knew her father loved her. She's played over and over in her mind the many scenes that proved she wasn't wrong to believe in his love. But after everything happened, he sent her away to America and died before she had a chance to see him again. So she's learned this: Shame was a stronger force than love.

Leo and her father had never liked each other. She had thought they would. Leo's mind had all the things her father admired. All the things she didn't have, the things that would make her father stop his explanations when he could see she wasn't keeping up, smooth her hair, and say, "Later, we'll continue." Smooth her hair, turn back to his book. Her father would never have had to wait for Leo to catch up, as he had to wait for her, the same way he'd waited when she was a child and they went walking in the hills. He'd stop and look back, smiling, encouraging her as she puffed up the hill on legs that were too short for such outings. How eager she had been!

Her father's face at the top of the hill. Smiling. Waiting for her.

My father's face. My father's smiling face.

So happy to see me! He has just seen me, but the sight of me always makes him happy. When he was walking ahead of me, with his back to me, he didn't see me. Then he turned around, at the top of the hill, and he could see me in the distance. Was he thinking: "Maybe she won't make it, maybe she's too young and too weak"? But no, he sees me, sees my effort, that I am a person who can persevere and overcome. I am someone like him.

My father's face. He smiles at me. His face shines like the sun with love for me. No one will ever love me so much.

There was a place where she could stand beside her father that was always safe. She had walked out of that place to be with Leo. And the kind of thing that could happen is this: He is looking down at her, her breasts are naked, her skirt is beside her on the ground. And he is saying, "You are the stupidest person who ever lived."

He is looking down at her. What does he see? She doesn't know the person lying on the ground, on the straw someone had meant for animals (she is an animal), wetness between her legs. Who can this person be? What would her father say if he were looking at her? She is looking down a long tunnel at a girl in shadow, lying on the ground. The girl isn't recognizable. It couldn't possibly be herself. This girl has nothing in common with anybody she could ever know.

What would her father say if he could see her? She has no father. She has given up her father to be here. What is this place where she is, this girl in shadow, whom she cannot recognize?

Leo turns his back to her. He puts on his shirt. His back is so thin, like a child's. She'd only wanted to tell him: "You are not so alone as you think."

She understands why he's angry. What she said *was* stupid. You had to make a separate place when you were having sex, where no one from your past could enter, no one from the rest of your life. Her mistake is that she keeps letting things in: her father. When she's with her father, she lets nothing in. She is with him in a clean space, doorless, or out of doors, perhaps an arbor, they might be sitting at a table, eating, drinking.

My body is not, can never be misplaced. I may die here, I may even be dead, and I would never notice. It would make no difference. Nothing will ever change.

There, on the floor, the wet between her legs, her breasts naked, their nipples pointing up like insects, is the place of change. Things change so suddenly: harsh noises and harsh movements. No one has ever lived as she has. She is the stupidest person that ever lived.

In this place that Leo discovered, where they can be together and not be found out, she is both things: the most loving, the stupidest. Also many more. In her father's place, she can be only one thing: his.

Riding in the train, first class, the dusty corduroy seats, with her son, and his girlfriend, she wonders who it is that she would like to be.

She thinks she knows what happened.

She was born in 1912, the daughter of genteel parents who had married rather late in life. Her father was an entomologist. They lived in a large, quiet house, surrounded by many trees. Her mother died when she was two years old. She was a quiet girl, gifted in languages. She wrote poetry. She was the apple of her father's eye.

Of all the girls in her class in *liceo,* she was singled out by her teachers as worthy of attention. She found it difficult to speak to other students. When she was fourteen, she became friends with Leo Calvi because of the poetry of Leopardi. Their passion was the thought and poetry of the Romantic Age. They wanted nothing to do with anything base or ignoble. The life around them was base and ignoble. Or Leo believed it was, and he convinced her that the only right way to look at life was his way. She did everything he said; her only thought was to please him, since she believed he was a genius. He was unstable and prone to fits of anger; he had no friends among the students (except her), and was often in trouble for showing disrespect to others.

One day he said to her, "Paola, we must think about becoming lovers." He said that the connection of sex and marriage was a base ideal tied to the love of property. He'd read Marx and thought he would become a Communist: He planned to go to Russia. Italy would fall to Fascism. Italy would get the ruler it deserved.

She thought of their going to Russia, married.

Then he decided life was not worthwhile. They were great souls like Shelley, like Leopardi. They must kill themselves.

His family had a house outside the city of Torino, in a hill town called Bardonecchia. The house was at the top of the hill; halfway up the hill was an abandoned tower. There were two guns in his father's house that he and his father used for hunting rabbits. Leo and Paola would take the guns out to the tower. They would make love. Then they would shoot themselves.

She must have agreed to it, but she has no memory of agreeing. Now, understanding that she is close to a death she will not have bidden nor be able to prevent, she needs to know if she was once a person for whom death was a desirable event. There are blanks in her memory, as if sheets of white aluminum had been nailed fast to an unstable wall. She has never worked to dislodge them: this would be the work of memory, which she has not done.

There are some things she knows: At some point, before the moment of his death, she had decided that she didn't want to die. She left him in the tower, running down the hill to get away from him. She heard the shot. The farmer ran up to the tower from the field. She and the farmer found him dead. Everyone blamed her. She was sent away to cousins in America. She studied nursing. At the age of thirty-five, she married. She bore three sons. Her husband died at seventy. She lives alone.

These are the things she knows. But what has happened to the things she must once have known, and now no longer knows? Where have they gone? What would you call them? And, not knowing what to call them, how can they be called back?

There was so much that neither of us knew. A whole body of ignorance, complete as a branch of knowledge: the science of what was not known, guessed at from books or paintings, things that didn't move or grow or smell or change. He was surprised at the dark tufts of hair between my legs, under my arms, the complications of my sex. And I at his. I wanted to say "I didn't think you'd look like this at all."

We were as ignorant as dirt. With all our learning, poetry, history, philosophy, music, art, neither of us had looked at a living body. Even our own.

I had no mother. I was afraid to touch any part of my body that seemed secret. I didn't know what could be wrongly touched, damaged for good. I got my information from the voices in the air: I heard things in the air that nice people could not have said. I felt that girls with mothers knew things. I had no mother and knew nothing.

But why did he know nothing? Why was he so surprised at how I was?

In the quiet houses all through Europe, the large dining rooms with the stone floors and walls that echoed, with the gentle lamps, the flowers, the long tables—what was said and learned and what was kept unknown? Night after night she sat with her father. How was your day at school, my darling girl, my precious star? And let me tell you how the leaves produce a substance that is known as chlorophyll, how water becomes the steam, forming the clouds, and what the rocks are made of. Did you dream last night, and are you cold, or thirsty?

But the things that weren't said! Seeing Leo's body, feeling what she felt when he touched her between the legs, opening and probing, she understood that she knew nothing. That in the world there were bodies of knowledge, and that all her life most of them would be kept closed to her, or she wouldn't approach them, out of weariness or fear, or she wouldn't even know to name them until it was much too late. When Leo touched her for the first time, she immediately thought of her own ignorance.

She was always feeling the depth and breadth of what she didn't know and couldn't do. Leo never seemed to feel that anything he lacked might be of value. This was what made him sure of himself and angry at the world for valuing what he didn't have. Her father wasn't angry, but like Leo, he was untormented by the things he didn't know. Her father thought it was funny when he didn't know the names of poets, styles of architecture, chemical formulae, the capitals of countries, old musical forms. The two of them looked the same when they read. They would squint at the book, frown at it, suspicious: it had nothing to give them. Then their eyes would devour it, still frowning. There were iron walls surrounding them and the book, yet at any moment someone might invade this territory, seemingly so well bounded. So how could they look happy when they read? They wanted to master the book and then be through with it so they could put it down, believing once more, reassured once more, that there was nothing important in the world they didn't know.

When she read, the border around her and the book was permeable. She was lulled and rocked; she was lively and yet somnolent. She could move as fast or as slowly as she wished; she could be anywhere she wanted. The joy of reading was a kind of sleep. What she learned would come to her without her will. She would approach a book in hunger and in trepidation since there was so much of such beauty she didn't yet know. Yet once she was in the book, taken up in the net of black marks on a white page, she wasn't afraid. Even studying for school, she never worried. She would look up from her book, surprised that the world had continued to go on outside the folds of clouds where she had been. Only when she put the book down, and went back into the world, she was ashamed at all the rest she didn't know.

Yet sometimes she understood that in this way of hers, this sleepy way, this pliant way, she had learned quite a lot. It always came to her as a surprise. Sometimes she caught Leo in a mistake, and she was shocked to realize that some of the information he spoke with such certainty was misinformation.

Like what he said about the troubadours. How could he speak with so much certainty and be so wrong? He had to say the things he didn't know weren't worth knowing. But he couldn't say that the troubadours weren't worth knowing about. Something would have collapsed if she'd caused him to see that there were things in the world worth knowing about—things she knew about—that he didn't know. He wouldn't forgive her. He might leave her. She was sure he would.

They climbed up the hill to the tower. He went ahead of her. She was bleeding. She didn't know how to tell him. He was speaking of the troubadours and their religion of love. He was so happy, for once he was almost young. He was running ahead of her, bowing, calling her "my lady." All time she was thinking of the blood between her legs, sticky as ink. Perhaps he liked it that she couldn't keep up with him. Perhaps he was imagining a feminine weakness: the bones of birds, delicate wings that fluttered, and a darling mechanism like the inside of a tiny clock. But she knew that what made up her femaleness wasn't any of that, but a dark mess of heavy meat, organs producing blood that seeped and oozed and stank.

"I am a troubadour, my lady, I salute the rose you are. A troubadour like my ancestors the troubadours who walked this very spot."

She knew troubadours had never walked here. She wanted to say, "It wasn't like that at all. The troubadours were in the south of France. They wouldn't have traveled this far north. They would never have been in these mountains."

The mountains were cold and hard. Her father had told her how the mountains had been formed.

There were many things she knew from her father that Leo would never know. She could learn only by being close to something that could comfort her. Her father's body. A kind book.

I was a loving girl, and I was hopeful, she thinks, seeing her son unwrap a chocolate for Katherine, take off the cover from the mineral water, and wipe the neck of the bottle with his handkerchief before pouring some into her plastic cup. Then I was not, and I have never been again, neither loving nor hopeful. I don't know what I've been. Something I can't name, pressing, for some reason I have never understood, to keep alive.

Something in her hadn't wanted death. And yet he had. Had she seen something he'd never been able to see, the endless spinning into emptiness, the endless strangeness, the fear (death means I will not be near my father's body)? Or did he see something her mind was too small and common to understand: that life was nothing and that death was glorious.

She wanted to keep alive for her father's face, his voice. In death, she would be bereft of them. Leo believed that in death he would be free, exalted. She could only imagine herself afraid. Like the time she'd lost her father in the market. She'd slipped her hand from his to watch a man who had a monkey. Then she looked and couldn't find him. Her eye flicked from one face that wasn't his to another. Each unknown face became her enemy, purposely concealing her father's face.

Where is my father's hat? And who am I among these faces? I can no longer place myself; I am afraid.

Leo wasn't afraid. In class, he stood up to the daunting teachers. "You are wrong, you know nothing," he would say. He called his fellow students ignoramuses. "Asses," he said at every turn, "you are all asses."

He didn't think she was an ignoramus. "You, alone, among them all, have the beginnings of a mind." He was sixteen, and he had no fear of saying things like that. In the overbright light of his judgment, only she stood acceptable.

If she hadn't discovered that sometimes he was wrong, would she have died with him? If he hadn't told her that the troubadours walked in the north of Italy, would she be here now on this train, *Milano a Torino*, comfortable, eating chocolates, her small feet in their white cotton socks on the seat across from her (she has laid down newspaper first) because now that she is old she has some problems with her circulation? Or would she be a skeleton, teeth, knuckles, hair grotesquely growing in the tomb, beside her father, underneath her father's name?

She isn't dead, and sometimes this surprises her. After Leo's death, she would waken in the night, in the unfamiliar room, on the new continent, the room with a carpet and a table lamp white as milk, and think for a moment that the place where she was waking wasn't her cousin's house, but death. Slowly she would recognize the objects, the new objects, none of them dear. The moon was kept invisible by the thin leaves of the trees whose names—*oak, maple*—gave her no nourishment, and never would. She would recover fully from the hope, still possible for her on her first wakening, that the objects in their cones of shadow would reveal themselves to be the ones in her old room in Turin: the ancient wardrobe, the table with her jug and pitcher, her bookcase and her writing table, the white shutters closing off the yellow leaves of the plane tree, the footsteps on the pavement and the noise of conversation in the street. The first shock of the unfamiliar things made her believe she must be dead.

Then it would come to her: the yellow chair, the plaid bedspread, the dark wooden knob of the closet door—this was her new room in America. She would remember that she hadn't died, she had been sent away. Her father had sent her away. She wouldn't see him again.

When Leo's father saw her on the street after the death, he spat on the ground as she passed. His mother went mad. She walked up and down the street in front of Paola's house and shouted curses of the purest filth underneath her window. Paola's father didn't know what to do. Within weeks, he had turned into an old man. They never went out of the house.

When he told her he was thinking of sending her to his cousins in America, how could she not agree to go?

My father was a weak man: he sent me away. He was a good man, but he was weak. Another man could have stood beside me at the door, raised his strong arm, encircled his shamed daughter. "Leave her alone," he would have said, and people would have felt they must obey. The two of them would have stood at the doorway, watching the accusers disappear, their backs receding down the leafy streets. Another man would have closed the heavy door and said, "Never mind, my darling girl, my precious." The grief, the shame might have been captured and contained by those words. But my father was weak. He died of it.

Never to see your face again.

Never to see his face again. She didn't know the right way to divide her life, by the death of which man. Leo, whom she had loved, to whom she would have given everything (but not, in the end, her life). Or her father, who had given her life, whom she would have been happy to die beside. After she heard the shot that was the end of Leo's life she knew that happiness was something she would never have again. She heard the shot, understood it not as Leo's death, but only as words, repeating themselves as she ran up the hill: *E finito.* It is over.

The sound of the gun meant I would never again live without shame. My father could have taken my shame, filtered it into another substance. Sadness, perhaps. Regret. Alone, the two of us could have sat in sadness, in the big dark house. We could have sat together, hour after hour, at the long table where we took our meals. We could have lit or not lit the lamp. We could have read, or had books beside us, our hands empty. The servants could have brought us meals in silence, somber and respectful. As if a corpse were in the house. There could have been no shame. Shame is a sin of the eye, and I would have lived in your eyes only.

So perhaps that was the point that marked the end of her old life; not her father's death, but the moment when her father could no longer meet her eye, and she knew that, from then on, when they were alone, they wouldn't be happy.

She had been happy with him: it's one thing she knows there's no reason to doubt. There was a night, a night that really happened, not one she only wishes had occurred. It was such a simple night: Quite warm, a summer's night, early in June. They'd just had a heavy supper of roast chicken and green beans; for dessert an almond cake from the baker's shop under the *arcadio,* where the women in their striped aprons wrapped packages of sweets so that they looked like hats. The store was devoted to making the edible appear permanent; the hard sugar flowers seemed to demand to be worn, not eaten. She and her father had chosen the almond cake.

They were heavy with the scent of roses and the happiness of food that they had eaten slowly. The light fell like milk from the white sky. Her father had gone into his library. She was meant to be reading in her room. But she was lonely for him, for his bulk in the heaviness of the warm night. She knew that when he closed the door of his library, she wasn't to disturb him. It was a sacred place, like a church, and she would no more have gone into her father's library than she would have walked onto the altar of a church. But this night she couldn't resist. The warm dampness of the air pulled her; her body was too light to resist the pull. She was too light without her father; she would be flung out of the orbit of the earth: a bird flung by a strong wind and tossed down. Or she would drop down into the dark leaves of the garden and become invisible.

The thought of invisibility wasn't unpleasant. It was neither one thing nor the other, neither pleasant nor unpleasant, neither frightening nor full of promise. But now she was being drawn toward placement, substance. Her father's body drew her, as a speck was drawn from your eye when something warm was pressed against it.

She would just stand in the doorway, very quiet. He wouldn't know she was there.

She opened the door. He was alone in darkness. She couldn't see anything at first and then she saw the red tip of her father's cigarette. He was lying on the leather couch, smoking and dreaming. For a long time they were both silent.

I am happy. I am very happy.

She pressed her palms tightly together as if she held dried petals between them and the pressure would preserve them. Delight, she thought, this is delight.

"Are you there in the darkness, little one? What are you doing in the darkness?"

"I was looking at the tip of your cigarette. It was glowing like a ruby in the dark."

"You say that because you are happy," he said.

There was no need to move toward him. What separated them was only air. He understood everything. For a long time they were both silent. The moon poured through the shutters and collected on the floor in even bars. She went over to the couch and kissed her father good night, as she always did, on his white forehead, in the clear space between the thick brush of his hair and his dark eyebrows.

When she kissed Leo, she never kissed him on the forehead. That was her father's place. Sometimes she kissed Leo's face, small rapid kisses, full of gratitude and praise. She was grateful to him for having chosen her. He told her that no one understood him as she did. In the whole city of Torino, only the two of them could understand a word of poetry.

She was grateful to hear what he said about Shakespeare, about Racine, about Leopardi. He read her his essay about unity in Homer. He had read Homer in Greek, so he could talk about the voice of Homer, the virility of Homer. "I am a poet in the modern

age condemned to a position of weakne
the fault of a womanized civilization. I s
virile poets. Every modern poet to be great
He had written this to her in a letter. But
he saw her breasts and he was weak and gi
he'd spent himself inside her. She knew his
wanted to say, "If you must hate women to
mean that you hate me? Who are you when ___ weeping or
resting? Isn't that a part of your greatness? Can there be no place
for that in your poetry?"

She began a poem:

> The boy left tears between my breasts
> Why not? He didn't need them, having
> No use for them in any of his poems.

She never finished it. He was the poet; he was greater than she
would ever be.

She wanted to say: "Do you have to hate me to be great? When
you speak of women, do you mean me? Do you leave me out of
the category? And what does it mean if you do or if you don't?"
But she knew that was the kind of question she wasn't to ask. She
knew what he would say. "As a woman, you are what I need for
my release. There is no great love between men and women. I shall
travel the world and have thousands of women, and you will be
only the first among many. I will remember you dimly. Many years
will go by and I will never think of you. And then, one day, in
some distant place when I am old, your face will come to me and
I will smile."

Yet the day she had the flu, he walked up and down the street
for hours, Concetta, the maid, told her. He was a scandal, she said.

Concetta money if she would let him speak to Paola
window near her bed. Concetta took pity on him and
ed him the window.

"I wanted to know how you were getting on with the Carlyle.
On Heroes and Hero Worship. I wanted to know what you thought.
Your English is better than mine. Have you finished it?"

"Yes. No. I don't know. My head is weak with this flu."

"Well, you've been out of bed long enough," he said, as if it
had been her idea. "Take care of yourself." And he went away,
smoking his pipe, which he smoked absurdly, like a boy playing
at being his father.

She felt that only she had ever known him. Even his own mother
hadn't known him as she did. But she could never tell what she
knew, so her knowledge was no good to anyone at all. Still, she
had it, she would never lose it; even if it had no purpose, it was
hers; it couldn't be taken away.

He could always convince her she knew nothing, she was ignorant, superstitious, sentimental. But he would tell her things he
told nobody else. He told her he was thinking of becoming a
Communist. She made the mistake of telling her father; she thought
he would approve and like Leo better for it.

"The little squirt knows nothing. Lives in the highest privilege
and preaches anarchy. Why, if a servant didn't set out his perfumed
handkerchief for him, he'd blow his nose in his fingers. He doesn't
know how to wipe his own ass."

What was that side of her father that could say things like that?
It was a voice she didn't know, language she'd never heard him
use. Never to her. But she'd heard him be cruel to the men he
worked with. "Imbecile," he called them. "Cretin." But never to
her. She was "my flower, my star, apple of my eye, light of my
life." She was everything to him.

"If the whole world turned against me, if I were ruined, penniless, out on the street, it would be no loss. It would be a holiday. You are everything to me."

At night when she closed her eyes she saw herself and her father walking in shadow. They are holding each other's hands. They perceive others in the dimness, other human beings probably alive but insubstantial and inert. The two of them are so light that their walking takes nothing from them. Only one thing is important: she mustn't let go of his hand. Vibrant as filaments, they walk through darkness, the two of them are the only bright things. But if she becomes distracted by one of the inert shadows, if she drifts away, all his brightness will be gone and he'll become one of the shades, unalive because she hadn't noticed, because she'd moved away, her eye on an allurement. Light as she is, she grips his hand. She won't allow herself to be heedless, like other women whose eyes had roved. Lot's wife, who looked back to see the small familiar things of her domestic life. She put herself to sleep with the good dream of her unbroken attentiveness.

She wrote a poem called "Eurydice's Lament." Eurydice weeps with guilt at having looked behind her, at having made a mockery of all Orpheus's efforts. Because of her, he is torn apart by furious women. Paola had written the poem in alexandrines: she was very proud of it. She felt it was good enough to show Leo. His eye flicked over it.

"The meter is excellent, excellent. And the image of the gray, blind lake beside which the shades are walking, and the patient cattle, that's very good. I had suspected, but I wasn't sure you had the makings of a poet. I feared you'd always be stuck on the level of a lady poetess, making up pretty verses. But the courage of your deliberate error shows you are not a lady poetess but a *poet*."

She couldn't understand what he was saying. Deliberate error? He was praising her for something that made a difference to him, something that separated her from other females, made her more like him, worthy of praise and the regard of equals. And she didn't know what it was. She went cold with fear. Should she pretend she knew what he was talking about, and take his praise and regard, living with the terror that one day he'd catch her out? Or should she tell the truth, losing his regard and her temporary place beside him as an equal.

She began to cry. "I don't know what you mean," she said.

"Mean about what?"

"Error," she said. "Deliberate error. I don't know what you mean."

"Switching the story, of course. Making it Eurydice who turned around rather than Orpheus. A brilliant stroke."

How could it be? That simple story that she'd known ever since she was a child. How could she have got it wrong? She'd thought it was the woman's fault for not paying attention, that lapse of attention she'd felt so often in herself: when her father spoke to her about beetles, when Leo spoke to her about the distribution of capital. She thought Eurydice must be like her. But in the story it was Orpheus, the man, who was forgetful. How was that possible? Her father was never forgetful. Leo didn't let things fall away. Their minds were tough and durable, and yet porous, like fertile soil. Nothing would slip from them. Her mind was watery and vague, like the terrain the shades walked, the terrain of after-death.

"Stop crying," he said. "You know I hate that. What would there be to cry about?"

"It wasn't a deliberate error. It was just a stupid mistake."

"So what? Poets aren't bound by fact. There is no truth for poets but poetic truth. What you achieved with the image of the blind lake. I hate it when you sniffle. Your nose gets red and you stop looking beautiful. It's your duty to inspire me by being beautiful.

Now you are a great poet. You are a woman poet. You do not know things from your brain, but from your womb. You are greater than I with your womb knowledge. You have the greatness of a child, or an animal. Together we are one great whole: One poet. And we will walk together, hand in hand, two poets among the honored shades."

How can she tell him that her dream of walking incandescent among the indecipherable shades is not a dream of him, but of her father?

She can't imagine the moment of her father's death; she has never allowed herself to think of it. She has allowed it to be possible that he has never died. But with Leo this wasn't possible; she was with him the moment after his death, Leo or whoever it was who was there, dying. What was it that happened? What he had thought would happen? What did he think he was doing, sixteen years old, shooting himself in an abandoned tower with a gun used for hunting rabbits? He lived for poetry; he believed he was a genius; he felt terribly alone; he thought no one had ever loved him. No, that wasn't it; he knew she loved him, but it didn't matter. He walked the streets in the evening; his parents were worried; they didn't know where he was. When he'd come in late, his father would strike him for making his mother worry. He was writing a history of consciousness, a history of the great writers of the world, a theory of literature, a play about a family in Russia after the revolution. He knew everything. He was the greatest writer *in Italia*. He knew nothing, he was lazy, nothing he wrote would come to anything. He walked the streets thinking of the greatness of writers, which he knew he would not possess. He sat in cafés, reading. He swam in the river. He walked with other boys occasionally, tiring them with his words. Always he believed of himself: "I am the loneliest of you all."

And so when her father said those cruel things about him, she only wanted to walk out of her house, to walk beside Leo on the street, on any street, anywhere he wanted to be walking, to protect him from her father. Her father who loved her above all things, but who knew nothing of the person she had become.

Her father thought she was good but she knew herself not good. He thought she was pure when she was impure, trustworthy when she deserved not to be trusted, sensible when she was foolish, learned when she was as ignorant as dirt. "You are as ignorant as dirt. You have the mind of a shop girl," Leo would say. And the next day: "Along with me you are the only poet writing *in Italia*." But her father thought she was only one thing: his shining girl.

She had never been.

Always, as long as she could possibly remember, there was the shame that she knew was hers, the shame her aunt had caught her at. One night, her aunt came in to leave some stockings she had mended. She can still hear her aunt's voice: "What are you doing there? Take your hands out from beneath the sheets. Get up and wash your hands. What would your father say?"

She had never been the thing her father thought. He loved a person that she never was. Her life's work: that he should never know this. Her fear: one day he will know. How could he think she was good when she had thought of the most dark lewdnesses? Parts of bodies, shameful, thrusting breasts, buttocks, private parts, torments, and she herself the center, being looked at by a thousand men.

I am lying on a slab in a high place. The crowd of men roars below me. I open my legs. They see everything. They want me more than anything but they can never reach me. They are stomping, slavering. They've become animals. I've turned them into animals, but they can never touch me. All they want in life is just to look at me. I close my legs and they have nothing left to live for.

Is this the girl my father loves?

She is an old woman, no one looks at her now. She never touches her body except to wash it or to treat some illness. Leo and her father are dead. She'd said that she would die with Leo. She had promised, but she had broken her promise. She had lived.

But he had died. What does that mean, that she is living and he is not? What is the difference between life and death? Between being alive and not alive. What had the first moment of not being alive been for him? Or the moment before that, when he was saying to himself: "Very soon I will not be alive"?

What were the pictures behind his eyes of where he would be after death? Did he believe he would be glorified, famous, free of sorrow? Why was life so intolerable to him? Did he think the two of them would be together in death? Was that why he wanted her to die with him?

She can no longer remember why it seemed a thing she might do: shut herself in a tower with a boy and his father's gun. She can't recognize the person for whom that idea was, even for a short time, a possibility. Is it the same person who rides the train now with her son? You would have to say yes. You would have to say that someone was born to a body, and that body, though changing greatly, had endured. She had come very close to death, the girl who was born with the body that had endured. Had that girl been planning to shoot herself? The woman on the train can't remember.

How would she describe that girl? Shy, most of the time, unhappy. Happy with her father, but really with no one else. Happy reading. Among people her own age, a stranger, an outcast. They spoke a language, they had customs she could never understand. She was miserable among them, an exile. Books were her home.

Also her father's body. And then Leo discovered her. He shone his light upon her. *I have chosen you.*

And who was *he?* She can't remember much about his body. The skin, soft as a child's. The fine hair in a line from clavicle to waist, the thin shoulders, the thighs, that weren't strong and great like columns, but feminine, unformed. That's all she can remember. He held her in his arms. She lay beside him. Then he decided he was through with life.

She can't remember what he said death would be like when he spoke about it. His interest seemed to lie only with the act of dying. He was interested in what he would represent: he had no thought for what lay beyond the representation. He had no interest in the thing he would become. Unlike her, he didn't imagine death to be a place he must inhabit. Only a kind of language. A strong sentence. Death would identify him, once and for all. He wanted to be seen as one who had taken his life. But what was it he thought he was taking?

He was terribly lonely. He lived for poetry: he feared that he wouldn't be great. Death in a tower was a great thing. Death after love: a poem. Perfect as Homer, Dante, Goethe. As Shakespeare. A sentence of absolute purity, like God on fire: I am who I am.

But who was that? She can no longer remember because she has tried not to remember. To call back Leo is to call back shame, his mother walking in front of the house cursing, "You are the whore who has murdered my son." And his father, spitting on the street when he saw her. The priests wouldn't allow Leo to be buried in consecrated ground: a suicide was defiled. She wished they had left him out, like Polyneices, the brother of Antigone, to be plucked by carrion birds so she could have given up her life to save his corpse from dishonor.

Yet she hadn't given up her life. An old woman, she is about to walk once more under the arches of her city, to drink coffee, to look at monuments. Will she visit his grave? And who is in that grave? A skeleton? A shade?

And what could it possibly matter?

When Carlo said, "Our first stop will be to see your father's grave," she was surprised.

She'd told him enough so that he'd wanted to see where his grandfather was buried. He thinks of his grandfather as a hero, standing up to Fascists, and a scientist, patiently cataloguing species of beetles. He'd thought that the grave would be in Turin: had she never told him her father and his people were Milanese? Or would that have meant nothing to him? So they had landed in Milan, rather than Rome, so that the grave could be their first stop on Italian soil.

She wouldn't have walked a quarter mile out of her way to see her father's grave. There was nothing there that had anything to do with her. To imagine that there was a kind of presence in those bones was to think in the way that priests forced you to, pretending that Christ was in the bread. They called it the Real Presence. There was nothing present in that grave that mattered. A grave was a witness that you had consigned the dead to the past, that you believed there was no chance you would see the living face, the living body, in the world again. She would not pay homage to her father's deadness: she carried his face, his living body, inside her still living body. She would not place flowers before bones, which were not her father: she would never kneel before an absence; she would go, to please her son, but that place meant no more to her than any other place.

Walking in the *Cimitero Monumentale*, in the section called Famedio, the section of the well-to-do, the family mausoleum sickened her. She stood silent before it for a moment, then walked away. She talked quickly, wanting to be far away from the display of wealth, her family's, to honor lies and an absence. All those years of cruelty, of putting aside money that could clothe and feed the living so that this thing could be built, this silent house of death that lay on living soil like a huge hoof on the chest of a still breathing person. There it stood among the other houses of defeat, bearing a name that was her father's, among the other edifices built on the unbreeding scandal of dead wealth.

He is not here. Nothing important in the world is here.

She didn't even know the sources of the family wealth. Her father despised money; to speak of it would poison the rich air he exhaled, the air that gave life to the space around him so that everywhere he breathed was fertile. He despised his brothers in their devotion to making money: he honored his father, but he spoke of him as someone from a different race.

Her father died in 1935. There was a mass arrest of people suspected of being anti-Fascists. Two men with Southern accents were sent to his house. They ransacked his library, looking for documents. They were throwing his books on the floor. He grabbed one of the men, younger than he, and called him a lout. "Put those books down," he said. "They're too good for your filthy hands to touch." The man, twenty years younger, forty pounds heavier, threw her father to the floor. She believes that her father took risks with the Fascist police because he no longer cared if he lived or died.

He never recovered from that fall. He had two heart attacks in a month. Then he died. Ailing, he wrote her that she was lucky to be out of Italy.

My darling girl. I think of you, fortunately living in a country that still has honor. I swim here in a cesspool, afraid to leave because I can't be without my books, my laboratory. You have learned that your father is a coward. I would give up almost anything to see your face. Even for one minute. Yet I could not arrive on my cousin's

*doorstep a pauper. All night I lie awake and think of you and the
days we were so happy. I do not believe that in my life I will have
happiness again. War will come and I will not live through it. But
I know you will live.*

She'd live the rest of her life because she thought he wanted her
to. She kept alive when living wasn't really necessary because she
thought her death would be one more shameful act committed
against him. And she had learned how hard it was to die. If she
went on living, she could feel he hadn't died in vain. She lived day
by day, watching, waiting, she has never known for what.

In the seven years—1928 to 1935—that she remained in America
while her father was still alive across the ocean from her, she had
no thought of her future. She lived quietly, first going to school in
Larchmont with American teenagers who left her to herself because
she wasn't one of them. She was foreign, with an accent and strange
ways. She studied her Latin. Sitting in her bedroom at her virginal
schoolgirl's desk, she knew herself not virginal and felt she was an
imposter as a schoolgirl. Sometimes she believed she defiled those
eager American faces by being around them. She had known death
and sex; they had known neither. She would run her finger over
the Latin syllables as if she were blind. The verses of Latin were
hope to her. The jokey boys and girls, on their way to football
games, laughed at their problems with Latin: it was their curse to
be forced to take it. It was a place that she could be and still
recognize herself. But gradually, she decided it was poetry that had
brought death, and she would give it up. One night she put the
books on a high shelf and decided she would not read poetry again.
She purposely did badly on her exams, hurting her Latin teacher,
who'd made special assignments for her.

Leo had loved poetry. He'd died of it. She wouldn't read it again.
But at first she'd needed it. She'd been alone for so much time,

and everything else was so unfamiliar to her. From the moment she boarded the ship in Genoa, her life had been mostly silent. Standing on the deck, or during the endless meals, Americans and English people asked her about Mussolini. They seemed to admire him. But her father hadn't admired him. He called him a buffoon, a lout, risked his job by refusing to join the party. Why had her father, who was not a coward in these things, sent her away?

The same man who could stand up to people in black shirts, people holding clubs and truncheons, couldn't protect her from shame. Perhaps no one could. Perhaps shame was the most powerful thing on earth.

On the ship over, with no distractions, and no one she dared speak to (although people were kind to the fifteen-year-old girl), she understood how her life would be. Alone, terribly alone on the ship at night, she both longed for her father's face and couldn't bear to call it up. It was as if the memory were a literal photograph that she unwrapped in secret, held against her chest, then moved an inch or two away from her to get a good glimpse of it. But at other times the shame was so great she dared not even unwrap the photograph. The history she carried with her was an acid that would eat away at the image of his face until what was left was grotesque: the eyes gone, half the nose, the mouth invisible.

In the black nights on the deck of the ship, she would feel cleansed by the rough smell of the salt air and the cold, polished stars. Among all the well-dressed people, and their dancing and their drunkenness, their costumes, and their funny hats, their sunglasses, their laprobes, their brisk walks ten times around the deck, she was entirely alone. She wished not to exist, but she had chosen to live, and now she must live for her father.

The rich house, where she was taken after her cousin and his wife had met her at the ship, was the place of her most deadly aloneness, where the effort simply to breathe nearly crushed her. The house of terrible aloneness. The cruel house.

It was big and dark and full of luxuries that brought no comfort and no joy. Her cousin was a doctor; his wife was the daughter of a man who owned factories. They had no children. This rich American woman had brought him to her home from Italy convinced that he would prosper. And he did.

Prosperity: a choking word. Now, sixty years later, her throat is thick with it. *Prosperous.*

It was a house of prosperity. Upholstered furniture and carpets, low ceilings, light woods, dark lawns and leaves that were never dusty, never lemon-colored. Quiet streets, soft foods: ham and baked beans, vegetables with butter, bread in slices, words for kitchen things sounding like the money that they cost: *percolator, Frigidaire.* On the wall were watercolors of bridges and trees with orange and yellow leaves. Outside, the sun hung sharp in the sky, fell straight on the white snow, the white fur on the women's collars. Her room had a plaid rug and a plaid bedspread: she looked out of her window on trees and lawn; she could see only glimpses of the other houses. In the morning, black servants walked on their low-heeled shoes, did their work without speaking, left at night; she could never imagine where they went. Only the church had no softness to it. The Irish priest who made the Latin sound like German, the vestments that looked brand-new, the stained glass in the windows that sliced the air like knives.

Her cousin and his wife didn't know what to do with her. She felt they wanted to hide from her every time they saw her. And there were so many rooms to hide in! So many other places you could be, halls you could walk down, corners you could turn, your shoulders hunched, your eyes turned downward.

Close a door so that you will not have to see me. Through your kindness I am kept alive.

She never wept. She was afraid of what would be unearthed once she began weeping: some hard soil packed around her roots would be dislodged by weeping. She imagined rows of trees fallen on their sides in a road, their roots shameful, disinterred by flood, with no connection anymore to nourishment.

She earned her bread through quietness, decorousness, constant apologies. They valued her quietness. Her wealthy American cousin moved with the effects of quiet wealth, pushing down the pedal of her Buick, putting on other furs—a grayish blue, a hazy red-brown—opening her soft leather purse, taking out her compact, clicking the purse shut with its tight gold clip, sitting at her vanity table with its perfume bottles, their rubber atomizers soft as licorice. She was very kind. It was impossible to know what she thought. She floated in and out, through her possessions, silent. Money flowed from her as if it were water from a stream she dove into and then stepped out of, silently.

Her husband drove to his office on Park Avenue (his specialty was ears and throats) then drove home, the silent purring of his car's motor like the silence of the house. Paola had been told he and her father were like brothers, and her father had trusted him enough to send her to him. But they never spoke of her father, and he seemed so different from her father she couldn't imagine they had once been close.

No one ever seemed to speak aloud in the house. Perhaps it was only that they didn't talk to her. Perhaps they had nothing to say, or they were too ashamed of her to speak.

Sometimes, her American cousin's niece would be sent for, to keep Paola company. The niece's name was Harriet; she was six years younger than Paola, and a tormentor. Why would they think the two of them would get on? Harriet's hair was wild and red; she wore thick ribbons woven into it; she loved chaos. Around her, glasses broke, china smashed, the keys of the piano played off tune, doors flew back on their hinges and from then on closed improperly, the smooth nap of the carpet stood up like the hair of an enraged animal. She would sit on Paola's bed, staring at Paola as she did her homework. One day she said, "I know what you did in Italy." That was all she said, and Paola never knew what she knew. But each time she saw the child, she was afraid. She would have given her anything: money, all her clothes, her books, her watch, keys to the house; she knew that Harriet was waiting for the right time, and when that time came she would get whatever it was she wanted.

Harriet was there the time Paola had the trouble with the shower. The child's malevolence with things was catching; you handled things badly when she was around. It must have been the disease of Harriet's presence that made Paola wait till she was there to use the shower bath for the first time. She'd never taken a shower, but had heard its sound, like the soughing of a gentle rain, delightful, stimulating, and mature. She heard Harriet taking a shower in the bathroom that they shared and decided she would follow. Then she heard Harriet screaming. She could hear her feet in their hard little strapped shoes running back and forth. "Aunty Violet, Aunty Violet, come and see, the house is ruined." Then, in a moment, her aunt decorously knocked on the bathroom door, and her voice like rolling coins said, "Turn off the shower, dear. Immediately."

She hadn't known that the curtain had to go inside the tub. She'd stayed in the shower twenty minutes and caused a flood in the kitchen. The ceiling was ruined. "Ruined," Harriet kept saying, her hard eyes simmering with joy.

Paola knew that the house would pretend to be friendly to her and to shelter her, but it too despised her for her foreignness, so she could never relax inside it: it was always waiting to turn her into the agent of its ruin. Ruin lay behind her: Leo's brains on the straw in the tower, his mother's crumpled face as she walked up and down the street, her own father's face which she sometimes thought she saw in the dark hallway.

Sometimes the objects in the house seduced her, for a moment, with their luxury, and she was able to believe that the velvet drapes were superior to the hard shutters of her home, that the carpets were better than the cold marble of the floors in her old dining room, that the light furniture you could sink into like a tired swimmer was better than the ancient straightback chairs in the *salone*.

Once, when her aunt and uncle were away, one day in summer, she came in drenched from the rain. The servants were preparing dinner. She was cold to the bone; she couldn't imagine ever feeling dry. Yet what her drenched skin hungered for wasn't wool or thick, absorbent cotton, but the cool satin of her cousins' bedspread. She stole into their bedroom; she left her clothes in a wet heap on the floor at the bottom of the bed. She covered herself in the pearl-colored satin, let it roll around her shoulders till its coldness and its inhumanity assured her sufficiently, she didn't know of what, and she turned out the rosy lights and lay on her back, letting the thick soft fabric rest against her nipples and the high arch of her hip bones. Fearful: What if someone came in?—a servant, her aunt home from Maine. How could she explain what she was doing, what she wanted? To be one with that luxuriousness they owned and prized, that so American soft thickness, that factory-made excess. She desired to be covered in it, to rub herself against it, so that she could be impervious, as they all seemed to be, to ruin and decay. The bad luck of Europe would fall off her skin; she would rub herself against the magic of America; she would not grieve; she would no longer, like her native continent, err, suffer, or do harm.

There were only a few months of this prosperity. She arrived in Larchmont in November of 1928, three months after Leo's death, and within eighteen months, her American cousin's money was gone, the bank had taken their house. They left it and most of the furniture inside it, moving to a small apartment in Jackson Heights, Queens. Her uncle still went to work, but there were fewer patients and money was scarce. Now it was the American cousin's turn to be silent and invisible. What had been mild lakes of genteel quietness became fathomless oceans of absence. She began drinking and Paola was left alone with her. They didn't have to feel bad about asking for help. She owed them everything, and they all knew it.

For the first time, things that were happening to many people, and not just to her, began to shape her days. She was the victim of history rather than fate. She was poorer because of the Depression, and she couldn't go back home because her father wouldn't have her live in Fascist Italy, where he was in danger. But these pressures never changed what life felt like to her; they only reminded her of what she knew: nothing was stronger than shame. As the war began, people she had known died in camps. But she was dead already. She wished that she could be like them, innocent victims, their fates visited upon them because of an accident of their birth. She knew they suffered monstrously, yet she believed they were more fortunate than she. She envied the dead, yet she could not bring herself to give up life.

In 1942, her American cousin died. Paola had been in America fourteen years, twelve spent caring for her cousin, hiding bottles from her, picking her up when she fell, listening to her accusations, her laments. She agreed that their troubles coincided with her arrival in America. How could she not agree?

When her American cousin died, Paola decided to train as a nurse. She had nothing to do with her time. When her father's cousin returned from the city, she would prepare him a meal, but as she no longer needed to look out for his wife, she had nothing to fill her days. Nurses were needed in the war effort. She specialized in rehabilitation. She moved people's limbs, then helped them to move their limbs on their own, and they improved. For a while she thought that perhaps she wasn't only a bearer of misfortune.

The time she worked in the hospital was the best time of her life. The work and its endless repetitions gave her a kind of peace, and the soldiers liked her. They were amused by her accent; they called her princess, doll. She was polite and distant with them, bending their legs, moving their muscles, making them walk steps she knew were agony, turning her eyes so they'd think she didn't see them weeping. When they cursed, she moved away and folded something, straightened something. At night she read books on anatomy and the new knowledge made her happy. No more poetry: muscles, bones, ligaments, joints, the flow of blood—not a metaphor but a real substance that could cause movement, whose failure could prevent movement. Speech with her colleagues was practical: speech, not figures of speech. At night, she came home tired and fell asleep after wishing her father's cousin good night: their only conversation.

She began going out occasionally for a cup of coffee with her colleagues. Nurses, mostly, and technicians, all of them involved in the work of broken bodies. She thought disdainfully of the conversations in the cafés in Turin where she had sat with Leo and their schoolmates. Conversations about greatness, about Homer, Dante, about politicians they knew nothing about and could do nothing to influence. Among her fellow workers in the hospital, there was quiet, engrossed conversation about what they did. "Let's try this with the Johnson boy tomorrow. Perhaps this kind of splint."

They were making up for the damage of the war.

She began noticing that Joe Smaldone tried to walk beside her on the way to the coffee shop, helped her with her coat and held the chair for her. She thought of him as a buffoon, good-natured, like a bear or a child. He ran the brace shop; he was remarkable with machinery. He could make what she needed; she would describe something, he would create a reality. He sang Puccini and Perry Como, every song vulgar and loud. He brought Sicilian food from his mother's kitchen, noisily unwrapped it, shared it loudly, its strong smells overwhelming the air in the brace shop. People's happiness with the vivid flavors made them laugh and forget that they were overworked and that they would never be able to keep up with the damage that the war had done, that they would go home tired every day and wake up tired in the mornings with too much ahead of them.

Joe had strong yellowish teeth and a brush of hair that was beginning to go gray. His eyes were hazel, and protruded, as if the pressure of too much health pressed them forward. He was never silent or unhappy. He pushed doors open like the wind; his step was heavy on the floor; each stride covered an inordinate amount of ground: he was across the room in a second, he was buckling straps, tightening screws, patting the boys on the back, telling them they were great, just great, they were in the best of hands, they'd be out of here in no time. They wouldn't be, but they continued to believe him, and it angered her that they believed him and that he went on every day with his loud lies. And she was angry that he'd even think of paying attention to her, angry when he passed the sugar or asked if she'd like a Danish or a bun, his treat. She wanted to turn on him with a hateful face that would have shocked him and say, "You know nothing about me. You don't know what I've done."

It seemed a part of his vulgarity and his stupidity that he didn't notice that there was no possibility of anything like courtship for her. How could he fail to see that she was as damaged as the boys in the ward? Would he have asked them to go out and play ball, to go dancing? Probably he would have.

She moved away from him and never met his eye. He didn't seem to notice, but he didn't try to be alone with her or ask her out. She didn't know what he understood. He was an annoyance to her, like a badly trained, ingratiating dog, good for certain tasks. Sometimes they shared elation at a new piece of equipment they'd dreamed up together. But she was careful not to smile at him with too much warmth, and to move away from the excessive heat and shadow of his too large body.

Then her uncle died, and she was shocked at the totality of her aloneness. She allowed Joe to marry her; she never felt that she had married him. She wants to turn to her son now and say, "I never hurt your father. I never told him that I loved him. I cooked his meals and gave him the home away from his mother's house that he had always wanted. I opened my legs for him. I denied him nothing. I gave him healthy sons. I wasn't cruel to him. I never returned his kindness with ingratitude."

She looks out the window at the white towers holding chemicals, possibly lethal, possibly poisoning the water that the children drink. She asks her dead husband's forgiveness.

You could have had someone who was good as you were good, and open, and full of faith in life. I'm sorry for you that you chose me, and that you were loyal to me. I'm sorry you saw something in me that was valuable to you. I was dead already when you met me.

She never thought he'd die before her. Life was so simple for him, and he was so effortlessly healthy; he never got colds or headaches; he'd never once broken a limb, he never seemed tired or out of sorts, he ate everything, digested everything, he liked all weathers, he was never purposelessly sad. He cried when John Kennedy was shot and when his mother died. Other than that, he greeted whatever life offered him with an alert forbearance, an eagerness that was never proud and never assumed he had a right to anything. He was at everybody's beck and call: his ten brothers and sisters, his widowed mother, dozens of aunts and cousins. No wonder his three sons loved him; no wonder they spoke to her as if she were a stranger, with kindness, not knowing what they could expect.

His family called him Bep. She hated that syllable; it meant they wanted something. And he would give it. The roof was leaking or a faucet didn't work or a child needed the doctor or someone had had a baby and was sick in bed and the husband didn't know how to change diapers. Or his mother was going to church.

If she'd loved him, she would have resented the time away from her. But even feeling only what she did—gratitude and respect— she was annoyed that they considered his life of so little importance that they believed he could drop it any time to be with them. She wanted to say, "What would you do if I took him away, back to Italy, or off to California. Or if I forbade him to do what you want? I'm his wife, the one he lives beside."

But she never said it, even though they were American and her saying something like that might be called "blowing off steam," might not create a rift that could appear geological. Sometimes, in the middle of some task, cooking some food, operating some appliance, she would say to herself: I live in America. I have lived in America more years than in Italy. And she would remember how she and Leo talked about America, or Leo had talked and she had listened. America was the world of the common man, a world of slang and new buildings as sharp and clean as needles. Negro men walked arm and arm with white women, people danced in the streets, everyone was free, the church was nothing, everyone went to movies all the time. When he finished with *liceo* he was going to America to tramp across the country with a rucksack. No money, speaking to whomever came along.

His ideas about America were as foolish as everything he thought about life, as wrong as the ideas Joe's parents had had when they came over, but they could be pardoned. Poor and ignorant in Sicily, of course they thought the streets were paved with gold.

Sometimes she took a spiteful pleasure in being among Joe's family because they proved so thoroughly that everything Leo had believed was wrong. The nonsense he had talked about the workers, never having met one! She'd like to see what Joe's brother Johnny would have made of Leo, or his sister Angela with her cruel, cynical tongue. They believed in work and money; they believed in nothing they couldn't see, though they thought of themselves as religious. The whole family inhabited their mother's house on holidays like a migration of hooved animals: loud, ravenous, and dangerous. Old hurts and resentments simmered, but they weren't people who allowed themselves to think of the past as something in relation to themselves, as something that accounted for the present. The past was finished, the future was for people with money. They lived, like animals, in the present tense.

From time to time, one of the sisters would break down: after childbirth or with too much to drink. One Easter, his sister Marietta cried because her mother had told her thirty years before she wasn't smart enough for nurse's training, and refused to pay for it, sending her to a six-month bookkeepers course when she hated numbers. They never confessed to having trouble with their children: when one of the sons died in a car accident after his senior prom, it wasn't spoken of after the funeral, except for the time that the boy's mother walked out drunk on Thanksgiving and lay down in the middle of the road. Perhaps the past existed only to accuse, and they were right to stamp over it with the herd's protective action. She wished she had their heaviness, to stamp over the past and render it infertile. They were always running, eating on the run. Sometimes it almost gave her strength to see them, so heedless. She could look at them and believe there was no past. The old world was simply that: old, obsolete, replaceable. There was nothing in America that couldn't be replaced.

Being in a room with them on holidays felt to her like drunkenness. The dining room table was heavy with dishes of food. "Good Italian food," they said, clapping her on the back, squeezing her shoulders. Never once did she say, "Not Italian, Sicilian." The heavy red sauces, the thick meatballs, sausages, fried peppers, everything with too much color, too much oil, too much fullness. She remembered the cups of broth, plates of cutlets on the long table in her father's house, dishes of vegetables, innocent omelets, quiet plates of fruit. The food in the Smaldone house clamored and crowded; it filled your stomach like a punch; it left no room for breath. They were happy when they had to unbuckle their belts, when food immobilized them, when they picked their teeth and leaned back, sighing. This was the men; the women labored duly in the dark kitchen; sometimes they laughed together, but it was bitter laughter. All their jokes were about the foolishness, the failures of men, the idiocy of girls to believe in them. Sex was a bad joke on women, an itch men had to be relieved of, like a bull who had to scratch his back against a fence.

What would they have made of what she'd believed in as a girl: love and death, losing her virginity at fifteen in a medieval tower to a boy who thought the troubadours had been there, when she knew they hadn't? How could she explain what her silence about the troubadours had cost her? All her silences. She imagined what they would say: "She thinks that opening your legs for some brat who can't even grow a mustache is about poetry."

She chopped onions for them, peeled garlic from its papery envelope, diced it fine until her hands were sticky, washed the pots, did anything to be subservient to them, of use, something that would help all the dark heavy food roll out of that room and fill those bellies to an overflowing silence. They thought she was snob-bish, uppity, she chilled their laughter and dampened their spirits or she sharpened their old angers; they would have liked to punish her for thinking they were not as good as she. She wanted to say to them, "I don't like you, but I know you are superior to everything I am."

She had to marry Joe Smaldone because, without him, with her father's cousin dead, she was alone. She saw her life as an empty boat drifting down a black river, illumined only by a slice of moon, then being swept to sea. Joe's clamor and his largeness, his thick webbing of familial obligations, his broad chest and legs and penis rubbing against her skin, opening her, coming inside her, his loud cries of grateful satisfaction, were like a stampeding herd that stood on the shore and blocked the vision of the empty boat, drowned out the reproachful soughing of the waves till there was nothing she could remember. All that death and that belief in things that weren't visible: poetry, love, greatness, history, all of that was nothing. There was only this business of living: getting food, begetting children, keeping them alive, keeping yourself alive until the noise stopped and your death was just another dreamless sleep after a meal you'd had a bit too much of but that, after all, you had been glad to have.

She looks at her son and the young woman sitting next to him, the young woman he's lived with but will marry now because she wants to have children. Even now, Katherine's thinking of what her children will be like, hoping she'll see Carlo's features in them. Paola was never able to think that about her sons because she didn't love her husband. She accepted maternity dumbly, as another price she had to pay. Anesthetized for the births, she stayed that way for their childhoods. The endless demands, just to keep them alive, brought her a numbness she couldn't help but welcome. Sometimes, they charmed her. She knew they waited for their father to come home to give them life.

She watches her son and Katherine talking. Talking easily. Having what is called a conversation. He says something; she laughs. She points something out, he looks at it, he waits to hear what it is she liked about the thing. All Paola's life she has been either listening or silent or caught up in a tumult that will drown the voices that torment her. She listened to her father; each word was a gift, bright-wrapped for her, but there was nothing she could give back, nothing good enough, no word of hers he needed. Leo had no interest in what she said, unless she agreed with him. He was interested in what she wrote, but not in her conversation. His bodily presence made her stupid; she became like one of those girls standing outside the cinema, staring at the pictures of movie stars, hypnotized by that hair, those teeth. The years with her cousins were years of silence. Then with Joe: clamor, drowning out the past so she could believe that when one part of the past was over she could fold it up, store it away like a sheet that had worn out and couldn't be repatched; there was nothing that could be done with that rent in the middle, so you put the sheet away in the closet, you closed the door on it, leaving it to lie folded in the darkness.

She watches Katherine talking. She wants to say to her: "How is it that you can speak? We weren't taught to speak." Paola's girlhood years trained her for silence. All the proverbs, the corrections, the rebukes: Walk silently, no one cares what you say, be quiet, don't you want people to like you? After a while there was no need to say anything at all.

She wants to turn to her son and his young woman, talking so happily, laughing, twining their fingers in and out of each other, leaning back in silence then making remarks. She wants to say to them, "Do you know I have never had a conversation? I would like to tell you something about me. I am not the person you think."

They know nothing about her. She can't even imagine how they would describe her. Would they say that she is quiet, responsible, and sad, that she hasn't much enjoyed her life, that she likes her garden, cooking, and domestic tasks? That she is kind to animals, but doesn't much care for children? That she reads surprising books, history and science, but doesn't speak about them? The pressure to say words fills her throat. If only once she could have said to someone, "I am not the person you think."

There is something she'd like to say, but she doesn't know how to begin. Or no, there are three ways she would like to begin, she doesn't know which is the right one. "Let me tell you what I'm like." "Let me tell you about myself." Or: "Let me tell you who I am."

She would like to feel absolutely free and confident in choosing the sentence to begin the conversation she wishes she would have. She'd like a sentence that would be like music: three lines simultaneously woven. She wants to say three things at the same time, but they all mean something different. Yet she wants to say them all. The air outside the window, the air through which she moves on this train, is saturated with a silver light. They go through tunnels, then there is darkness, then they see a mountain. Then a pile of stones, children looking out a doorway, a dog asleep beside a house. Her eye takes in all the things at once: she can hold all three images simultaneously. Why can't she say three sentences at once? "Let me tell you what I'm like. Let me tell you about myself. Let me tell you who I am." The first would be as if she drew a picture of herself and her surroundings; the second would be a story of herself, standing in the shadow of her past, a figure in a pool of darkness. In the third, she would be who she is: the past inseparable from the present, but not dominating it, as the hills that rise from a lake and the lake itself make up a whole bordering each other, joining without separation.

But she has lived so quietly. And in her quietness, too deep to sadden her any longer, only something she has always known: "No one is listening to what I say."

She would like to practice speech. Perhaps by naming: "House." "Children." "Stones." "Dog." And then go on from there: "I like that dog, but no, that house doesn't please me." Or "That child is sad. Perhaps I could do something to help him."

Could she begin now, with these two, sitting across from her, who brought her over the ocean, after all, so she must mean something to them. Could she begin this way: "Why have you brought me here? Who did you think you were bringing? And to what?"

She is traveling across the land of her birth. And what does that mean? She wants to say: This accident, my life, began here. This is the spot where I saw my first sights. My first experiences were here. I hardly remember them. I left quite early. What can it mean to say 'the land of my birth'? To say it, I must believe in my own existence as an event worth speaking of.

I had a childhood here, a girlhood. What does "a girlhood" mean?

She sees that she has before her an important task: to understand that all the things that happened in her life happened to *her*. That she is the same person who was born, was a child, a girl, a young woman, a woman, and now she is old. That there is some line running through her body like a wick. She is the same person who was once born. All the things that happened to her happened to one person.

She wants to turn to the two sitting across from her and say, "I'm trying to understand what it means to have had a life. I would like to tell you who I am. This would require both a knowledge and a faith that I am far from having. It may be too late. I don't think you can help me. There are things that I would like to say, but I have no experience of saying things like them."

.   .   .

213

If only for a moment I might think you could help me. If just for a little while I could believe I wasn't alone.

There were times when I wasn't alone. Most of the time, I didn't know exactly how to be. I wasn't sure that what I did was the right thing to be doing. I often thought that I should be doing something else. I didn't know what. Except for moments with my father. I would like to describe to you a time that I was sure I was in the right place.

I am sitting on a marble floor. Reading English picture books. My woolen stockings irritate the soft flesh on the inside of my thighs. I am reading English names: Margaret, Joan. The colors of the pictures are dull and smudged: orange, ochre, sea green. These people know how to live. No one dreams of correcting them—Margaret and Joan—as my aunt corrects me. They have never been ashamed since they have never once done the wrong thing. They are always with their fathers, who own great lands. Their curls are reddish gold and fall like water down their backs. They hand their fathers cherries they have plucked from trees whose leaves are blackish blue. The mothers, in elaborate hats, pay no attention to the daughters. All the animals can speak, but the children are the only ones who know it. All the food is precisely one taste and one taste only: sweet, salty, bitter. The sun is orange, the moon is silver like a nail. The branches are black against a cutting blue. I look up at my father who is smoking, writing. I am in the place I need to be. I will stay with him forever. What he doesn't know, what I will keep him from knowing: without me he will die.

Her father is no longer alive, and soon she will no longer be alive. What words she has said to her son about her father have been spoken grudgingly: to speak of her father is to allow him to be no longer fully hers. When she speaks to her son, she never uses the words *your grandfather*. To name him in that way would be to give him an existence apart from her. He is "my father." Those other words would propel him into the present without her. The present, where he is only a ghost. She can't let him be a ghost, apart from her. She can't even let him be in the present accompanied only by her son. So she can't use the words *your grandfather*. She can only speak of her father if she accompanies him in the sentence that could describe him for her son.

When she tries to speak of him, she realizes how little she knows of him. She knows him only as the father of a child. Who was the man who walked apart from her, when she was somewhere else? She has no idea. She doesn't want to know. She has no interest in her father's life apart from her. And so it is impossible to speak of him, except superficially: he was a scientist, an anti-Fascist. She can only speak the truth of him as if she were still a child, and that would be, at her age, and speaking to her own son, grotesque.

But if it's difficult to speak about her father, how can she even begin speaking of Leo? Is there anything she could describe? She thinks of telling Carlo something about sailing in a boat. She could begin by saying, "A friend of mine had a little boat which he very much enjoyed rowing down the River Po, the river of our city, which you soon will see. Sometimes he would take me with him, and I very much enjoyed the boat as well."

But after that, there is very little she can say. If the problem of her father is that she doesn't want to speak of him without her, the problem with Leo is the opposite: she doesn't want to speak to her son of a dead man, who was her lover, in relation to herself.

If she began to talk about the boat, what could she say that Carlo should know? If she said he was happy in his little boat, she would then have to let him know that this was rare, that most of the time he was unhappy. Then she would have to tell him why, and she doesn't know how to do it. Would it be dishonest just to talk about the boat? Would that mean her first conversation would be a lie?

There is nothing she can say. She can't even tell him the story that is in her mind, that seems so innocent.

He was happy in his little boat. And when he asked me one day would I come out in the boat with him, I was nearly crushed with happiness. He kept his boat near a little wharf near the Porta Isabella. Underneath his brown trousers he was wearing a pair of old black woolen trunks. My suit was heavy black wool as well. We were both shy taking off our street clothes. We didn't look at each other. He gave me his hand to get into the boat. A shock went through me when any part of our bodies touched. His legs were thin and his nipples were dark and soft-looking like a baby's. There was almost no hair on his chest.

We hadn't yet made love. He hadn't even kissed me. We had talked of poetry, of the Italian language, of the disorder of the state. About America. Or he had talked. I was so brimful of joy I was afraid to meet his eye. Whenever I looked at him, his face seemed angry. As we went out on the river, he was happier. He rowed well. He put the oars down, let the boat drift a while. He began to sing. He made a hat for himself, like a pirate, from a handkerchief. He made another kind of pirate hat for me out of a newspaper. He put it on my head and caressed one of my curls, tucking it behind my ear. He smiled at me. This gave me the courage to lie down in the boat, which pleased him.

I lay back in the boat, my hands behind my head. The sky was light blue: clouds swam like fish above us. The river was the color of green marble. I could smell the sweetness of the grass. I was thinking, "I am a pretty girl. He likes to look at me. All I have to do is lie here with my hands behind my head, and he's happy."

Everything seemed simple. We got out of the boat. He'd remem-

*bered to bring a towel to dry my feet. I didn't tell him that I'd
brought one. We walked up the street along the river, tired from the
sun, like sleepy animals.*

*I know we were happy that one day. But most of the time we
were unhappy. Why weren't we happier? Why didn't I remember I
was pretty? What was wrong with us?*

She remembers coming upon photographs of herself recently,
or no, not many, only one. She has only one. And she thought to
herself: What a pretty girl I was. Why did I have no joy of it?

Another question with no answer: *What happened to all the
photographs, to all my father's things?* In that bad time, 1936, when
her American cousin was staring out the window of the apartment
in Jackson Heights, struck dumb with mourning for her lost wealth,
and her husband walked around wringing his hands, wondering
what would come next, how could she say: "What has happened
to the furniture, the dishes, the books, the little lamp we read by,
the vases with their narrow necks for tight bunches of flowers?"
The heavy truth of the material: things do not become ghosts. My
father is a ghost, but the things we had are not. She'll never know
what happened to their things.

There are too many explanations, any of them plausible. Perhaps
their fate was political. Perhaps Fascist hoodlums threw their things
out in the street. Or took the furniture to their own houses: the
harsh settee with its itchy, berry-colored upholstery, the rugs, the
crockery. Were they touched and sat upon by glamorous Fascist
wives with wavy hair, or poor souls beaten to submission? Did they
eat with what had been her father's spoons? Was Il Duce saluted
underneath her father's prints of the Acropolis? Were executions
planned at the dining room table where her father had called out
to her, "My princess, my star, my treasure." Calling out to her at
her place, the wife's place, at the other end?

The most likely explanation, though, isn't political. The most likely explanation is that her aunt took the furniture. She wonders if there will come a moment, even one, before she dies, in which she will be able to forgive her aunt. That would mean something she almost wants. But not entirely. Forgiveness would mean giving up that grain of sand, that dark irritation around which she formed her idea of who she was. *I am not her.*

How could she know herself? All of her aunt's ideas of how to be were ideas of transgression.

A proper girl does not:

Speak out

Run

Wear her hair like this

Or like that

Read that kind of book

Refuse to put a pleasant look in her eyes when an older person is telling her something that is, after all, for her own good

Have that kind of ink stain on the knuckle of her middle finger

Spend so much time with her father, who is, after all, a busy man and has more important things to do in this world

Think she is so important

Think anyone cares about what she likes or doesn't like: no one wants to know her preferences, which are of no importance

Let anyone know that she cares for one thing more than another

Put too low a price on herself: she knows her price

Act as if she's been robbed when someone who has her interest at heart looks through her papers, for her own good

Let herself be used

Let anyone know about her menstruation

Criticize the government

Refuse to join organizations for young ladies
Think about herself

She hears her aunt's voice saying all these words, again and again, like a curse or a hypnosis. Surely her aunt is dead. She never heard from her: her aunt had said she'd never wanted anything to do with Paola again. She'd brought disgrace upon the family, a family that had been without a blemish for a hundred years.

The terrible thing is that her aunt had been right. Everything her aunt predicted because of her father's indulgence, their mutual insistence on flaunting convention, on not listening to her—all the bad things had come true. If they'd respected conventions. If she'd not read, not written poetry, not given in to herself, Leo would be alive, an old man now, and her father would have died in honor.

Her aunt was eaten up by law. By the spite which the law bred. The spitefulness of the law-abiding was a burning bush that burnt and burnt and never was consumed. Her aunt's sallow skin. The circles underneath her eyes. Her feet in their little boots. Her fingers, knitting. In her aunt's eyes: "I know everything you are. I know what you will become."

Paola and her father had tried to live more hopefully. More openly. To please themselves more. In the end, no one had been pleased and everyone had been shamed. The dead had died shameful deaths. The living mourned them in shame. Only her aunt, living by law, died in peace.

Did she steal the furniture? She might have said, "They left me dishonored, it's my right. She'll never come back to get it. She owes it to me, she owes me as well endless remorse, endless apologies."

The last words her aunt said to her were: "You have disgraced us all." Cold pleasure in her light eyes. Could those eyes have been my mother's? They were sisters. Were those my mother's eyes?

She can imagine her aunt's spiteful face, ordering the men to move the furniture to her apartment, her lips pressed together, her white face cold as death saying: "Put this down here. And this and this. I want this lamp on the table. I will put that vase away for now. And the rug, which I never liked. But this dish, this picture, give them to me now."

She can imagine her aunt reading a pious book, moving her lips by the light of the lamp she'd always coveted, the lamp Paola and her father had read by, a calm smile on her face, the calm smile of the murderer who can't be blamed because he'd taken life where it was meant to be taken. But she can't imagine what her aunt might have done with the photographs.

Did she hide them, or put them with the rubbish? Did the hoodlums throw them on the street, or lock them away in their cellars? She sees a holiday photograph of her father's face, staring at her accusingly from under the wheels of a tram. Or looking up at her remorsefully in the dark shop of some antiquarian. She is seized by the poignance of intimate objects ripped from their origins, like widows untrained for the harsh world, living on sufferance, by chance. She grieves for her father's face in the lost photographs. And for her own. He wrote in one of his last letters: "I think it would be better to be dead, but I live so that just once more I can see your face."

What was this face that he so loved? White skin, dark eyes, circles below them like bruises when she'd slept too little or was sick. Thick, dark hair she usually wore in a braid. A nose: too big. A mouth: the lips too wide, smiling rarely, usually at him. Was that what he wanted to see before he died?

If that was what he wanted, it would have been impossible. After the shame that she had brought, she no longer deserved the face she used to show him. The face of the one who belonged. She no longer deserved to belong to him. She couldn't look into his eyes, the dark eyes identical to hers.

She has no photographs of the two of them together, but she knows there were photographs. She thinks of one she would very much like to have, of her and her father at the sea. They're holding hands, both wearing straw hats. There may have been a donkey in the picture, also wearing a straw hat.

She has only one picture of her father, his composed and thoughtful face looking out at her formally, assuring her that she is right to be alive, yet accusing her of not being with him.

Who, she wonders, of the people that she knew in Turin, is still alive? Leaving in shame, she left behind her silence, darkness. Why should she try to fill it up? The past to her is a dark rectangle, framed by a lighter, grayer rectangle. Why should she fill the empty shape with faces? None of the faces would be happy. For a minute, just a while ago, she was able to think of a time she and Leo had been happy in the boat. But again she remembers: most of the time they weren't happy.

This is why she hasn't spoken much. How could she begin a conversation about Leo in a boat and expect that someone would follow her through her aunt's prayers, her father's face beneath the tram wheels, until she comes to the place where she is now, ready to speak about the boat again? Ready to talk about how they couldn't be happy if any other person was around.

In front of other people, he couldn't be proud of me, nice to me. Why did he invite his friends to be with us? He knew how shy I was. It made him furious. "Now don't act like a white mouse in front of my friends. You've known them as long as I have. You're far more intelligent than any of them. Your English is much better, and as for writing a line of poetry that's a patch on yours—none of them could. I've told them so. Don't go acting like a mouse of a shop girl. You know I hate that. I won't respect you if you act afraid that my friends will eat you up.

But I was afraid, and when they spoke to me I smiled and blushed. I couldn't speak, even the idea of speech was painful. Afterward, when his friends suggested we all go to a café for an ice, he walked away angrily. "You take her," he said. Then everyone separated: he'd made them remorseful, they didn't know about what. So I was alone with him once again, and he was even angrier. "Of course you didn't talk, you were too busy displaying your legs so they'd look at you. I'm surprised at you! I'm surprised you can look me in the eye."

And how could she tell Carlo about the time they passed the three girls in their boat, those sisters who lived alone although they weren't much older than Paola or Leo. Their parents were dead. The older sister was in charge, she must have been twenty-five.

The girls were waving to him, challenging him to a race. He was telling them that they couldn't possibly beat him. He was so happy, with his handkerchief on his head like a red Indian, teasing those girls as beautiful as movie stars, with their long legs and their golden hair that took the light. I touched my own hair. It was dull and thick, my skirt was heavy against my white legs. He was laughing. "I will never let a woman beat me." He was rowing and laughing as if his heart might crack, but if he died, then it would be of happiness.

The girls got tired of the race; they just gave up and started drifting. They forgot about him. He said to me: "You'd never be able to live like that, on your own, or with other girls, like Americans do. You'd never be able to leave your father."

But they have no father. I am the fortunate one. I wanted to say: I have my father. Why would I want to leave my father to sit laughing in a boat?

He watched the blond girls in their white dresses drifting down the river: white, golden, green. I saw that I would never please him.

"Perhaps you could make friends with those girls," he said. "They seem very intelligent."

Then I said the words I knew would do me anything but good. "They have quite a bad reputation."

"Among shop girls, certainly. And your father. I'm sure he wouldn't approve."

He turned his back so he wouldn't have to look at me and watched the lazy laughing taunting girls who had forgotten they had ever seen him. They always would forget and he would always love them, as they floated by, glimmering on the water.

How could she tell her son any of this? The train has stopped. Now they are in Torino. There is no time.

They are getting off the train. Now who will she be? Her son, this nice boy, raised in health and plenty, wants her to fill the dark shape with faces. "Not just for you, Mama. It's my past as well. I don't know anything about your early life."

"But everyone is dead. I'm sure they must be dead now."

"Yes, but they weren't always, Mama." His insistence, in what he doesn't say: "Let me have your past. My past. The imprint of your past is on my fingers, in my eyes. Why won't you say the words?"

And she, answering him in silence. "Why must I relive the past for you? I created something for you—fog, indecipherable voices in the distance—to replace the assault of words, accusations that scalded my skin. They might have scalded you. A boy died; I was supposed to have died too, but I didn't. And everyone blamed me for being alive.

"The boy's mother walked up and down the streets, up and down, cursing me. She had been a proud cold woman, but when her son died she became a witch. Nothing would have made her happy but my death.

"And now, my son, in this city, where I have come because you asked me, because I have refused you so much and have perhaps grown tired of refusal—what will I see now? And who will I become? Who have I been, between the time I left this city, a young girl, and now?

"A numbness.

"People lived a life outside me, they were shadows. I have helped the sick, cooked meals, opened my legs over and over to a man, kept house, and cared for children. Everyone, everything has been a shadow to me. Life has flickered near me: a film of shadows being run off a reel. Click, click, the snapping sound of film broken off has been the sound of human voices to me. Clicks in the dark air.

"And you call me mother, so you ask me for a past that you can know and use.

"You think you have a right to ask me to remember things, because I am your mother.

"As if the pain of giving birth to you weren't enough.

"Now, because you asked me, I must ask myself: What did he see before he died? What was behind his eyes in the moment when the bullet hit his brain? What message did his brain give him? What did his eyes know? And did I ever mean to die?

"And was my face the last thing in my father's eyes?

"You are asking me to live through all that again. You don't know what you ask."

"Surely, Mama, there can't be dark secrets that you need to cover up."

Words spoken from the certainty of a fortunate generation, brought up in the light.

The words not spoken. "Who were you, Mama, before you were mine?"

The question never answered, by more words never said.

"What can I tell you that would nourish you, that wouldn't

poison your life as it has poisoned mine? About my father, whom I loved and whom I shamed and caused to die? Of the day I stood at this station? I was fifteen, my father was sending me away. I would sail from Genoa; he would travel with me that far. All the way he didn't speak. He bought me chocolates for my journey. Black shirts were everywhere. It was normal to be afraid. I had grown up afraid. But now I thought, 'My father, I will never see your face again. What will happen to me when I no longer see your face?' "

She'd seen Leo's face in death. The farmer said, "Is this your friend? You came here with him all the time. He came here with you before today."

Like Peter, she wanted to deny him. He had no face. He had done away with his face. He would never again be recognized.

"Is this, my son, what you insist I see again? In your ignorance, in your childish hunger for a past that will be of no use to you, will you make me see these things again? Should I tell you the story, simply in plain words? Should I say: I was fifteen years old; I wasn't a virgin; I was menstruating, my boyfriend and I had pledged to kill ourselves?

"We went to a small town outside of Turin, Bardonecchia. It took two hours by train. His family had a house where they went only in the month of July. It was September, so the house was empty. In July, he'd made an impression of the key on a little piece of wax, and then he'd had a key made from that."

She couldn't tell Carlo that once Leo had brought her to his parents' house to have sex in a proper bed. Like a married couple? she asked. No, he said, like a couple who doesn't have weeds poking up their ass every damn second.

She was the one who lay on the ground. She was the one who felt the straw. Was he worried for her? Or did he just want to defile his parents' bed? She was ashamed, taking off the dust sheets to expose the law-abiding bed to the unlawfulness of what they did. He laughed in a way that made her scared for the coldness inside him.

Then his remorse on the train home! He moved away from her as if she'd soiled herself and might soil him. It was his dirt she was carrying, and if he carried her filth on his body, it was because his body had searched it out. She wanted to say to him: "Don't hurt me this way. All I want is to make you happy."

He was reading Goethe, reading Byron. Each day he awoke miserable. The country was in the grip of brutes. The Italian language was impossibly corrupt; the literature was written by the dead hands of old men: nothing could bring it back to life. They both had the potential to be great poets, but the age would not permit them to be great. The only great thing was to kill themselves. If she didn't agree to kill herself with him, he would despise her and regret that he had ever spent a moment with someone so undeserving of his attention.

Up to this point, she knows that what she is remembering is right. But after this, her vision dims, figures appear like tiny dots against the landscape, then they blur and disappear.

Had she believed that only his regard made her honorable? Whole, actually whole, in a way her father's love did not? Knowing her body, Leo really knew her, knew her in desire, in a way her father couldn't know her. Did she believe Leo was great in a way that her father wasn't great, and that Leo's loving her was the one great thing that had happened to her, and in honor of this greatness she should die with him as he had asked? Or was it that she didn't want to die, but thought if she went along with him, it would be like his other enthusiasms, learning Russian, or becoming a vegetarian: he'd eventually grow bored with the idea.

The day they traveled to Bardonecchia to die together and they walked up the hill, she much slower, behind him, she wasn't thinking of death, but of menstruation. They'd had sex four times in six months, and he'd never really looked at her. He'd never had to understand anything about her body, only his. Now this would remind him of everything she doesn't want him to think of: that she is weak, that her body was meant to bear children, that whatever she does she can't keep herself from smelling bad.

Her aunt had made her terrified of smelling bad. Her aunt who prayed all day and lit candles to the saints, who gave her the box of rags that she must wash the blood from. And she must wash herself with great care: three soapings, then three times in clear water. Men can smell the blood on you; they have a nose for it. They sniff it out like dogs. (Even my father? Will he know my filth?) It reminds them of what you don't want to remind them of. A good man is disgusted by the very thought of it. Even in marriage, your husband must have no hint.

How do you know? she wanted to say to her aunt, you have no husband, you know nothing about men.

But suppose her aunt was right? She always spoke with certainty as if everyone knew the truth of what she was saying, only a fool wouldn't know.

I was so alone. Why didn't some kind woman, someone's mother, say, "Don't be afraid. You're a pretty girl, a good girl, no harm will come to you." I needed someone to say, "This is the way of doing this, of doing that. Nothing is wrong with you. You are not committing crimes. The world is large and will absorb the errors you innocently make. Don't worry."

She worried all the time. As they walked up the hill together, he was thinking about death. She was thinking, "He'll call me a dog, a pig. Any minute he'll say I smell bad. And suppose he sees. He won't be able to forget; he'll always be disgusted."

He was singing a song about death in German. He had hidden the gun in the tower. As he came near her, desire made him childish, weak. He was so pleased by her; he only wanted to please. No harshness, no criticism, no comparisons, no cataloguing of her faults. She was beautiful, a goddess of love, a great poet. They would go down in history: people would speak of them for centuries. Theirs was a great love.

She couldn't hear what he was saying. She was waiting for him to stop talking so she could say the words she had to say. She stepped back from him, her eyes fell on the straw covering the dirt floor, the straw that animals had lain on, that they were meant to lie on.

"I can't do it today."

"Do what?"

"I can't lie with you. I'm not well."

"What do you mean? You climbed all the way up the hill. You look perfectly well. What's the matter with you?"

"I have my menses."

She used the scientific, the archaic term, as if it were happening to somebody already dead or in a book.

"Oh, I know all about that. I've read about it. It's a good time to have sex, you can't get pregnant. Only ridiculous bourgeoisie are stopped by this sort of taboo. Or superstitious peasants. We're above all that. Now, come on."

Something about his saying, "Now, come on," causes a flooding in her brain, water rising to the top of her skull, a rushing, drowning out his words. All she can hear is one word repeating itself: "Cannot. Cannot." She has never refused him anything. But he will not see her blood. She has the right to her own hiddenness. The flood grows to an ice mountain, one no axe can break. She is stubborn now, as she was when she was a small child. No one can make her do what she doesn't want.

"I'm sorry. I just can't."

He paces around the tower; his feet, stomping, kick up dust from the dirt floor.

"On this day of all days you refuse me."

She doesn't know what she said then. She can't imagine anything she might have said.

"You okay, Mom?"

How strange, his easy slang, his short American words on this street which represents to her nothing so much as formality. They have only to cross the street, then a square, to be at their hotel, but he calls a taxi because he can't carry all their bags. How foolish! They'll drive across the square in a taxi. She begins to laugh.

"Why are you laughing, Mom?"

"To take a taxi to cross the street!"

All three of them begin to laugh. Anyone but her son might be offended. But she knew he wouldn't be. She never has to worry about his taking offense. This makes him different from all the people she knew when she walked on this street, this street in which it was so easy to have someone take offense.

She wants to say to him: "I must tell you. I have been afraid all my life."

Instead, she laughs and says, "You are a real American."

In the middle of the street, thin trees grow high, their leaves are yellowish and dusty. She hasn't seen these trees in sixty years; she's forgotten the look of them. And yet, her forgetting them had no effect on them. In her mind they were consigned to oblivion, yet they did not cease to exist.

But what happens to the faces of the dead? She has let them go, purposely, as you would open your hand and let something drop from it. As if you'd caught a small fish, kept it, and only half attentively opened your hand and let it disappear again into the water. Sending it back to where it came from, after all. Darkness. Forgetting, simply this: a relaxation. What could be easier than to let the fingers open, trail in the cool dark water? Nothing is easier than forgetfulness.

Is that what she'd accomplished, simply a relaxation? Or had she hurled the past from her as a thief would hurl the useless part of what he'd stolen, vengefully, into the river?

What is it that she's done? How can she know?

She sees the high trees of her childhood, looks at Carlo and Katherine laughing, and wonders if she can give him what he says he wants: her past.

And even if she could, she wonders now if she would want to.

He was the one born happy. He was the one her sadness didn't touch. Now he teaches children games and dancing. "Some life, Ma, they pay me to do that." She's seen him in a circle with children. "Mr. S," they plead. "Stand next to me." They're so happy when they see him, they jump for happiness. "Mr. S is here."

How has she brought something like this into the world? This life he lives, so free of sadness. Is this the life she wanted, so that she refused to die, refused to see death as beautiful?

Her sadness crushed the other children. Sadly, they looked up at her from the table. "Mama, tell us what we've done that makes your eyes look at us without smiling. Tell us so that we can atone." It must have been her sadness that bred in her children this impulse to atone. They walked through life heavily and the words were always on their lips: "I'm sorry. I will try, try not to, try again." Their heaviness, which she knew to be of her own making, defeated her. She had to turn away. But this boy, her youngest, looked at

her and said: "Watch this, Mama, and this, and this. Forget whatever it is that has made your eyes like that. Look! Look at me."
He could make her laugh. Funny faces, funny hats, jokes, dares,
nicknames, shortcuts, secret passages. All the things she'd never
known about or had.

She looks at her son and Katherine, still laughing. An important
question occurs to her, one she *can* ask.

"I've always been so serious. Why have I always been so serious?"

He opens the taxi for her, almost lifts her out. His small bird-
mother. He takes her arm, walking her to the door of the hotel.
"No more. No more serious Mama. That's why I've brought you
home."

And to remember?

He speaks English to the desk clerk and the desk clerk immediately loves him. He says, "This is my mother. She is from Torino.
She's been gone for more than sixty years. And now she's back
home."

The clerk comes out from behind the desk to shake her hand.
A stranger. She hopes a stranger, she'll make herself believe he is.
She freezes in fear. Everyone here is dangerous. Anyone she meets
could be her enemy. Anyone who knows anything about her is her
enemy.

Why did she come? Her son's laughter, his daring, she sees now,
is a deep offense. As if you laughed in front of an uncovered corpse,
its eyes plucked by crows, unrecognizable.

What does it mean to be recognizable?

Leo had been unrecognizable. His face was gone. No one could
know him. It had come about because of her.

"What was your name before you married?"

She wants to lie, but that's impossible, she has to tell him. She
says her father's name.

He shakes his head. "I don't know anybody by that name."

Her son says: "Too bad. But we'll keep looking."

She says, "I told you nobody is left." She prays that this is true. What can it mean that all of them are gone?

It means that she has gone on living, that she is old, has been spared sickness, violence, accident, political upheaval, war. That she did not take her own life and it has not been taken from her. She still has that thing: her life. What is it that she has?

She looks at the buildings and the trees. They're the same as when she left. Branches have been lopped or fallen, leaves have dropped to the ground, new ones have grown. Yet you would say: "That's the same tree." She is grateful to them for their constancy. And the buildings: She wants to honor them for their having been in one place for so long. Thank you, thank you, she wants to say, for having been the same for hundreds of years, and being silent. Seeing the trees, the buildings, which are voiceless, allows for her a past that cannot hurt her. Thank you, beautiful stones, curves so like one another, constant shapes. There's no need for me to erase the memory of the pleasure I took in you. If I want, I can empty the square of people. I can have merely architecture. I can be in the square alone at dawn. The birds will wheel above my head, accusing me of nothing. The violet fog of dawn will lift and the morning light enliven the yellow of the buildings. The sun will pull moisture from the stones of the street. The dew on the chairs left out in front of the arcades will disappear: I can be alone in a city which, after all, I have not stopped loving. The buildings and the trees have never harmed me. They were not what I had to drown out. I only had to silence the accusing voices.

They've left their bags in the hotel room. Carlo and Katherine share a room, of course. She's grateful they don't even try pretense. The water in the shower tastes a little bit of sulphur. She is cool and clean and she can walk with these two young people up the street to the piazza, show them the small green square with its old wooden branches, the statue to a writer nobody has read, point to a hundred-year-old shop, still selling, as it did the day she left, canes and umbrellas. She is alive. She has her face even if the others are the faceless dead. She looked in the telephone book to see if there was anyone by the name of his sister and her husband. No. Dead? Moved away? Is it possible that simply by the accident of having lived this long, she has arranged that there is no one else still left who can remember?

Both Leo and she had parents whose families came from some-where else. In that they were unusual. Her father and his family were Milanese, Leo's family were from Trieste. His brother had died in the First World War. Perhaps Leo had wanted death so that he could be honored like his brother: the honored and spotless dead. Leo had been spoiled by his parents and his sister as their only living son. His parents were old when he was born, but even if they'd been young, they would be dead. Her father would be one hundred ten years old.

Perhaps Leo's sister had moved away. To Argentina? To Aus-tralia? Someplace with an *A,* she thinks she remembers they'd been planning that. His sister had married a Jew. Perhaps they died in Auschwitz, that also has an *A.* No, she won't believe that. She doesn't have to. There's no one to tell her anything: she can make the past whatever she wishes. She'll believe that Leo's sister and her husband moved to Argentina. Who will contradict her? The trees? The buildings?

In the whole phone book of Torino, none of the names she fears can be found. Perhaps there is a school friend, but she won't look any more than she needs to. She feels grateful that the house in which she lived has been destroyed. Carlo was disappointed when he heard the house was gone. "Don't you want to see your old neighborhood anyway, Mama?" She answered, "My old neighborhood, the Crocetta, is dominated now by Fiat and the concrete blocks put up to house the workers. No, my dear, we won't go to see that."

He understands that she doesn't want to go back because it would be too painful for her. But he's wrong, or he's wrong about the sources of her pain. She doesn't care that the house is gone; she's grateful that it's gone. She's come back to Italy hoping that everything has changed; that stones have collapsed on stones, that there is emptiness where the dead walked, ate, were cold or tired. The houses of the dead were nothing but accusing witnesses, silent in their pride: We know what you have done, and nothing is forgotten. If she can see that the cold pride of those stones has been mocked, she can believe that what happened to her has been blotted out from everybody's sight. A blankness exists in the world: she is the only edifice, containing both the cold bones of the dead and their still living bodies.

That the way of life that formed her and of which she was a part has died brings her no grief. It died because it carried in its flesh the seeds of death. The quiet mumblings of the servants, the silences of wives, the children cowed behind closed doors, the fathers raising up their hands in anger, or hiding their heads in shame: these were the seeds of death that bore such dreadful fruit. A dead boy in a tower. The dead eyes of the Fascist thugs, the dead eyes of the crowd, stupefied by worship and by terror. She is glad it is all gone. So when she said to Carlo, "It would be difficult for me to go back to the place where I once lived," she allowed him to misunderstand. It had been settled long before they got onto the airplane: she would not go back.

She never got the money that should have come to her from the sale of her father's house. It must have been left to her. Her aunt had cheated her of it. Knowing that in her shame she would contest nothing. Her aunt had died without issue. Where had the money from the house gone? Into endless Masses for the dead, into dark convents and monasteries, the coins trickling down to the wet soil of all those dirges, thousands of times repeated, every day for fifty years, and all for her aunt's soul: "Eternal rest grant unto her, O Lord, and let perpetual light shine upon her"? Every day, the silent money, stolen calmly, righteously, perhaps growing in a bank vault behind the sacred name of some dark monastery: my money, my father's, stolen, buying her eternal rest. Better that than piles of stones: at least what it bought was invisible, would disappear, as if it never was, as false as money itself. Let it be used to feed the nuns and priests her father hated: at least nothing could be searched out and seen: her father's money had become words. She'd had no good of it, and so it was one less thing for which she must atone. She can be here with her son; she can show him the trees, the buildings, and not a word need be said about what she wants kept hidden. She can be like an impoverished owner of a great estate, who must show strangers around the grounds, the house, but can keep some of the rooms locked, some wooded areas off limits. She can give him the objects of the past without the stories of the past. The past can have large areas of beautiful emptiness, like the great square at dawn: the birds wheeling and cawing in the silver light that will surround it for an hour, unclear as moonlight only without shadow or surprise.

"You never told us your city was so beautiful, Mama."

Did I ever know it? Was I happy here? Did I walk these streets and let the warm air blow around my face, look in shop windows, eat an ice cream with a silver spoon? I did with my father. We walked the wide streets; we saluted statues of men on horseback, we rode the tram, which we caught in front of the building shaped like a triangle; we sat in the public gardens when the roses were full out; we walked by the water when it shone green in the clear light of noon.

Since everyone who knows the story is dead or gone, since there are no words left to accuse her, she can now say (grateful to her husband for leaving her the money), "Let's sit in this café and I will buy you sandwiches and champagne."

She doesn't have to stain the whole of the past with the blood of a dead boy. Objects are stone: impermeable. The blood will not adhere to the rough bark of the old trees. She toasts her city with its millions of dead, mostly unknown to her. She toasts the buildings and the monuments and the dusty trees. She toasts her son and his pretty happy girlfriend. She will try to find exactly the right things to tell them.

But not now. Now toast the trees, the buildings. She can tell or not tell the story. It's up to her. For now, her eyes feast, her tongue delights, her skin exults at the warm breeze around her.

"Thank you, children. You have given me so much."

"You seem like a new person, Mama."

"Come, let's explore. Let's see what I remember of my old city."

She may be a little drunk. When she gets up to walk, she isn't sure how steady she is, but her feeling is pleasant. Perhaps when she walks she'll float or fly. She's so happy she could be taken up to heaven, like the Virgin in the picture near the altar of her girlhood church. She walks quickly, in her sneakers, a girl's shoes, and here she is an old woman. Has she tricked someone? She's so light and carefree; the weight of her life is off her shoulders. All her life she's been wrong to carry it. At any moment she could have put it down. Carlo and Katherine hang a little behind her, swaying with love, singing to each other. She walks past the fountain, into the arcade, pointing to the pretty sweets in the shop windows. The girl makes her stop to look at shoes and says to her, "Paola, should I buy these gold sandals?" "Yes," she says, "like Artemis, for running swiftly." Katherine leaps down the arcade, and Carlo follows her. "Tomorrow, first thing, I'll buy them."

At the end of the arcade, they turn right down Corso Re Umberto. She remembers a photographer's studio, and an automobile showroom. She remembers the cars that used to be there, cars you couldn't believe human beings would own, never mind buy. Cars for gods or plutocrats. Or Fascists. Il Duce, standing up on the back of one, the top down, crying: "Worship me. Obey." The people did. She is reminded of the fear in which they lived, which everyone took in with every breath. A people, a whole nation, breathing fear. She walks up the street looking at windows, trying to find the old photographs, the monumental cars, but of course they're gone. The lights of the arcade are far away. The buildings cast long shadows on the pavement. The light loses its comfort. Men with grizzled faces appear, slinking from the small streets, out for no good. Whores in parked cars flash headlights on and off.

All the buildings look the same, windowless behind their shutters like the eyes of those long dead. She walks up and down the streets she doesn't remember. None of their names means anything to her. She has no memory of ever having lived in this city. She can't have lived here. Some mistake has been made. This is not a place where anyone she knows has been.

Behind her, Katherine and Carlo are beginning to lose pleasure in the walk. They'd like to know where they're going. But she doesn't know. She's lost. She'll try to keep it from them if she can. With a false smile, she turns up streets, down streets, pretending she knows where she is. The sign reads *Via della Consolata* but she is very far from consolation. The wires overhead menace her; suppose they are carrying information, she doesn't know to whom, suppose they are carrying electric impulses that could shoot through her and eliminate her in the darkness, all her particles absorbed into the air, as if she never was? The shadows of the wires on the streets, the bluish light of the lamps hanging from them, seem to exist only for purposes of malice. Malice is all around: she takes it into her lungs with the sooty-tasting air. She is beginning to stink with fear. Suppose they should wander all night? Suppose someone should pretend to lead them home, only to take them someplace for purposes of malice?

She remembers things people whispered about the secret life of Turin: It is a center of black magic, people always said. Another thing she heard in whispers: There is a little city within the city just for freaks, the misshapen, the ill-starred, ill-born. They live inside walls in their city within the city: they aren't allowed to see the light of day; they've been banished by their families from ordinary sight. But perhaps mothers, guilty, apologetic, arrange secret meetings with their horror children by night in streets like this. At any moment gargoyles with human bodies, cyclopses, faces without noses, arms that are stumps, backs hunched over, figures in postures that make them indistinguishable from animals, will reach out to kill her and her son for sport. They've been heard speaking English; their throats will be cut for their travelers' checks and their running shoes. Drunks, dope fiends, maniacs, everyone lurking against the cold shoulders of the buildings, hiding behind trees, is ready to spring at them for only one reason: the malice in the air.

"Is this road right, Paola?" Katherine says, thinking she's speaking in a kind voice. But the question can't be kind.

"It will be all right."

"Let's ask someone, Ma."

He still allows the possibility that there could be benevolence. He doesn't see, neither of them sees, the red eyes in the shadows, the masks that will lift at any moment, the handsome face only a lure used by the grotesque marauders hiding a few feet behind the arch. If they asked for directions, every answer would be a snare.

Each step takes her farther away from knowing where she is. She's been told that she was born here, lived here, but the person who walked these streets can't be anyone she knows. Or ever knew.

"Here we are, Mama. There's the statues, there's the church. The hotel is just up here."

He believes they aren't lost. But she doesn't know how they got here, so it doesn't matter. It was chance, it was a lucky chance, but chance is too often cruel, and it might not happen again. Nothing she did helped them. Nothing she could have done would have been the right thing. Nothing good that happened came from her.

"Good night, Mama."

"Good night."

She lies on her bed and falls into a sleep that feels poisonous, like the sleeps of fever. Soon she wakes under the rough sheets that chafe her elbows. Her eyes open wide with horror. What has she done? She had thought she could pretend that the past didn't happen. Of course it happened. She felt freed from it because she hadn't found three or four names in the phone book. But that meant nothing. Around any corner there could be the waiting face, speaking the words she dreads: "Why would you think we had forgotten?"

The faces crowd around her. She can't see them any longer; there's no way of telling who they are. She would cry out, but she has long ago given up hope that crying out will do the slightest good. She's known for years that she will always be alone.

But now she's not alone, they crowd around her, they breathe on her, their breath is horrible, they can do nothing but accuse. "You have brought death and shame." The past is a knife under her flesh. For years it lay flat, cool against the bone, its sharp point meaningless since it lay still, a parallel layer, steel on bone, but pressing nothing. This was called forgetfulness. Now the point flashes up, cuts organs, a hole in the white of her eye. Blood is drawn; she sees the faces in a veil of blood. The faces of the dead: "We let you stay in life, but we have not forgotten."

Is there no way of putting them to rest? She thrashes in her bed, as if the movement could banish them. But every movement causes the blood to swish, the knife to pierce through a fresh inch. She moves her head back and forth on the pillow.

If only she had her large American pillow so she could cover her head to drown out the distorting voices! She hears only fragments of words. The voices are coming through the membrane that once sealed the barrier between the living and the dead. They are evil voices, repeating parts of words: "Death. Shame." There is no fresh wind of health to clear the air of their perversion. There is no voice of God. Life is not stronger than death. And shame, as she has always known, is stronger than anything on earth.

She hears the voices and she senses faces near, but they aren't discernible. But what are the faces of the dead? Perhaps they are indiscernible. Death has transformed them.

What is her father's now? All rot has been accomplished. What is Leo's face? Skulls, two skulls. If the two of them were lying side by side, Leo's skull and her father's, she wouldn't be able to tell whose was whose. How can she know if she remembers what they really looked like, if what she calls her father's face, what bobs up like the head of somebody only pretending to be drowning, could be just an image she's responded to from looking at it in a photograph. She doesn't even have a photograph of Leo. His face was obliterated through an act of his own will. In death, he was unrecognizable. Does the face in her memory bear any resemblance to the face that was once his? Or has she put together, here and there, the features of many people she has known?

She knows that the faces, indiscernible in the half-light around her, are the faces of the dead. She believes that she is still alive. If she has a discernible face, she must be still alive. She tries to imagine what she looks like, what she would look like to someone standing at the door looking at the woman lying on the bed. If she could describe the woman lying on the bed, then she could believe herself free.

She begins with a simple sentence. "A woman is lying on the bed." The simplicity of the sentence relaxes her. What it describes hurts nobody. She feels a little safer, and she wants to make herself feel safer still. She tells herself to describe the woman on the bed.

"The woman on the bed is old and small, but youthful for her age."

The breathing around her is quieter now. Because she has made herself into something she can describe. Something that language fits. Something that language can explain.

"The woman on the bed has skin that is normally very pale, but at this time of the year it has been darkened, because she's spent time outdoors in the sun."

She touches her own face. She recognizes it. It is still alive. It's something about which someone would say, and not be wrong: "The sun has darkened it."

"If you looked at the woman's hands, you could see that she's worked outdoors, probably in a garden."

Yes, my garden. Thinking of those living things, healthy and growing, doing no one harm. Hard work. Sore hands, weary knees. I have done all this. *Not I,* the woman on the bed.

Describe the woman's eyes.

I can't see them in the darkness.

Come closer. Turn on the light.

Dark brown, gray-green circles underneath, when she is very tired. A large mouth. She still has her own teeth. Remarkable at her age. A fortunate woman, never to have lost a tooth!

She gets out of the bed. She has made the faces and the voices disappear, go silent. She looks out at the window that faces the piazza. In the piazza is a little park with a small fountain. She's grateful to someone for having thought of and then built this pleasant place. The fountain is dead, but the air is soft and quiet. Now and then she hears a car's noise as it breaks through the dim air. She can see two stars, distant above the trees whose leaves sway only a little in the light breeze before dawn. She will sit at her window, waiting for the sun to rise. Then she will wash and dress and make her way across the street to the railway station. She will buy her ticket and have a *caffè*. She will take the train back to that place. Not forgetting to leave a note for Carlo, sleeping happily in Katherine's arms, in the rank smell of their armpits after their night's exertion. Happily asleep encircled by the girl who loves him freely, without fear, and whom he freely, fearlessly embraces, just as if this were an ordinary thing.

Everything proceeds as she had hoped. She boards a train at six fifteen, having had a coffee and a brioche, eaten as she leaned against a pillar. She believes that the tracks have been moved, but the station is the same building, the same place she always left from in her itchy woolen clothing, when she went with her father to visit his parents in Milan, the same place where they boarded a train for Genoa, barely speaking to one another. *Father, in a little while I will never see your face again.*

The pain of those words as she remembers makes her want to run away, run back to America, to her large flat wooden house with its appliances and garden, the tomatoes ready for harvesting. How can she trust her neighbor's daughter, who has said she'll water them, but may forget? Better perhaps to leave now. To get on a plane right now. Already too much has become unsealed, so that she feels her mouth is full of words. If she opened her mouth to speak, what would come out but words as dangerous as poison?

Why did she come back? Because of her son, who could make her smile with his jokes, his dancing. So gifted, Mrs. Smaldone! Your son has great gifts. He would stand on a stage dancing, singing, acting in a play, and people clapped and clapped, they didn't want to let him go, they were afraid of what life would be after he disappeared from the stage, they would simply be who they had been before: frightened and hopeless, overworked. On the stage, he suggested life's goodness: "Things will be better. Think of me and there can be a better life." Each of them in the audience heard him say that to them. She most of all. This gift, this shining gift that nothing in her had darkened. Now he's going to marry this girl, whose parents come from Africa, from Nigeria, this girl who dances so beautifully with him, and laughs and quiets him, this girl who is his boss, the head of his department, he works under her. Not a girl, she shouldn't call Katherine that, but she wants to say: "You are a boy and a girl. You are standing at the beginning of a road. Ahead of you is hope, behind you is memory. You have much more hope than memory."

They're grateful to her for accepting what is called an interracial marriage. For standing up to Joe's family (if he were alive, she'd have had to stand up to him, but no one says that). For indicating by the refinement of her carriage (which she'd tried to hide from them, but never could, so that they always resented her) that her approval of this marriage meant it was right. She used the thing they resented and feared, appearing before them in the tumult of their gatherings, a woman who knew the important dates of history and the Latin names for plants. She walked into the din, her daughter-in-law-to-be on her arm, doing what she'd never done: subduing them. Saying nothing, but they knew: they couldn't dare be cold or excluding or harsh or coarse or cruel, all the things they can and want to be. For once in forty years, she said, by holding her spine exactly straight, with every moment of her history for bulwark and justification, what she had never thought of saying aloud: "I am above you. You will not dare, not in the slightest way, to thwart what it is I want."

And it worked. In this small thing, she has conquered.

So Carlo and Katherine wanted to thank her, to give her this gift: an airline ticket, something they were sure would make her happy. "You must give me some of your memories, Mama. Something we can give to our own child."

She couldn't say no to them. You didn't say no to two who said by their lives that perhaps life could be better, different, they would show you how. So she allowed them to take her back here. She thought she'd do what she had always done: cover over, simulate, be quiet, change the topic, speak only the pleasant words. Or perhaps she thought something would come to her, something truthful, in the nature of relief. Most of all, perhaps, she thought she would find nothing, that nothing was left and therefore nothing could accuse. She thought this until the buildings loomed around her in their malice and the faces came to her in the dark room, breathing their foulness on her, saying they had never left her, they will never leave her now.

So she must go back to the place. Bardonecchia.

She can see from the window of the train that everything is different. The vineyards are gone; the small white houses of the peasants have disappeared, telephone lines, television aerials, factories whose signs shout out the names of products she's never heard of have replaced them. But the mountains are the same, and the wind on her face as she stands at the window looking out and is surprised suddenly by darkness when the train goes through the tunnel. That too is the same. Even the surprise.

Leo mocked her for liking to stand by the window looking out.

He always sat in his seat, reading. That day he was reading Leopardi. "Leopardi was one of us. He understood the uselessness of life. Listen to this," he shouted at her, so the other people looked at him as if he were mad. He was declaiming Leopardi's poem to the moon right on the train in front of everybody. In the middle of the day.

> Dim and tremulous
> Seen through the tears that rose beneath my eyelids
> My life being full of trouble—I would remember
> And reckon up the cycles of my sorrow.

Tears came to her eyes because he was so unhappy. She knew that all his suffering meant he was superior to her. People made fun of him and said his cult of melancholy was absurd, but she understood his sadness. Which was why she agreed to go with him, so they could shoot themselves in the tower. She believed that he needed to think of himself as someone who would do that.

But did she mean to die? This is what she can't remember.

She gets off the train, sixty-three years later, remembering the wetness of the cloth between her legs, her body's heaviness, her determination that he won't see her like this. Sixty-three years later, and the station is the same. The floor is smudged with the ground ashes of cigarettes; dilatory sweepers with nothing at stake clean forty percent of the dirt. The floors are polished concrete with stones imbedded in it like pigs' knuckles. The floor is the same as when she came here last, and the same men lounge, even at this hour, at the round tables of the café, nursing cups of coffee, smoking, smoking, making guttural remarks about the bodies of the women who pass by.

But as she walks into the cool day, which already has the dry taste of autumn, she sees that the rest of the town is unrecognizable.

All the structures—the stores, houses, and restaurants—seem to be new as though the whole town had been bombed. She knows it wasn't. Part of Turin was bombed, but not this place, and she can see that the building occurred more recently than that. The 1960s, she imagines.

What happened to the small shops like caves, the low white houses where the merchants lived? Everything she sees seems to be imitating something else, something German, Scandinavian, as if the whole town had crossed the Alps. Ornamented wooden fretworks. Houses made of unpainted wood, rather than stone. Cleanliness. Prosperity. Where did this wealth come from? Then she understands: everywhere shops are selling skis, clothing for skiing. This town, which had been a place where the Turinese bourgeois came in the summer—one month here in the mountains, then one at the sea—where the hills surrounded the dry farmland with a vigilant ungiving harshness and the farmers tended their vineyards and their sheep, is now a place where people come, perhaps from everywhere in Italy, to have fun in the winter. She's distressed by the cheap architecture, the slapdash imitation, the impermanent and makeshift look of things. She thinks to herself: None of this will last.

But what *has* lasted? The buildings, the vineyards that were here sixty years ago and seemed eternal, all are gone. The material world can be made to disappear for good; nothing can bring these things back.

But she can bring back the feeling of heaviness in her body and the stickiness of blood between her thighs. Only now she is old; her bleeding is long over. The heaviness in her body is the heaviness of age. If today she has difficulty climbing up the mountain, it will be because of a permanent infirmity, not a monthly weakness that will disappear in a few days.

She walks up the street, past the church of San Hippolyto whose bells will ring the Angelus at noon, as they did on that day. Or will they? Perhaps even in Italy the churches are empty and the Angelus no longer rings. Passing the houses with their climbing roses that look so unfresh and badly placed, the cars, the aluminum chairs with green plastic webbing, she stops at a spigot that brings water from a mountain stream. She lets the cold water run over her fingers, but she doesn't take a drink, as she used to. The harsh mountain refuses, as it always did, a welcome. Nothing about that has changed. The look of the dry soil comes back to her.

She can remember Leo walking, shouting Leopardi over his shoulder, telling her to hurry up, calling her a slowpoke, so happy on the day of his death. She can remember the feel of the stones through her shoes, the look of a fly as it landed on her hand. But one thing she can't remember: Did she actually mean to die? Did she believe that this would be her last day on the earth?

The thick, clean line that divided the present from the past has disappeared and spread, like ink in water. She feels she must answer the question—Did I mean to die?—but to answer it she must be in the past. But what would she go back to? There's no such thing as a past she can go back to with certainty, sure it was itself, not her invention. The past is gone, like the low white houses replaced by Swiss chalets.

But it isn't gone. It's lived with her, she's lived her life according to its word. Hiding it, like a shameful relative in a cellar. And now she's here.

Because she will die soon. Because she wants to know whether, at fifteen, she meant to die. Because she must know if Leo's death is due to her. Because perhaps she'll see him here, not dead, not with his face blown off, but recognizable, aged, full of wisdom, sadness, withered, but in this life. Or perhaps he'll be here exactly as he was the minute before he put the gun in his mouth, and he'll tell her nothing happened, she lived her life as though something happened, but it never did, she can go back now, she is still a girl, she's done nothing to be ashamed of, she can start again.

She is walking up the mountain behind Leo. He is thinking of the uselessness of life, the nobility of death, and she is thinking of the stain between her legs. He takes her to his parents' house. They get the guns, making sure they're loaded. They walk halfway down the hill to the tower. He takes off his coat for her to lie on. He unbuttons his shirt.

"No," she says, "I can't."

He doesn't believe that she doesn't want to because of her bleeding. He says she doesn't love him, she is selfish, stupid, a shop girl. Now I know, he says, oh yes, now I understand. You've been with someone else. He names the names of all the boys he knows she's been with. He insists that she tell him which ones.

She is a girl who is so rarely angry that this anger takes her by surprise. Someone is sawing off the top of her skull; the sharp pain may make her head explode. She says every bad thing to him she's ever thought of.

"You're ridiculous. You're a pompous, self-indulgent fool. No one takes you seriously. Everyone laughs at you but me, and I'm tired of you now. To hell with you."

She runs out of the tower, down the mountain, feeling nothing but her skull on fire because of the words he said.

And then she hears the shot.

It is the moment of his death. It is the uncrossable line between the time of his existence and of his failure to exist. She runs up the hill. She knows without doubt that this is the end of all that part of her life that went before it, that the rest will be different, she will divide her life between what went before this moment and what she will call the rest of life. The farmer, tending his vines in the field, hears the shot as well. He gets to the tower before she does. He tells her not to look, but she insists. She can't remember any more. She can't remember what she saw, in the seconds before the farmer (of a lower class, but still a man, therefore having authority over her) pushed her away from the door.

She doesn't know what she did next. She must have sat in the farmer's house, waiting. His father came, also her father. She doesn't remember taking the train home to the city. Did they come in cars? No one she knew had a car. Did the police drive them? The police were her father's enemy. Would they have helped? Or gloated? Or made more trouble, to rub his face in his shame?

She remembers a rushing: furtive whispers as if an explosion had just happened and people, in shock, were unable to raise their voices or to walk from one place to another. They walk aimlessly, their hands open at their sides. She remembers Leo's mother's cursing. The news that she must be sent away. Her father turning from her, unable ever again to meet her eye.

From that moment till this: never again to meet my father's eye.

Sixty-three years later. The tower is half-demolished. By history? Nature? She could ask someone, but she won't. The remains of the tower are surrounded by rubble. A cyclone fence has been built around it, PERICOLOSO, says the sign on the fence. But a hole has been cut through. Boys play in front of the tower, throwing rocks at each other. Plastic bottles are wedged between the larger rocks where they stand. She wants to say to the boys, "A boy like you died here. It might have been because of me."

She looks at the boys, pelting each other with lumps of cement. No, he was never like them. He was never playful. He would have adored these boys, longed to be one of them, but they wouldn't have let him. He was always alone and always sad. He had sweetness, also cruelty. And a brilliant mind, that shone like a bright star through all his sadness.

She sits down on the ground. She puts her head in her hands and weeps. Because they were so young, children, and there was no one to say to them: "You are beautiful and gifted and in a dark time you are the world's hope." Because no one would talk to her afterward, because they treated her as someone who stank of death. Because her growth stopped here, like a flowering bush frozen by a cold wind. She was a young girl, a pretty girl, her mind was full of knowledge and the desire for knowledge, she loved her father and her city, she loved the boy who held her in his arms, and thanked her for her body's beauty. Why did no one say to them: "You are good children. Live your lives."

Sixty-three years of frozen life. Now she will weep. She longs for someone to embrace her, to answer her cry. To tell her: "You have atoned enough." Or "There is nothing to atone for."

The boys throwing stones at the foot of the tower look at her and move away. An old lady, they think, gone crazy. They run down the hill, their sneakers kick up pebbles. She weeps until she can barely see the mountain. She doesn't know how she'll get back to her son, how she'll take up the small amount of what will be the rest of life. She is seventy-eight years old. Soon she will no longer be alive.

How can she have wanted to die? Even now, she doesn't. A fly settles on her hand, overlarge, amber, intricate as a ring. She hears the boys shout down the mountain, feels the pebbles she is sitting on through the thin cloth of her trousers. She can't bear that she must give this up: this world of information—seeing, touching, hearing. And for what?

I didn't want to die. I didn't want you to.

I wanted you to be happy. That's why I said I'd die with you. Just to make you happy for a little while. I didn't think you'd do it.

Or maybe it wasn't like that. Maybe she wanted to be famous, honorable. Perhaps she thought it was a way she could be with him forever, and that nothing in life was worth more than that.

She looks down at the ground. She takes some pebbles in her hand. She wonders if it matters, what she wanted on that day. Death can't be undone. She had a fate. She lived a life. He died. What did it matter if she meant to die or not, or if he meant to, if he died from spiteful anger or mistaken nobility? He died. She didn't. She lived a life. There was more to her life than his death. She paid too much. Only she knew what happened, only she can remember, and she doesn't know how. The work of remembrance is too hard for her. She doesn't know what she's forgotten, or invented, or told wrongly to herself, or silenced, or made up.

She understands that after her death no one will think of Leo. He will vanish in the pocket of oblivion, faceless again, this time for good. She should tell the story of his death to someone. Yet whom could she tell? She can't imagine any expression on any face that would be bearable to her, anyone who wouldn't fix their eyes on her and think that now they finally could understand her. That would be wrong; that would be unbearable. She would still be the woman they had known before they knew the story. She doesn't want to look into anybody's eyes and see pity or new-minted comprehension. She has made something of herself: a quiet woman with a husband, children and a house, a garden. Something was salvaged of a life. That salvage is all anyone should know.

She reaches into her bag. She picks up the notebook with a plastic cover that her sister-in-law gave her as a going-away gift. MY TRAVEL DIARY, it says, in gold letters against red. She opens the book and rips out a piece of paper. On the top of the page she writes, "For my son, to be read after my death."

She begins: "I would like to tell you about something that happened to me when I was very young." She looks up at the mountain: the severe outcropping, the folds of rock like a wrinkled curtain. It is late August and the soil is very dry. Down in the meadow a few cattle graze reluctantly, wishing for better times. The sky is cloudless with a hint of punishment in its unmixed blue. She thinks of Carlo reading this. And Katherine, whose parents fled murder and starvation in Nigeria.

"It happened when I was fifteen years old," she writes.

But what was *it?* She sees the small word—*it*—the enemy, hard as a bullet. Was it the death, their history, the history of Italy, the history of poetry, the history of men and women? Whose name should be included: Goethe, Leopardi, his parents, her aunt, Mussolini, a host of female martyrs, the Virgin Mary, her dead mother, her father whom she loved above all things?

It.

She puts the pencil down. She rips up the paper she was writing on. She blames her son for suggesting by his hopefulness that there could be a story she could tell. There is no story: she has forgotten Leo's face. She has lost it; she has allowed it to be lost.

She can't bring him to life in any way so that his life won't seem merely a preparation for his death. She can't tell the story in any way so that his death won't seem the only real thing about him. She can only remember him without his face.

There is nothing to tell her son. If she told him something it wouldn't be true, and it would cause him to pity her. Even after her own death she won't allow herself to be pitied. He would understand everything in her life as springing from only one thing: Leo's death. Each act of her life would be reduced, overshadowed by death. It had been hard to resist death, the strong seduction of oblivion, but she had done it. Because she had wanted life.

What was it that she wanted? Perhaps only this: not to have it stop. The stream of sensation. Taste. Smell. Sight. Perspective. The feel of cloth. Of cold rain.

Not to give in to nonexistence.

Most of her life is over. Soon she will be among those who have no more sensation. Fiercely she lifts her face to the hot sun. She stoops and picks up pebbles, pressing their sharpness into the palms of her hands. She pulls up tough grasses, resistant as wire. She listens to the sounds of the cars, the light wind soughing in the skinny pines. *After all, I have refused to give this up.*

But soon she'll have to give it up. When that time comes, she doesn't want her son to feel that he must be beside her to make something up to her because of something—one thing—that happened to her. She will face the hour of her death alone, like Leo, like her father. She starts down the hill. When she gets back to the hotel, and Carlo asks her where she went, she'll say, "Somewhere I used to go. It wasn't worth your while. That's why I didn't take you."

"Oh, Mama," he'll say. "I would have gone, so that you wouldn't be alone."

"I know," she'll say, as if she believed, like him, that such a thing were possible.

She walks to the train as if she walked among the dead. No face arrests her, nothing in a shop, no detail of a building. Only one thing impresses itself on her eye: the floor of the station, disgusting with the greasy ash and butts of cigarettes. The walk up the stairs to the platform makes her heart beat heavily. *One day it will beat too heavily, one day it will stop.*

She gets into the train, one of the first to board. Everything is still and quiet. Then the train starts up with an insulting lurch. She leans her head back, feeling the paper antimacassar stiff against her hair. She doesn't want to see the mountains, the green of the trees, the houses, the countryside's inhabitants, stupefied by the passing of a train. She closes her eyes.

When she opens them, she is in darkness. The train is going

through a tunnel. In the middle of the tunnel, it seems to stop. She's all alone in her compartment, and she wishes she weren't. She would be happy to be with anyone, but particularly someone younger, practical, quick-witted, strong. But no one appears. She can hear in the other compartment muffled grumbling, indistinguishable words, as if she were at the sea. The train is still; there isn't even the smallest movement.

What will happen if it never moves? Who are these strangers, and how can she expect them to behave?

She hears a child cry at the other end of the corridor. The conductor walks back and forth, begging for patience. A young man passes in front of her compartment: he tells the conductor he is out of patience. He bangs a rolled up newspaper against the wall, then disappears, closing the door behind him with a furious proud click. The sound makes her feel even more alone.

What is it that I have, she wonders, that cannot be taken from me? She touches her knees; she cups her elbows in her hands. She listens to the sound of her own breathing. But what does any of it mean, in this small box of darkness where she sits, and what can it protect her from? How can she prevent herself from being swallowed up by all this darkness?

She sees it's useless to resist it: no, she won't do that. She'll give in to it. She's resisted it for all this time, but not now, not again. She allows herself to be absorbed by darkness and at the same time to penetrate it. She waits for something. It would have to be some face. Her father's face appears, but it isn't the face she needs. The face she needs eludes her.

She is trying to remember Leo's face. If only it would flower in this darkness, like the faces of Rembrandt's or Titian's young men, emerging from the blackness like a flame. But it refuses to be bidden. Emptiness spreads like a fresh stain. Emptiness takes on volume, weight. Then it is no longer just one thing. Broken lines appear, then curves, and then thin crescents filling out, moving toward each other in the dark.

After a while, various faces form and break the surface. She knows none of them is his. His has been swallowed up. The faces that she sees are faces of other men, young men, some she's known, some she's seen, soldiers, doctors, actors playing parts onstage, faces in great paintings, her sons, gray photographs of prisoners, colorful photographs of athletes striving for a victory. The darkness seems to rise around her like a wave. She hears the voices of the other passengers, indistinct yet alone. The empty words fly up, then burst. Voices separated from bodies fill her all at once with a terrible sympathy. She wants to tell the voices: You are not alone. She feels the need to pray, to use words that might attach to something and cohere. She doesn't know who would hear the words. She doesn't care. The God that people pray to is an empty word, a husk, lighter than air. Only the rhythms of old prayers are called for now. She clasps her hands.

O brave boys who died in foolish wars, who died for nothing
Boys with ideas, murdered on streetcorners for a heedless
    word
Boys who threw themselves from windows for the shame of
    history
Boys driving fast cars, taking others with them
Boys who stood up to brutal men who were bound to over-
    power them
Bands of boys hiding at night and springing out at soldiers
Boys dying for their mothers, for their fathers, to save a child
    they never knew
Sickly boys, living in their youthful beds the life of endless
    yearning
Boys killed feeding furnaces or in the teeth of powerful
    machines

Boys dead in ships, by drowning
                              forgive us, all of you, for you
                              have died and we
                              have lived.

She sits back, in the stillness. Not knowing what will happen next. She closes her eyes. The train starts. They leave the tunnel. Everyone on the train applauds. For a moment, she thinks they are applauding her. Then she remembers: it happened to no one but herself. She falls into a sleep she only half believes that she will wake from.

But she does wake, the conductor calls "Torino" and she steps onto the platform. The high ceilings of the station make her breath feel easy. She walks into the street. She is only steps from her hotel, but she decides she'll walk a while.

At a stand, she buys a pistachio gelato, green as a sea creature or a jewel. She touches things with her fingertips: she feels things as her feet strike down: everything is terribly distinct: rough, smooth, hard, soft, silky, cold, sweet, light, uneven. The leaves showing their silver undersides in the breeze fill her with joy.

In the shop windows, many expensive things, desirable objects, are for sale. Pots of Persian violets, seasonless chrysanthemums, Greek heads, English watercolors, grapes, short dresses, dark shoes for winter, woolen jackets, tinned asparagus, breads in a variety of shapes, silk scarves, umbrellas, bracelets. An African has watches and earrings, cigarette lighters, spread out on the pavement. There is nothing she wants to buy. She is excited and expectant: she doesn't know for what.

And yet she knows something has happened. Just a hint, a possibility: a suggestion of a face to whom she will tell her story. All the different stories. All the different ways it could have happened, each of them true. As all the faces were the face of Leo. As all the dead are one.

In the darkness, she found not one face, but many faces. She invented a face from darkness. From within darkness. Something was knowable. It was not a replica of what once was. It was distinct, but multiple, and liable to change. Leo's face was swallowed up in darkness. Yet there were things that she could see. The most important thing was this: The dead, being one and many, knew there was nothing to forgive.

She is full of gratitude, it doesn't matter that she doesn't know to whom. She lifts her heart in thanks. She thanks the red glow of her father's cigarette, the almond cake they ate, the feel of stones through the thin soles of her espadrilles, the fly resting on her hand, intricate as a jeweled watch. She thanks the safety of the journey that brought Katherine's family from Africa to New York. She thanks Katherine and Carlo and their singing and their dancing, and Katherine's gold sandals. She thanks her sons for allowing her to teach them to read, the men whose limbs she helped to straighten, the globes of red tomatoes ripening thousands of miles away without her, her cousin's satin coverlet, the harsh sheets and thin towels of the Turinese hotel, the water in the fountain in the square, the birds at daybreak, wheeling high above the roofs, all that has gone before us, everything, all things, the living and the dead.

She opens the door to the hotel. The doorman says, "Your son, his friend, are waiting."

Yes, thank you, she says.

Sì, grazie.

FOR THE BEST IN PAPERBACKS, LOOK FOR THE

In every corner of the world, on every subject under the sun, Penguin represents quality and variety—the very best in publishing today.

For complete information about books available from Penguin—including Pelicans, Puffins, Peregrines, and Penguin Classics—and how to order them, write to us at the appropriate address below. Please note that for copyright reasons the selection of books varies from country to country.

In the United Kingdom: For a complete list of books available from Penguin in the U.K., please write to *Dept E.P., Penguin Books Ltd, Harmondsworth, Middlesex, UB7 0DA.*

In the United States: For a complete list of books available from Penguin in the U.S., please write to *Consumer Sales, Penguin USA, P.O. Box 999—Dept. 17109, Bergenfield, New Jersey 07621-0120.* VISA and MasterCard holders call 1-800-253-6476 to order all Penguin titles.

In Canada: For a complete list of books available from Penguin in Canada, please write to *Penguin Books Canada Ltd, 10 Alcorn Avenue, Suite 300, Toronto, Ontario, Canada M4V 3B2.*

In Australia: For a complete list of books available from Penguin in Australia, please write to the *Marketing Department, Penguin Books Ltd, P.O. Box 257, Ringwood, Victoria 3134.*

In New Zealand: For a complete list of books available from Penguin in New Zealand, please write to the *Marketing Department, Penguin Books (NZ) Ltd, Private Bag, Takapuna, Auckland 9.*

In India: For a complete list of books available from Penguin, please write to *Penguin Overseas Ltd, 706 Eros Apartments, 56 Nehru Place, New Delhi, 110019.*

In Holland: For a complete list of books available from Penguin in Holland, please write to *Penguin Books Nederland B.V., Postbus 195, NL-1380AD Weesp, Netherlands.*

In Germany: For a complete list of books available from Penguin, please write to *Penguin Books Ltd, Friedrichstrasse 10-12, D-6000 Frankfurt Main 1, Federal Republic of Germany.*

In Spain: For a complete list of books available from Penguin in Spain, please write to *Longman, Penguin España, Calle San Nicolas 15, E-28013 Madrid, Spain.*

In Japan: For a complete list of books available from Penguin in Japan, please write to *Longman Penguin Japan Co Ltd, Yamaguchi Building, 2-12-9 Kanda Jimbocho, Chiyoda-Ku, Tokyo 101, Japan.*

FOR THE BEST IN CONTEMPORARY AMERICAN FICTION

☐ **IN THE COUNTRY OF LAST THINGS**
Paul Auster

Death, joggers, leapers, and Object Hunters are just some of the realities of future city life in this spare, powerful, visionary novel about one woman's struggle to live and love in a frightening post-apocalyptic world.
208 pages   ISBN: 0-14-009705-8

☐ **BETWEEN C&D**
New Writing from the Lower East Side Fiction Magazine
Joel Rose and Catherine Texier, Editors

A startling collection of stories by Tama Janowitz, Gary Indiana, Kathy Acker, Barry Yourgrau, and others, *Between C&D* is devoted to short fiction that ignores preconceptions — fiction not found in conventional literary magazines.
194 pages   ISBN: 0-14-010570-0

☐ **LEAVING CHEYENNE**
Larry McMurtry

The story of a love triangle unlike any other, *Leaving Cheyenne* follows the three protagonists — Gideon, Johnny, and Molly — over a span of forty years, until all have finally "left Cheyenne."
254 pages   ISBN: 0-14-005221-6

You can find all these books at your local bookstore, or use this handy coupon for ordering:
Penguin Books By Mail
Dept. BA Box 999
Bergenfield, NJ 07621-0999
Please send me the above title(s). I am enclosing _____
(please add sales tax if appropriate and $1.50 to cover postage and handling). Send check or money order—no CODs. Please allow four weeks for shipping. We cannot ship to post office boxes or addresses outside the USA. *Prices subject to change without notice.*

Ms./Mrs./Mr. _____

Address _____

City/State _____ Zip _____